Douglas Lindsay was born in Scotland in 1964.
It rained.

By Douglas Lindsay,
available from Long Midnight Publishing:

The Barney Thomson Series

The Long Midnight of Barney Thomson

The Barber Surgeon's Hairshirt
(aka *The Cutting Edge of Barney Thomson)*

A Prayer For Barney Thomson

The King Was In His Counting House

The Last Fish Supper

The Haunting of Barney Thomson

The Final Cut

Other Novels

Lost in Juarez

21 Years On The Back of
Dixie Klondyke's Spanish Guitar

21 Years
On The Back Of
Dixie Klondyke's
Spanish Guitar

Douglas Lindsay

Long Midnight Publishing

This edition published in 2010 by
Long Midnight Publishing
PO Box 4445
Wells, BA5 9AL
United Kingdom

e-mail: office@longmidnightpublishing.com

www.douglaslindsay.com

A catalogue record for this book is available
from the British Library

ISBN 978-0-9561466-8-7

Cover design: Iza Swierad
Copy Editor: Patrick Davies

Printed in Great Britain by the MPG Books Group,
Bodmin and King's Lynn

for Kathryn

1

We've all got our reasons for joining. We like to think that every liberal on the planet is a loony-tune, but they're right; it's a control thing. The need for power, to be above the law; so you can manipulate it, or break it. And there has to be a massive S&M streak there or else you'd become a traffic warden, or umpire co-ed softball on a Saturday afternoon.

I never fitted the mould. I joined the police for two reasons. One was Jean Fryar, a sixteen year-old shop assistant from Stepps; and the other was Jonah Bloonsbury.

Jean Fryar left school at the first opportunity. No 'O' levels, no common sense. Started working in a newsagents up the old Edinburgh Road. I used to go in there sometimes on a Saturday for my twenty Silk Cut Extra Mild. Fancied myself with the ladies, although the only experience I had with women's underwear was from Kay's catalogues. Jean was all right, if a little canine in her appearance, but I was young, rampant and desperate. Asked her out, she coyly unwrapped a bar of Dairy Milk and accepted, and that night we went to see *Sauve Qui Peut (La Vie)* by Jean-Luc Godard at the GFT in town. I thought it might impress her, but she fell asleep after ten minutes and I spent the rest of the film furtively trying to touch her breasts without waking her up.

Three weeks later on a wet Saturday night in her front room, I succeeded in having sex for the first time. In all the excitement the condom got left behind in my jacket pocket. Along with my brain.

Within a couple of months, two things happened. Jean found out she was pregnant, and a young detective constable in Glasgow called Jonah Bloonsbury cracked a murder inquiry which had defeated the most senior detectives in the city. The guy was nine years older than me and he had his fifteen minutes. Front page news, dick of the month. He'd acted alone on a hunch all the others had ignored and had nabbed his man after a long chase on foot over open moorland up beyond East Kilbride. In the end he'd banjoed the bloke over the napper with a guitar. Thrilling stuff, and as I sat in the sixth year common room contemplating my upcoming wife and child, I decided the police were for me.

We got married on a staggeringly warm summer's day in 1980, and three weeks later Jean had a miscarriage. So the child was gone and, immature and insensitive beyond reason, I immediately contemplated losing the wife as well. The police no longer seemed necessary. However, on the day I was to withdraw my application there was a follow-up report on Bloonsbury in the Record. Two months later and back to normal – but in the meantime the guy had received one hundred and twenty-three proposals of marriage. All those women, for solving one bloody crime!

By the time I joined I had met Peggy and was seeing her behind Jean's back, and by the time I finally met Jonah Bloonsbury, Peggy and I had been married for fourteen years and the marriage had long since drifted into disinterest. By then Bloonsbury was a drunken detective chief inspector, living on past glories and suffering the same sort of marriage as the rest of us.

That first murder case wasn't his only big success. There were several others, though none so high profile. But somewhere along the way the pressure became too much for him, and he drowned in alcohol. Very last century. I don't know when he hit the downward spiral, but by the time Bloonsbury reached thirty-five he was wasted, viewing everyone with suspicion through the dregs of a bottle of cheap blended malt.

There was one last crowning glory over a year ago, plucked from nowhere, to temporarily save his wretched career and wasted reputation, but since then his life has been nothing but a fast drop to the bottom of the ocean. And now he's just a guy, drifting through his forties; overweight, ruddy-faced, bleary-eyed. A waste of a good man, but there are many more where he came from.

So I joined up for two illusions. A child that never came, and the continuing chimera that is the career of Jonah Bloonsbury.

I bumped into Jean Fryar again a few months ago. She slapped me across the face, we went for a drink, compared divorces and children – three and two for me, five and seven for her – and nearly ended up in bed. I like to think we both thought better of it in the end, but really the decision was all hers. And that's all there is to say about Jean Fryar.

However, the story of Jonah Bloonsbury limps on, while the rest of us watch it pass by – mourners at a wake – as he reaches for one last success; or perhaps merely hangs on, hoping to receive a full pension, with as much dignity as a man with a bottle of whisky attached to his face can do.

2

He sits on the train and wonders. What would you call that scent in the air? Wild flowers? Freshly cut grass? Spring meadow? He prefers not to think about it and looks at the window, at his reflection, imagining the smells of the tunnels through which the train is passing. Rotten cabbage, sewage, decay, instant noodle snacks. They should bottle those. He glances over his shoulder at the woman three seats back, and imagines her dabbing herself with the scent of instant savoury noodles. Cool.

(In one respect, we'll cut to the bottom of the ninth. Our lad is a little messed up, and has a thing about women with long, straight auburn hair. A big thing.)

The train rumbles to a halt, emerging from the tunnels into the drizzle and cold dark night of Dalmarnock station.

He doesn't turn all the way round, but looks at the woman's reflection, catching her eye in the window. A fleeting glimpse then she looks away. He smiles at her too late, but can feel her shudder.

He looks along the length of the carriage. Two old women, doing that old woman thing; a single man, sleeping happily, a line of green drool working it's way down his chin; and four teenagers, discussing dialectical materialism and passing around a bottle of cheap wine.

He sucks his teeth, runs his hand across the stubble on his chin and looks at his reflection in the window. Five days growth. Every murderer should have five days growth on their chin. It says something. His mind rambles on, a trail of confusion, his eyes attracted over his shoulder every few seconds to the woman behind.

The doors fizz slowly shut. He looks up at the route map above the window. Seven stops to go, and she'll have to get off at one of them. He wouldn't do anything on the train. Too much chance of Postman Pat coming along and interrupting things. Well, if Postman Pat had been a ticket collector, that is. Ticket Collector Pat.

A quiet back street, with a gentle drizzle, broken street lights and a dog barking half a mile away. That was the place for your first murder. A fifteen-piece orchestra playing eerie music would also be handy, but unlikely nevertheless. Fifteen-piece orchestras accompanying murder scenes have been outlawed on the streets of Glasgow for several years.

He imagines the newspapers, seeing his photofit picture, and wonders what *nom de plume* they will honour him with. Fancies something biblical. Bible Bob. Bible Bill. Bible Ben. Bible Belt. Bible Butthead. Whatever. He hadn't thought of that before. What would he have to do to get a cool biblical-type name? Scrawl something suitable in the victim's blood, perhaps. Or leave a hand-written note. Some religious nonsense, although he'll struggle to think of anything appropriate. *Jesus said, and the Bland shall inherit the world of television*?

He looks out of the window, at the lights and wet streets of Rutherglen, as the train crawls towards the next stop. He laughs to himself, as if he was in an episode of *Wacky Races*.

His eyes slither round again and he looks straight at her. She avoids his gaze. Long auburn hair, the way he likes it. The way Emma had it. Twitches at the thought of her, pushes it from his mind. Bloody Emma.

The woman bites her nails, looking round at the first damp run of the platform as the train shudders slowly into Rutherglen station. Pretty face, slightly overweight, small nose, glorious pink lips, getting very frightened by the geeky guy two seats away who is staring at her. She's seen the movies on Channel 5 at nine o'clock. She knows the score.

Too late now, the thought of Emma is in his head. Beautiful long auburn hair, and all for what? A travesty, a disaster, o woe! as the old fella Shakespeare would've written.

The train comes to a halt. He looks over his shoulder at the woman as the doors open. He keeps his eyes on her. Why should he hide it now, she knows what's coming to her.

There's giggling from up the carriage as the four teenagers drunkenly make their way off the train, pushing, laughing, arguing about Marx's contribution to 19th century stand-up comedy.

He looks back to the woman. She's staring at him now, and this time looks away more slowly. Hey, hey, hey, he thinks. She fancies me. This is going to be even easier than I thought.

He turns away and looks up the carriage, feeling a bit of a buzz. He's a strange little man, remember. The two old women are looking at him as well.

'What?' he says, a bit disconcerted. 'What?' he repeats, and their eyes avert.

The sleeping man's head bobs up from a silent slumber, then flops back onto his chest. The doors start their slow fizz. There's a stamping on the floor behind. Still engaged with glaring at the two old yins, he is slow to turn. Then he suddenly realises what he's missing. Turns quickly now, but she's already out the door, the doors already closed. He runs to them, stands at the glass looking out at her. She waits on the platform, crying out for the train to move off; breathless. He starts pulling at the rubber between the doors. Makes some headway. An inch. She doesn't wait. Two inches. She sees the teenagers disappear through the door into the waiting room, one other passenger making the slow walk along the platform, and runs after them. The train starts to move off. He's tugging desperately at the door, but he's not getting any further. He's still there pulling at the rubber as the train pulls past the woman hurrying to the exit, and their eyes meet one last time. He drinks in the auburn hair, hoping he will remember her, but all these women look the same. She shudders then feels like crying with relief as he steps back fro m the doors and then is gone as the train accelerates away into the rain, the still of the night.

He returns to his seat. Looks at the old women, who stare back this time, and he feels intimidated. His eyes drop.

'Bloody Emma,' he mutters.

The woman climbs the stairs up to the bridge over the railway tracks. A lucky escape. She feels the relief, and already she is beginning to put it out of her mind. Men. They're all the same; and she starts again to construct her defences for when she has to explain to her husband where she's been all evening.

3

Monday morning, three days before Christmas. Sitting at the desk with a colossal hangover, the memory of the weekend still burning. Partick Thistle lost three-nil at Ross County, and I ended up in bed with this bogmonster from Castlemilk. It was female, but I'm not sure if it was human. Don't remember a thing about the night before either, so I don't know if it was worth it. At least I wasn't called in, and any weekend without that is something of a success.

Taylor isn't in yet, not that he cares. It's just me and Herrod and a collection of maladroit constables. The Superintendent's in of course, doing that woman in power thing. Letting all us men know who's boss and quoting obscure literature at us every ten seconds so that we know she's not just some totalitarian uberbabe; that she's got as much brains as breast. Very commendable and don't we all just respect her for it.

Passed Alison on the way in this morning. I was married to her for twenty-nine days a couple of years ago – something which I did in a fit of idiocy after my divorce from Peggy came through. She was working downstairs somewhere, walking by with a criminal on her arm. He looked good on her. We smiled. Very cosy. We get on a lot better since the divorce, although we avoided each other for nearly a year afterwards. She's marrying

Sgt McGovern in June, which is unfortunate.

Herrod lifts his head from some paperwork, tossing the file into the out-tray as he does so.

'It's all a load of bollocks, Lumberyard,' he says.

Can't argue with that.

'That you found the meaning of life again?'

He sticks his feet on the desk, and lights a cigarette. They recently introduced a no-smoking policy, but there's no one here to police it. The man smokes B&H same as everyone else. That's why he never gets the women, same as I do. That and he's ugly. And he doesn't smell too good. Women hate that. And Bernadette nearly killed him two years ago when she heard about him and WPC McGuire and he's kept his bayonet securely locked away ever since. Under the thumb, our Herrod, no mistake.

I light a Marlboro to show him who's superior. I bought into the Marlboro man image because virtually no one else has in Britain. Women love it. I had a friend once who smoked Woodbine because no one else did, but it didn't have the same effect. Whoever heard of Woodbine man?

'Got this guy, right?'

Herrod's always got a guy. Don't think he believes in arresting women. Too much trouble.

'The bampot says he was at his sister's all night. Who the fuck spends the night with their sister? I haven't seen my sister since she was twelve. I vomit on my sister.'

I'm fully prepared to believe that Herrod has in the past, at some time, vomited on his sister.

'But not this guy. This eejit spends the night with her. Very cosy. The sister backs him up, of course. Best buddies and all that shite. And all the while, as they're tucked up under the sheets, or whatever they're doing, his warehouse is going noisily up in smoke. Full insurance, nothing to do with me, mate, I was in bed with my fucking sister.'

So what? You get a million of these a day. But you always know with Herrod that he's going to turn it into some conspiracy or other. But there's no way he'll get anywhere near investigating some small time insurance fraud anyway. Bloonsbury or Taylor will stick some cretinous Detective Constable on it for ten minutes, before they move onto some other crime they'll never solve.

'Your point is?'

He sucks on the cigarette. Like he's sucking a nipple. Although I suspect he's forgotten what that's like. I don't think Bernadette's got nipples. I'm betting on her having green scales under all those crimplene polo necks.

'It's all a load of shite.'

'You said that. We know. We're not here because it's fragrant. What are you saying?'

'That's my point. It used to make sense. You came in here on a Monday morning, you did you're job, you took from it what you could, and every now and again you arrested some eejit and kicked fuck out him. Tell me that didn't make sense.'

'Get to the point. You sound like an advert for the polis in the Sunday Times.'

He shrugs, spits out a sigh, shakes his head.

'I don't know. I've just had enough, you know. All this crap, all these eejits. I've had enough of them all. Every last fucking one of them.'

He finishes his lament, stubs the cigarette out in an overflowing ashtray. My heart bleeds for him. I almost want to give him a hug.

'Shut up you stupid prick, and stop feeling sorry for yourself. You're talking pish.'

He grunts at me and moves another report from in to out without looking at it.

The door opens. One of those joke constables walks in looking like the before half of a Clearasil advert, followed by DCI Bloonsbury – a man who hasn't slept for a month – reeking of alcohol. The model detective. We nod at him, he ignores us, walks into his office, and slams the door shut. A couple of shots of J&B, two cups of coffee, half pack of Bensons and he'll be ready for us.

The man's downhill slide has picked up some momentum in recent months. Word is the Super's on the point of kicking him into touch but, for all that hard bitch act, you can tell she's soft on stuff like that. Likes to take care of her men.

Bloonsbury's door reopens almost immediately, half an hour before schedule. Got a face on him like a flat tyre and a piece of paper in his hand, which he waves in the air. Looks like Neville Chamberlain.

'Herrod?'

'What?'

Bloonsbury looks at the piece of paper and gives it another shake.

'Rape case. Stonelaw Road. Mean anything to you?'

Herrod nods. Looks moderately sheepish, if so grotesque a man can even remotely resemble a sheep.

'Well, what the Hell are you doing sitting about when there's some poor lassie to get interviewed? Get you're arse over there.'

The door slams shut. Herrod stares at the floor, then looks up as he fumbles for another smoke.

'See what I mean?' he says.

I ignore him and feel sorry for the victim. If getting raped wasn't enough, the poor girl has to be confronted with Herrod the following morning.

*

Quarter to three. Dispatched to the hind end of Rutherglen Main Street, Detective Constable Morrow, PC Kelly, and WPC Bathurst in tow. Spent most of the day working on a big theft – two hundred TV's in a lorry up at Bothwell services – and I get called away to come and hold Morrow's hand while he does his best to ask the right questions. And it's a no-hoper right from the off.

Fight broke out between three morons not far from the town hall. Two against one, rather than all three for themselves. The one comes off worst, ends up on the ground getting his head beaten to a pulp. He'd already been whipped off to the Victoria by the time we got here, but there've been enough people to tell us what he looked like after the attack. Massively swollen head, face bloodied and purple, no teeth left to talk of. Horrible. A few of them thought he might be dead, but apparently he survived it. Probably because they didn't hit him anywhere near his brain. Seen enough of these stupid bastards who've had too much to drink, think they're Clark Kent, and end up with heads the size of basketballs.

So at two fifteen in the afternoon, three days before Christmas, when there are more people on Rutherglen Main Street than you'd get on a Vietnamese refugee tanker, no one sees a thing. Plenty of folk have seen the guy lying on the pavement looking like dog food, but no one saw the incident take place or the assailants in question.

There are two things to do at a time like this. Forget it and go back to the station; or hang around for five hours questioning everyone over the age of three, all the while getting absolutely nowhere. If the bloke stiffs, of course, then the papers will get hold of it and all of a sudden you've got to look as if you're doing something. But if he walks, then bugger it, what's the point?

Now I would have had Morrow down as a sad young bastard, keen to make his mark, thinking he was Starsky and Hutch and shooting his mouth off. That's what I was like at that age – I was going to be the next Jonah Bloonsbury. Thank God that didn't pan out. Anyway, Morrow turns out to be human. Seems as disinterested as I am. Asking the right amount of questions; looking concerned, being seen to do his bit, but fully aware that it's pointless; just dying to get back to the station for a slash and a cup of tea. I admire that in a young detective. Look good in front of the public, then forget about it half a minute later. The way forward.

Not that anyone cares. No one seems to know the guy and you can bet when he gets out of hospital he won't be seeking the help of the law to gain his vengeance.

Constables Kelly and Bathurst do their bit. Kelly looks moderately perturbed at the obvious lack of interest from CID, but he ought to know better. Hard to tell about Bathurst. A closed book. A very impressive cover mind, although perhaps too young for these old hands.

DC Morrow appears from a shop, looking like a man who wants to be somewhere else. I detach myself from an old wife who claims to have seen everything. I was hopeful at first until I realised she had obviously been on another planet when the assault took place and was merely glad of the excuse to talk to a man all afternoon.

‘What’s the story, Tom?’

Consults his notebook. Very efficient.

‘Got a bit of a description from the shop assistant. Not great, but enough to stick into the computer, see what we can get. Apart from that, not much at all, sir.’

I nod, turn away, look up and down the street. Cold, grey afternoon, the Christmas lights on and looking pathetic. A thousand shoppers and they all look miserable.

Still haven’t bought anything for Rebecca. I have no idea what you buy twelve year-old girls these days. Don’t want to look like an idiot. Buy her some toy they advertise on the TV, when for all I know she’s already busy doing drugs and men. Tough decision. I’ll do my usual and ask one of the women at the station.

Already got the boy his Rangers change strip. Nearly choked in the shop when I had to buy it.

I shrug. ‘Fancy a cup of tea, Tom?’

Morrow nods. ‘Sounds brilliant.’

A last look around the scene of the crime. Kelly and Bathurst appear to be running out of people to interview. Nothing much else to do. You might never know an incident had taken place.

‘Right then, constable,’ I say to him, and off we go.

4

The auburn hair obsessive loony sits in the cinema, enjoying the dark. Skywalker and Vader. Good and evil, the eternal struggle. He itches. His head twitches with each swipe at the Jedi, he cheers when the hand is severed, his shoulders move in time with the beating of his heart. He kicks the chair in front, imagining he’s been taken by the Dark Side. Which is more or less accurate. (He’s actually been taken by a combination of poor genetic material – his father used to be a stuntman on Bill and Ben the Flowerpot Men, and no one knew who his mother was; poor upbringing, being raised mostly by a convent worth of sadistic nuns; a disastrous first sexual encounter at the age of twenty-one; a good stiff kicking at the hands of a gang of mutant forest pygmy women at the age of twenty-three; and a lifelong belief in mermaids, fairies, Santa Claus and the flatness of the earth, which have left him open to ridicule by all but the most tolerant. But the Dark Side will cover it.)

Every few seconds he glances at the woman in front, though she doesn't notice. Auburn hair. Followed her into the cinema. At first he thought it was Emma, there in the flesh, but he knew it couldn't be. The more he looks, the more he sees the differences, the more he convinces himself of the similarities. She sits alone, and he wonders what kind of woman goes to the cinema unaccompanied? What message is she sending out?

And so the film lumbers on and he sits and waits and revels in it, and cannot keep his eyes off the hair of the woman a few seats away.

It will be dark when they get out, the streets will be quiet, of that he is confident. His first target, the first auburn haired woman who he had randomly stumbled across, had managed to get away. But this time, Bible Balthazar will not be thwarted.

And as the credits roll, and the woman who might well be Emma rises from her seat, he bides his time, and listens to the thumping of his heart.

And the woman of his temporary obsession, contemplates the call she will make to her boyfriend when she gets home, and the stupid argument that is to be continued, unaware that this night she will never reach her front door.

5

Monday night, Christmas bash. Private room at the Holiday Inn in the centre of town, well out of our patch. DJ playing rotten music and the horrors of the karaoke to come. We're all expecting to hear Bloonsbury's drunken rendition of *Can't Help Falling in Love* for the three hundredth time, and a lot worse besides. I've always managed to keep my vocal cords to myself, except for four years ago when I inadvertently performed *Brown Eyed Girl* half naked, with an empty bottle of Budweiser stuffed down my boxers; but Bloonsbury is out there every year, running the gamut of easily murdered Elvis songs.

It's just after midnight and already the party's beginning to break up. You get the sensible crowd who disappear home early, then you can guarantee the remaining hard core will be here until it's time to go to work tomorrow morning. There's always a lottery to get the day off, which I never win, but since Peggy kicked me out I spend half the year going into work straight from a long night before anyway. One more day just before Christmas doesn't make any difference.

The Super is long gone. The chocolates were hardly off the table and she was out the door. Her old man gets in from Washington tonight, so she's off back to the castle in Helensburgh to warm up the bed, though from what they say she'll probably be asleep by the time he shows up.

Herrod looks miserable. I expect Bernadette's got a chastity belt on him and has melted down the key. She's got her two weans and now there's no need for any further sex. She's got the classical skelped arse face and every time I meet her I wonder all the more what the hell he was thinking. Not that the first Mrs Herrod was any better.

'Same again, Sergeant?' Dragged from people watching by the familiar chant. Smokey room, bloody noise, *Girls Just Wanna Have Fun* and a few poor saps making an arse of themselves on the dance floor. Including, I can't help but notice, WPC Bathurst, stunning in a skin tight white number. She's got a few of her type running after her but I think I might make a go of it myself, nearly twice her age though I am. Not quite drunk enough yet.

'Aye, no bother,' I say to the boss. He asks the same of Herrod then plods morosely off to the bar.

Taylor has been on edge all evening. Seems to think that if he lets his concentration slip he might end up in the same position as last year, i.e. up to his armpits in bed with DS Murphy from Clarkston. Don't think he's ever told Debbie about it but it's plagued him ever since. I've said to him; if you're going to screw around behind your wife's back then it's the same as anything else. You've got to give it a hundred percent or it won't work out. He never listens. One drunken shag, then he fended Murphy off for a couple of months until she lost interest. He's spent the last year feeling like a total bastard, hoping that the missus never finds out. I suspect, however, that she might not even care.

Herrod drains a Bacardi and coke. I mean, a thirty-nine year old man drinking Bacardi and coke, for God's sake.

'Jonah's been saying all month that he's not singing this year. It's offensive to the King, he says.'

Light a smoke and laugh. Have to admit to it being a snort by now. That's vodka for you.

'So what's he been doing for the last ten years?'

'Blaspheming. Says he's repented. Never again. The King is God, an all that shite.'

We both look over at Bloonsbury, the great Elvis apologist; three tables away, spectacularly fucked out of his face on cheap whisky and in the process of making a monumental idiot of himself over some young tart from out of our patch, who none of us has ever seen before.

'Who's that he's drooling over?'

Herrod shrugs and lights up. 'Some stupid bitch from Springburn. Wee scrubber.'

'He's got a chance though.'

'No way. The man can't get it up when he's sober, never mind in that fucking state. His penis hasn't seen any action since Beattie walked out. Even then, it hadn't got behind enemy lines for about eight year.'

Bloonsbury rests a hand on the scrubber's knee, doesn't take long before he slips it under her skirt. The scrubber does not protest. Herrod grunts, shakes his head, and turns away. Jealous.

'Bastard.'

Taylor, the white knight, returns with the alcohol. Notice, with dismay, that he's moved onto orange juice. He parks himself, distributes the booze, looks morosely around the dance floor. In the midst of the tumult the DJ has stuck on *Lady in Red*, sending most sane men running to the toilet to heave; and everyone else onto the floor in rapturous convulsions of concupiscence, slabbering all over each other and practically having sex where they stand.

Standard format every year. The arrival of the slow crap means that in a minute we'll be subjected to an hour of karaoke, before we get three hours of house rubbish, followed by twenty minutes of *Wonderful Tonight*. After which they'll toss those of us who haven't managed to fix up a shag out into the streets. I hope to be in the fixed-up-a-shag brigade and notice with some satisfaction that WPC Bathurst is sitting out the slowie.

'What's the matter with you?' I say to Taylor.

He doesn't notice. I repeat it. He looks round, shrugs.

'Just thinking about Debbie,' he says.

Have a horrible feeling that if I pursue my line of enquiry he's about to get maudlin and am in no frame of mind to listen to that. Change the subject.

'John says that Jonah isn't going to do Elvis this year. Blasphemy, apparently.'

Taylor grunts. 'Fucking Elvis,' he says.

We look at Bloonsbury, his face now surgically attached to that of the scrubber. If she sucks all the alcohol out of him he might wake up to what he's letting himself in for. As it is, even if he doesn't submit to the full horrors which await him, he's still going to suffer the ridicule of all fair minded men for snogging a pit bull in front of us all. Bloody idiot.

'If we're lucky, he'll be too carried away with Lassie there,' says Herrod, 'an all the singing will pass him by. What do you think?'

Neither of us answer. There's no way he won't sing. We descend into morose silence and watch the doings on the dance floor. I could be wrong, but it seems that Police Constable Hodson is having sex with some minging tart from Shettleston. Hard to tell and I strain to see properly. They're clamped pretty close together,

her skirt's bunched up and I'd swear he's got his dick out. I laugh, take a large drain of the vodka tonic and sit back.

The music comes to a halt, couples detach, apart from Hodson and his tart who waddle over to a dark corner, and the DJ starts exhorting idiots to go up and sing. Everyone looks at Bloonsbury and the man does not disappoint. Accepting the rapturous and ironic applause, he removes himself from his hound dog and makes his way towards the microphone. Mumbles something to the DJ and turns to his audience. Winks and points at the wolf. Herrod and I burst out laughing. This could be even funnier than usual.

And then, as if Elvis is watching and can't stand to be blasphemed, we are treated to some divine intervention. A sober polis with a moustache walks through the room. Everyone looks at him. He stands out a mile. Makes his way towards our table. Me and Taylor look at each other and mouth 'fuck', just as Bloonsbury fluffs the first line of his song, smiling at the Rottweiler as he does so.'

The moustache arrives. Detective Constable Comedian. We are not impressed. Bang goes my tryst with Bathurst. He stands at the table, looks down at us. The lot of the polis. To get your life constantly interrupted by work, even when you're not having a good time.

He bends forwards, starts shouting into Herrod's ear. Herrod's face drops onto the table and he looks morosely over at Bloonsbury. 'Shall I stay?' he's warbling, and no you bloody well shan't is the reply. You're obviously out of here, mate, with crime to investigate. Taylor and I nearly reach over and kiss each other. No pleasure greater than thinking you're about to be dragged off then finding it's some other poor sod who's in the soup.

Herrod gets up, head shaking and looking like a pishing wet day in Largs. Taylor and I clink glasses and watch him trudge over to Elvis and mutter something at him. Then with a 'Fuck's sake' shouted into the microphone, Bloonsbury removes himself from the stage and starts the long trudge back to work. Grabs his coat, gives the stankmonster a grimace and he and Herrod troop out to the ribald cheering of the rest of us. It's times like this that make it all worthwhile.

I survey the scene with renewed good humour. Constable Edwards gets up and starts a passable Prince impersonation, taking his top off as he goes – really, these young polis should learn to keep everything undercover until they've got some chest hair – and I, flushed with unexpected romantic bravado, decide it's time to make my move on Bathurst.

I stub out the smoke, excuse myself from Taylor. He nods, doesn't mind – he's smiling at last – and I worm my way over. She's standing with her back to the wall under a picture of John Lennon in a policeman's helmet – some wanker's idea of a joke – and looking gorgeous with a glass of white liquor in her delicate little hands. She smiles at me and she's alone. Good start. Like scoring a goal in the first minute. I manage to stop myself doing that drunk thing where you lean on the wall next to the bird and drool on her. Keep a respectful distance.

'How you doing, Evelyn?'

A reasonable opening. Nothing fancy, nothing smart. Nice and easy does it.

She smiles and nods, not intimidated by having a drunk, thirty-nine year-old detective sergeant hitting on her.

'I'm fine,' she says. 'You? That's a nice jacket you're wearing.'

Two-nil.

I smile – there's a lot of smiling going on. I hope nobody's watching or they'll vomit. It's got to be done, though.

'Thanks. You're not looking too bad yourself.'

'Do you like this dress?' she says. No, not says, gushes. Her lips are moist, her nipples are hard and straining against the material, her eyes are showing glorious signs of intoxication.

'Like it? It's fucking stunning, Hen.' Hesitate, think about it; might as well jump in head first. 'You're fucking stunning.' I'm all charm, me.

She laughs. Three-nil. Think she's going to say something, but doesn't. Her eyes say it all though. She's gagging for it. Probably heard about me from at least fifteen other women at the station. I'm drunk, horny, and I feel about eighteen years old. There's no stopping me now. Caution to the wind.

‘I was thinking of leaving here. You know. All this karaoke crap. Fancy coming back to my place?’

She laughs again. I could shag that laugh.

‘I don't think so.’

What? Three-one.

‘Why not?’ Try not to sound desperate.

‘Well, it wouldn’t be right.’

Three-two. What’s she talking about?

‘Why?’ Maintain control.

‘Well. You’re old enough to be my father.’

Oh.

An equaliser, a winner and at least fifteen more goals just to rub it in.

She has the decency to look a bit embarrassed after that remark but once the ball’s in the net, it’s in the net. Contemplate a rearguard action, possibly a scorched earth policy, decide the better of it. Everyone’s interests will be best served by a quick withdrawal.

I shrug. ‘Right enough, then,’ I say.

She laughs, looks embarrassed again, doesn’t say anything. The final whistle blows, I turn my back and walk off. Imagine that every other git in the place is laughing at me. Find Taylor sitting alone at the table, looking morose again.

‘No’ get a lumber, then?’ he says.

I nod, sneer, start to make my way to the bar. ‘Want something stiffer this time?’

Taylor thinks. ‘Why not? Johnnie Walker.’

Right. I mince off to the bar, feeling like I’ve had my balls cut off and determined to get even more tanked out of my face than usual. Look to the middle of the floor to watch Edwards nearing the end of his Prince performance. Not surprisingly, he’s bollock naked and making a total arse of himself. He may have no chest hair, but at least his pubes are in fine form.

Fucking idiot.

6

Tuesday morning, the top end of Cambuslang, nearly to Halfway. A cordoned off road, with the usual ghouls a few hundred yards away.

The body's long gone, and will currently be under the knives of Baird and Balingol, the pathologists from Hell. Butchery with a sharp knife and a smile. I didn't see it, of course. Only got here this morning. Herrod said it was horrific; a bloody mess. Shredded. Glad I missed it. Dead bodies still give me the willies.

Crawled in, massively hung over, just after eight this morning, to find the place had gone berserk. A major murder three days before Christmas. All hands on deck, with Bloonsbury in charge of the sinking ship. Very brave. He's back at the station now, co-ordinating all the crap that has to go on. Taylor's been roped in as well, not too happy about having to answer to the whims of drunken Jonah, but that's the polis for you.

They didn't do much last night, but the shit's flying this morning. House to house all the way up this street, and back out along the main road. They'll branch out soon, see what they can get from the surrounding streets.

At the moment they're estimating the time of death between half ten and half eleven. Most of this lot were in their beds by then, or watching TV. The drudgery of normal life. The body was found by some bloke about to take the dog for a walk. Didn't recognise her, such was the disfigurement of her face, but we've since learned that he knows her. We'll ask the right questions. You never know what these idiots will do, but instinct says it wasn't him. The guy's in shock. He'll probably need therapy – it's the modern way. If he can find someone to sue, he'll do that as well. In the old days you'd bugger off down the pub for a pint with your mates, have a laugh and forget all about it. Now, you can't solve anything in life without employing a psychotherapist and a solicitor and a life coach. The supermarkets'll be offering those services soon, wait and see. Bastards.

Herrod's up the other end of the street, house to house. In a better frame of mind this morning. He enjoys murder. Thinks it justifies his existence. Sometimes you'd think he'd commit murder, just to give them all something to investigate.

Bathurst is out there somewhere, going house to house. Saw her briefly this morning, and she was decent enough not to give me a 'made a dick of yourself last night, didn't you?' smile. Very professional, although she just looked miserable. Regrets turning me down, I expect.

PC Edwards approaches, closed notebook in hand, looking like a man who stripped naked in front of his peers last night, and regrets every minute of it. He was another one to make an attempt at Bathurst, I believe, and was no more successful than I.

'Didn't get much sleep, eh, Constable?'

He shakes his head. Daft bastard.

'Nice y-fronts, by the way. Think you'll ever get them back?'

He shifts uncomfortably. Itching to tell me where to go, I suspect. Can't, of course. He goes for the quick change of subject, which is all he can do.

'There's a woman over here you might like to speak to, sir. Knew the deceased.'

Fair enough. Can't spend too much time laughing at prepubescent constables when there's murder to be investigated. I nod my head and follow him to a terraced house, not far from the close where the body was discovered. Perhaps the street won't be such a barren desert of non-information after all. Don't feel up to interrogation, and hope that the woman wasn't a close friend of the victim who'll spend the interview blubbing. Can't cope with emotion after a big night out on the piss.

Walk into the front room. Ground floor house, where the sun never shines. Maybe in late afternoon. A drab little room, a few desultory Christmas decs, and a drab young woman sitting in the middle of it, looking as if she's upset because she's run out of Frosties. A cup of tea held between the hands, TV on with the sound off.

I sit down opposite her and she notices me for the first time. Constable Edwards stands by the door. Hope I don't look as bad as he does.

‘Detective Sergeant Lumberyard,’ I say.

She nods, drinks a noisy sip from her tea, looks at the silent television.

‘Mrs Eileen Sprott,’ volunteers Edwards from the door.

Hold my hand up to him. Constables should be seen and not heard. See him nod and retreat further behind that rough exterior. Other things to think about, such as how to explain to his fiancée all those photographs of him naked which’ll probably start turning up in the post. We polis are an unforgiving lot.

Mind on the job.

‘Mrs Sprott, I understand you knew Miss Keller.’

Wonder who’s been detached to inform the parents. Hope it’s not Bloonsbury himself. Feel sorry for them. Jonah breathing all over them, telling them they’re daughter’s mince.

She looks at me, another noisy slurp.

‘Well, aye. Not that well, but. Used to get the same bus from town sometimes.’

‘And when was the last time?’

‘Last night, you know. She seemed happy, so she did, and now she’s dead. Can’t believe it, so I can't.’

‘Where d’you get the bus from?’

‘Buchanan Street, you know. I work in a jewellers in the arcade, and she worked in Frasers or something like that. Part time, I think. Saw her about town sometimes, but it wasn’t as if we were that friendly.’

That’s good. The automatic distancing. Doesn’t want to associate too closely with the victim. A little bit of dishonesty never did anyone any harm, and it means she’s less likely to go to pieces on me.

‘And did you ever go out much in the evenings or weekends?’

‘Do I go out much? Of course I go out, what do you think I am? Some sad bastard with no friends?’

‘No, not you. Did you go out with Miss Keller?’

‘Oh.’ Dozey bitch. Pay attention. ‘Naw, naw, not much. Every now and again, you know, but not often.’

‘When was the last time?’

‘A couple of weekends ago, but I can’t really remember.’

Nod the head, look serious. Pretend to think.

'Did she say anything on the bus yesterday about what she was going to do last night?'

She looks at me, nodding. Face like a kid who wants to tell the teacher who threw the piece of chalk.

'Aye, that's the thing. She says she was going to the pictures, you know, that wee one along the road. The one that's showing *Return of the Jedi* twenty years after everyone else.'

'And did she say who she was going with?'

'Aye. Some bloke.'

'Any idea who it might have been?'

She shrugs. Difficult to know if she's telling us everything.

'Not sure really, you know. Some guy she's seen a few times. Think he's from around here somewhere, you know Cam'slang, but I'm not sure, you know.'

'And had you ever seen him?'

Big shake of the head. Drawing back before she gets too close.

'Naw, naw. I was always joking with her about getting a look at the guy, you know, but I hadn't seen him. Says he was good looking, but you never know, do you? One woman's Chateaubriand is another's tin of spaghetti hoops with sausages.'

Just what I was thinking.

She slurps her tea, then her eyes light up and she looks at the TV. Follow her gaze. It's some sad looking guy I've never seen before, and you can tell she's itching to turn the sound up. Leave her to it.

'Well, thanks very much, Mrs Sprott. We'll need you to come to the station later to make a statement.'

'Why? What have I done?'

'You haven't done anything. It's just procedure.' I love that innate trust of the polis. Course, she's right.

'Oh.' Looks back at the TV. Time to go.

I nod at Edwards, he opens the door and out we go, back into the cold of early morning. As we close the door behind us the TV is turned back up loud, and Mrs Sprott goes about the business of forgetting everything she knows about Ann Keller.

We stand outside the house and take a look up the street. At least twenty polis milling around doing the thing. Most of them will come up empty, but every now and again you get something like I just did. Put it all together, and you never know. There's a long way to go, and most of it'll be pretty boring. I start to trudge off, head down, wishing for once that I had a cup of tea, rather than a vodka and tonic.

'Why didn't you ask about Mr Sprott?' says Edwards, one pace behind.

I stop and look at him, shaking the head.

'Get me a cup of tea, will you Edwards?' I say, doing my best to look superior.

He looks chastened and walks off.

Because I'm hungover and I forgot, that's why I didn't ask about Mr Sprott. But he doesn't need to know that.

7

Almost four thirty and there's ten of us in the room. What will become the daily roundup, assuming this thing isn't solved inside the first day. Waiting for Bloonsbury to arrive and take charge. He's in with Miller giving her all the latest, and probably getting his bollocks torn off for not having caught the killer yet.

So he'll get shredded in there, then after this briefing he'll have to go out and face the hounds of the press, when he'll probably get shredded again. He'll consider this a pleasant interlude, if discussing this kind of thing can be pleasant They've got the photographs on the wall. Before and after, and it's not noticeably the same woman. Sure, we get murder in these parts, although this is Glasgow not Detroit; but not like this. Domestic, casual, accidental, thuggery, we get them every now and again, a few a year. But this; violent, savage, psychotic. I'm out of my depth, I have to admit, and happy I'm not in charge. I bet Bloonsbury's shitting his pants over this one, and God knows what state he's in, given the alcoholic abyss into which he's been plummeting these last few years. Poor bastard.

There's some muted conversation, but not much. Not with this on, not with those pictures on the wall. We're all waiting for Bloonsbury so we can go out and get on with it, or go home for the day and think about it all. Be thankful it wasn't our wife or daughter or whoever that had their entire body slashed to pieces, and hope that it doesn't happen again before we catch the animal who did it.

The domestic stuff keeps intruding there as well. Still no idea what to get Rebecca for her Christmas. Seeing them tomorrow, although at this rate I might have to cancel it. Pizza and presents, and I'll hand over the gift for their mother and hope I get something back. Gone a bit over the top this year. Diamond earrings, just under three hundred quid out of some place in the arcade in Buchanan Street. Money I can't afford for a present for my ex-wife who's shagging someone else. I don't think I'm trying to get her back, but then why else am I spending so much money? I'm confused, but that's the best way to be.

The door opens, and I am torn from the worsening morosity and pointlessness of my reflections. DCI Bloonsbury, looking as if he's just been savaged himself. Think he needs hospitalised. He's a big man, six-five maybe. Back row forward in his day, played a Scotland trial. Nearly made it, although in those days all you got for playing rugby was a lot of sore joints and goofy ears. Well, the way he walks now he certainly got the sore joints. I'm five ten and I could head butt the guy without needing to stretch. He's got the ruddy face of the alcoholic, and looks way beyond his forty-eight years. The man's a disaster, but somehow he's been managing to get by the past couple of years.

There was a time last year when he was almost kicked into touch. His wife had just upped and left him for Wee Alec, a plumber from Dundee, taking the kids and everything else of worth in the family. So the guy went over the edge, but somehow he clawed his way back. Got a lot of help. He's a bit of a hero round here, for one reason or another. Used to be the star, and people still want to look up to him, even though more and more of us are seeing through him.

So this was his crowning glory from last year. Just as he was at his lowest ebb, he came up with a beauty. Big murder case out this end of Glasgow. A poor wee woman bought it from some ski-masked weirdo wielding a kitchen knife and a multi-pack of bite-size chocolate bars. (You just don't want to know what he did with those.) So, the feeling was that he was going to be a repeat murderer, women all over the city were shitting their pants, and us lot were looking like a bunch of lemons. Bloonsbury was in charge, seemingly getting nowhere, then boom, out of nowhere, it suddenly all fell into place. The big man put it together, made the breakthrough, and we got the guy. Some sleazoid from the west end who denied it all the way to the joint, but we had him. Enough evidence to put away a thousand murderers.

Bloonsbury was the hero, feted in the papers, got that ugly mug on TV, had all sorts of people queuing up to suck his dick.

And he's been surviving on it ever since. Don't know how he did it, given the state he was in at the time, but it was good to see. Trouble is, of course, he's been getting all the big ones ever since, and not been doing too well. This'll be the last chance, and all you can imagine is him hitting the bottle even harder, and maybe, if he's lucky, his liver'll give out and he'll die before he can blow it.

He comes to the front of the room, looks like shit. Stares at us, we stare back. You can see he would rather just be down the pub staring at a full bottle of Glen Ord, or one of these other single malts he occasionally fancies himself as being able to tell the difference between.

'Right then, gentlemen,' ignoring the three women, 'all the facts. What have we got? You first, Herrod.'

Herrod nods, looks at his notebook.

'Victim, Ann Keller. Auburn hair, twenty-seven, bit of a looker. Had two part-time jobs. Ancillary at the Victoria, sales at Frasers in Buchanan Street in the town. Worked in the shop on Monday, was due in the hospital today.' He pauses, looks through the notes. Try not to let my mind wander, having heard all this stuff already. 'Went to the Classic cinema to see one of they *Star Wars* films. She was due to go with her boyfriend, one Christopher James from

Cambuslang, although the usherette remembers her as being on her own. He claims to have cancelled the date.'

Bloonsbury blurts in, Herrod doesn't look impressed. 'You been speaking to him, Jack?'

Taylor is roused from his perpetual melancholy. Either thinking about Debbie, the continuing depression over DS Murphy, or Rangers' failure in Europe.

'Been in with him most of the afternoon. No alibi for last night. Stayed in, watched tele. Can describe what was on, but he could have set the video. Looks pretty upset.' He shrugs. 'Don't know. Forensics have been over his flat, we'll see what they come up with. I'm guessing it'll be nothing. Don't think he's our man.'

'Why did he not go to the pictures?'

'Said they had a fight. Something to do with a necklace given to her by an ex-boyfriend.'

'Got a name?'

'Aye. Looking into it. We'll find him, get him in.'

'Could he have made the story up? Deflect attention, and all that?'

All right, it's not brilliant, but believe me, this is Bloonsbury a hell of a lot more switched on than he's been in months. Maybe he's going to go for this one. Wants to be the hero again. Get his name in the papers.

'Don't know. We'll talk to the guy, see what we come up with.'

'Right. Herrod, what else?'

Herrod looks pissed off. I can never decide whether he reveres Bloonsbury as the god-king of detectives, or whether he thinks he's an idiot.

'She leaves the pictures, walks home. Ten minute walk, she never gets there. Somewhere along the way she is accosted, strangled and stabbed.' Looks at his notebook. 'A hundred and twenty-three times, mostly in the face and chest.' Jesus. Who the fuck stabs someone a hundred and twenty-three times? Herrod looks at the women, slightly embarrassed, as if they might be delicate in some way. Old fashioned, Herrod. 'He pulled her into a close entrance before he did it, then left the body where he killed her. Found by some poor bastard who lives on the third floor. The deed couldn't have been done more than three or four minutes. The guy checks out, by the way.'

There's a bit of a silence. We're all mad, tough bastards here, but this kind of thing is always going to stick in the throat.

'Why do you suppose he did that?' says Bloonsbury.

'What?'

'Stab her over a hundred times.'

Herrod shrugs. 'I don't fucking know, do I?' he says.

'Aye, right, fine. Any ideas people?' says Bloonsbury looking around the room.

Keep my mouth shut on this one, I think. He wants to ask some idiot doctor with letters after his name and a mind for lunatics, not a bunch of polis more used to dealing with car theft.

DS Harrison speaks up. An attractive woman in her way, if a little brutish. Reminds me of my Aunt Maureen. I've heard tell she wears a chain around her waist, although have never had the desire to try and see for myself. Anyway, there's a rumour that she prefers the company of women, which is something I have to admire, because so do I.

'He knew her, hated her, got carried away with an act of vengeance.'

'Maybe,' says Bloonsbury. Never know with the guy if he's being cagey or slow.

I shrug, and decide to participate. 'The guy was hardly rational. From the ferocity of the attack we know that he absolutely lost it. You stab someone over a hundred times, you're not thinking straight.'

Bloonsbury sighs, shakes his head. 'Aye, I suppose you're right.' Starts rubbing his eye. The man needs a drink. 'I'll speak to that doctor, what's his name?'

'Arkansas,' volunteers a voice from the floor.

'Aye, right, how could I forget a fucking stupid name like that? All right, anything else? Did the ghouls at pathology have anything illuminating to tell us?'

Herrod. 'Aye. Apparently she'd had sex yesterday afternoon. There were still traces of semen in her,' and he looks shyly around the women folk again, 'you know, inside her. Unrelated to the murder. From that we've got male, mid-thirties, blood group AB neg, and that's our lot.'

I tell you, Baird and Balingol are something else. How did they manage to work out that the guy's male just from his semen?

'Ties in with the boyfriend, presumably,' says Bloonsbury, looking at Taylor.

'Aye,' says Taylor. 'Did it in the afternoon, in the toilets in his work in town, so he says. It was after that he told her about the present from the ex. She went ape, he kicked her out, the usual thing.'

'Right,' says Bloonsbury.

He looks around the room, not sure where else to go with this. Building up to his Lou Grant speech.

'Right,' he says again, 'this is a sick bastard we've got here. People are going be shitting their pants, so we need this guy off the streets before Christmas. So, I know we've all got things to do at this time of year, but the quicker we get this out the way, the more time we can spend on enjoying ourselves. So let's give it everything we've got for the next couple of days.'

Very inspiring.

'Right. We've got descriptions of the lassie going out on the news, phone lines open, and all that. You all know what you're doing, so get out there and get on with it. I've got to go and speak to the fucking papers.'

The meeting starts to break up. All hands on deck. Let's hope there's no more crime in the area for the next few weeks. Bloonsbury leads the way out the room and then we all start to shuffle after him. Taylor puts his hand on my shoulder.

'I need a drink, Sergeant. You coming?'

Where better to increase pressure in the investigation than from the pub? I nod and lead the way. The group disperses around the station, each with things to do. Not much conversation. All this is a little freaky. The thought that at some stage we're going to come face to face with this guy. And if we don't, it's because we'll have failed to do our jobs.

Almost out the door when Sgt Ramsey stops my steady progress towards the first vodka tonic of the day.

'Got something for you, Dallas.'

'What?' I don't look impressed.

'Aggravated assault in Westburn. Your show.'

Bugger. Bugger. Bugger. As Hugh Grant might say.

Taylor shrugs. 'See you in a couple of hours, Sergeant. I'll still be there.'

Aye, right.

8

Doubtless the world is quite right in a million ways; but you have to be kicked about a little to convince you of the fact.

Not number twenty-one from the book of Useful Police Philosophy. From the writings of Robert Louis Stevenson, in case you didn't know. Now, I'm not denigrating the guy, but really I don't give a shit. Books are not my thing, particularly ones which were written way back, when making love to someone meant that you sat on the end of the bed and told the woman how good she looked in pink. And I think I speak for most of my colleagues when I say that. If any of us ever has the time to read a book – and with all the detecting and drinking that has to be done, it isn't often – we like to settle down with a good crime thriller. Pick up some handy detective-type hints. *Literature* just isn't on the list.

However, there are dark forces which conspire to thrust it down our throats, whether we want to hear it or not. The dark force, in particular, is Superintendent Charlotte Miller, BA Hons in English Lit. Not that she charges around saying, 'Hoi, Lumberyard! Get that crime solved, and did you know I got a first at St Andrews?' She is a little more subtle than that, although not much. Lets her erudition spill out all over the place. Makes you want to punch her in the face. I'm a smart bastard and you're an ignorant little pleb, so do what I say. The attitude that launched a thousand rebellions.

Stevenson is her favourite. Always throwing in quotes, or

giving us some other little homily from his life. Very inspiring. My heroes are the Partick Thistle team who beat Celtic four-one in the League Cup final. Difficult to quote them however, any more than we would normally in life when we're beating up Catholics.

The woman is forty-four, and therefore younger than all the chief inspectors at her fingertips. This is, as you will imagine, a source of friction. Most of these guys are in their late forties, they're not going anywhere else, and they're from the 'women should be in the kitchen with the washing up' generation. Confronted with a woman who is a) smarter than them, b) in a position to tell them what to do, c) going places they can't even dream about, and d) much, much better looking, most of them spend their days in a foul mood, dumping on delinquent constables. Point d) may seem the most trivial and sexist of the lot, but you have to be realistic. If this woman looked like a Czech shot putter, modelled for Hound Monthly, chewed tobacco and bent iron bars with her teeth, I'm sure they could cope with it a lot better. But she's a dream. I'd have her before any of these strapping, ball crushing constables that pass through here – even the good looking ones like Bathurst – but there's no way Miller is going to go anywhere near the likes of me. It's not because she's married, because faithful she ain't. It's a power thing. She goes for people in power, people that can do things for her. And note that – people. Not just men. This woman would have fought on both sides of the Spanish Civil war, if you know what I'm saying.

She's married to a boring suit called Frank, who sells oatcakes or some shit like that abroad. So the guy's never here, which gives her plenty of time for bridge building. Met the bloke a couple of times and nearly fell asleep talking to him. One of the camel coat Ibrox brigade, turns up there about once a season and talks as if he knows a shit load about Scottish football, when in truth he doesn't know any more than any other comedian who supports the Rangers. Believe he's got designs on becoming a director, and they're welcome to each other.

It's nearly ten o'clock and me and Taylor are sitting in the pub. I've just arrived, he's been here since about five. Given that, he's remarkably cogent. Probably been making a pint last a few hours, since there was no one here to buy him a round.

The aggravated assault was the usual thing. Domestic, brothers, one of them ended up in hospital, the other's in a holding cell back at the station. They were fighting over a woman, which is no surprise at all, and she played the innocent, concerned bit of tottie throughout. Playing one off against the other, and if any of them should be in the slammer, it's her.

'Your round,' says Taylor, with the detective's eye for detail. I think I could dispute that but choose not to bother. Stub the remains of my seventieth smoke of the day into the McEwan's Lager ash tray. Make my way to the bar, catch the eye of the sultry barperson, Lolitta.

'Vodka tonic, and a pint of heavy,' I say, and she nods and goes about her business. It's a quiet night, there's no one else within hearing range and I wonder whether I should go for it. She's wearing a tight white top, displaying adequate amounts of cleavage, and as she bends down to retrieve the tonic from the fridge, I get a good view of her massive buttocks. Very sexy. She stands up, slightly flushed around the chops, not a bad looking girl. Nevertheless, decide against. Go for idle chatter.

'Can you no change the tape, Hen?'

She listens to the music for a second and shrugs.

'It's Christmas,' she says, pouring the pint.

'Aye, but it doesn't mean we have to listen to *I Wish it Could be Christmas Every Day* a hundred times, does it?'

She watches the smooth brown liquid slowly fill the glass, the light reflecting off its deep hues. Sound poetic? Can't stand the stuff myself, tastes like pishwater.

'If you don't like it you can go and drink somewhere else,' she says. 'That'll be five sixty-three, please.'

I can't go and drink somewhere else because every bar, restaurant, supermarket, shopping mall, airport, train station, telephone box, coal mine, whorehouse and public toilet is playing the same bloody tape. Decide it was just as well I didn't go for it and hand over a twenty pound note to piss her off. Then, drinks and change in hand, make my way back to the table. Sit down, suddenly occurs to me it's a few hours nearer Christmas and I still don't have anything for Rebecca. Look at the watch. Have to have something by five o'clock tomorrow evening. Bugger.

'What do you think of Bloonsbury?' says Taylor, licking the froth from his lips.

'What do I think of him?'

'Aye. Has he still got it? For a big case like this, I mean.'

'Fuck knows,' I say. 'I doubt it, but he seemed a bit more switched on this afternoon. But let's face it, the Addison case aside, what's he done in the last five years?'

No answer. There is no answer.

'So why,' I say, 'did she put him on this one?'

Taylor shrugs. 'So's he'll screw up, maybe.'

'Why?'

'It's like James Bond in *The Man With the Golden Gun*.'

I look at him. I have no idea what he's talking about.

'You'll have to explain that to me. You mean there's an Asian dwarf involved somewhere?'

'No, not the film, the book.'

'Never read it.'

'James Bond is washed out, at a dead end. He's been brainwashed by the Russians, the Secret Service have no more use for him. But, fuck, he's James Bond. They can't just pack him off to a desk job. So they send him after Scaramanga, the deadliest assassin in the world. If he kills him then he's proved his worth; if he gets killed then they don't have the problem of what to do with James Bond.'

'Oh, aye. So what happens?'

'What do you mean, what happens? He's James Bond, you idiot. What do you think happens?'

I nod and think about the analogy. He could be right.

'But Jonah Bloonsbury ain't no James Bond.'

Taylor lifts an eyebrow.

'Fucking right he's not. She's sailing him down the river and when he fucks up, he's history.'

Take my first drink, screw up my face. Put in too much tonic. How do I manage to still do that after seven or eight million of them?

'So then what?'

'We get it,' he says, shaking his head. 'Would have been Evans, but now that he's buggered off to his one bedroomed ruin in Arocher, we'll get stuck with it. And it'll probably be after he's killed again, and the press are baying for blood. Bloonsbury's won't be enough.'

'So?'

'So, we'd better start thinking about how we're going to get this guy.'

'Oh.' Work. 'So that's what you've been sitting here thinking about, is it?'

'Not just that,' he says, and I'm not sure I want to know to what he is alluding. 'Anyway, someone's got to do it, 'cause Jonah's probably face down in a ditch by now.'

'So what have you come up with for your five hours ruminations?'

He takes an especially large drink, licks the froth from his lips, lays his hands on the table.

'Bugger all. I was waiting for you.'

Very funny.

'I'm serious,' he says in reply to the look on my face, and I believe him. 'So, what have we got? Some weird bastard who slashes a woman to pieces. Total rage, cutting her up to the extent that she is unrecognisable.'

'Why not just leave it to the profilers?' I say. They have these sad folk who just sit there all day inventing people. Someone pishes against a wall and they spend three weeks compiling the psychiatric profile of the man, before deciding his brother stuck a carrot up his arse when he was three. It's their job, let them do it.

He points his finger at me. I hate it when he does that. 'Because they don't know fuck all, son,' he says.

He's right.

'So why so brutal to the face?' he says. It's like being at school.

'Personal grudge.' Think about those photographs. 'Deep personal grudge.'

He nods. 'Either against her, or someone who looks like her.' Fits the bill. 'I'll go for the latter. If he knew her we'll find out about it, but it doesn't feel right.'

'Could be some psycho who sort of knew her. Worshipped her from afar and all that shite. She didn't know anything about it, he makes his approach one night after the cinema, she rejects, he slashes her to pieces.'

He shakes his head. 'Maybe, maybe. I don't know. I like the sound of it being some fuck-up with no previous relation to her at all. Completely arbitrary. If she hadn't been there last night, she would never have got it. She was in someone else's place.'

'So, what? We're looking for some guy who's been dumped by a bird with auburn hair? That could be me.'

'Aye, well you've been dumped by just about every size, hair colour, personality type combination, so I'm not about to drag you in.'

'Thanks.'

'Don't mention it.' Another drink from the glass. Funny how he's managed to speed up now he's got someone to buy him a round. 'What we need is a description of the guy. She was walking along a main road, for God's sake, just come out of a busy cinema.'

'There were fourteen people at it.'

Shrugs. 'Whatever. You'd think the bloody usherette would be able to remember a few more faces.'

'You just can't rely on people,' I say.

'Ain't that the truth,' says Taylor, then with another long pull at his glass, he finishes off his pint. 'Buy you another, Lumberyard,' he adds, to general astonishment.

I nod, mouth partially open in surprise. Jack never buys a round at home. Now; two nights in a row.

Taylor makes his way to the bar, I look around the pub. The usual crew. One or two others from the station, but never too many. Most of them prefer the Whale, and they're welcome to it. Spit, sawdust and Slavic-style women with excessively hairy armpits.

The door to the pub opens, and with a portentous gust of cold wind, in walks Charlotte Miller. Raised eyebrows from the polis, and then we all try to pretend we haven't noticed.

Try not to choke on my vodka when she walks over to our table and sits down. Smile at her, but seem to have lost contact with most other forms of communication. Smell her perfume, breathe it in, try not to imagine her naked. She's wearing a fuck off blue trouser suit and, as usual after fourteen hours in the office, looks as if she just got dressed five minutes ago.

'It's a cold night,' she says, rubbing hands. Her own, not mine.

I look at her and nod. Feel like I've got a hand on my throat and on my bowels. Classic feelings of intimidation.

'What happened with the assault? Brothers, was it?'

'Aye.' Try to talk normally. 'We've got one at the station, and the other's in hospital.'

'Over a woman?' she says.

I nod. It's easier than having to open my mouth. She smiles at this and shakes her head.

'You men are all alike.' Wait for the literary quote, but Stevenson mustn't have written anything about men only thinking with their dicks.

Taylor returns with the drinks and nearly drops his pint. Makes a quick recovery. Give the guy his due. He's suspicious of her, but she doesn't turn him into a quivering blob of jelly, the way she does me.

'Hello, Jack. Been here long?' she says. Bitch. Must know exactly how long he's been here. Now me, that would have me in a tangle of deceit and idiocy, trying to explain why I'd spent so long in the pub. But so what if Bloonsbury had given us this big Jock Stein speech? It was the end of the day and if we had nothing else immediate and wanted to sit in the boozer, we could. But I would still be trying to justify myself. Jack's too cool for that; or past caring.

'About five hours,' he says. 'Can I get you a drink?'

She nods. 'Whisky, neat, thanks.'

He turns back to the bar. She taps her fingers on the table. Long fingers, and I imagine them all over my body. Swallow, and try to think of something else.

'What are you doing for Christmas?' she says.

'Working.' Stick to one word answers.

She smiles, almost looks understanding. 'Someone's got to. Frank and I are going to Braemar.'

I nod, not surprised. Braemar. Brilliant. Eat some smoked salmon for me.

'When are you seeing the children?' she asks.

'Tomorrow evening.' She asks about the children every now and again. I think she learned to do it on a management weekend. One of these things where they pitch twenty people into a bog on Benbecula with a box of matches, a pot noodle and three sheets of toilet paper, and tell them to survive for a fortnight.

'Oh,' she says. Taylor is labouring behind a guy at the bar trying to decide between cheese and onion and dead goat flavour. 'You won't be late, though?'

I kind of gawp. What's she getting at? I don't see this coming at all. She almost sounds nervous, except that it's not a word I could possibly associate with her. I sort of shake my head and say, 'I doubt it.'

She taps her fingers.

'I was wondering if you'd like to come over later. To the house, I mean. Frank's going to Aberdeen on business for the night. Just like him, Christmas Eve, for God's sake, but you know what he's like. Meeting him in Braemar on Thursday morning.'

Various thoughts flash about my head. Vague things about Aberdeen and Frank. Push them to the side. She's inviting me to dinner, at her place, when her husband's going to be out of town. Fucking hell.

I nod. 'Aye, I think I could manage that.' Hope I don't sound like an idiot.

She smiles. I could eat that smile. 'Great. I'll speak to you tomorrow.'

Taylor returns, glass in hand, lays it down in front of her. Wonder if he notices how pale I've become. Feel white, but I may not have descended that far.

She smiles at him, lifts the glass. 'Cheers,' she says, and before we can make a grab for our drinks she's downed it in one. Looks at the two of us. Having said what she came to say, and realising she isn't about to get any meaningful conversation, she stands up.

‘Right,’ she says, ‘thanks for the drink, Jack. See you both tomorrow.’

We nod, she turns and walks out, leaving a trace of French perfume in the air. We watch her go, then the door is closed behind her and we turn to alcohol, our only friend.

‘What the fuck was that all about?’ says Taylor eventually.

I’m not sure, and shake my head.

‘I think she wants to dominate me even more than she does already,’ I say after a while.

9

Early morning. Auburn hair-obsessive loony man stands in the newsagent. Looking for a present for his aunt; through endless boxes of chocolates. Presented with a glorious array of enticing packages, and every one, everything he looks at, reminds him of Emma, and reminds him of that bloodied body. He sees blood spraying into the air, he feels the knife damp in his hands, he feels the soft flesh of the face splay under the force of his stabbing. It all makes him feel vaguely unwell, nauseous, but he decides it’s because he hasn’t had any breakfast. He wonders if he should go for a cup of tea. Looks at the watch, almost time to get to work. Plate of Cheerios would sort him out.

He can’t get the vision of what he did out of his head. It was supposed to give him relief, but he is beginning to accept that it wasn’t Emma under that frantic knife. And he still wants to see her, but doesn’t want to do to her what he did last night to that woman. That would be...unnecessary.

He looks over the middle row of books, feels a flurry of the heart, a coldness in the blood. Then he realises it’s not her, not Emma, the auburn haired woman on the other side of the shop. She looks up, notices him staring at her, and looks away. The hair’s the same. Maybe a bit shorter, and curlier.

He starts to follow as the girl walks slowly out of the shop. Maybe it is Emma. Those eyes, he saw the light in those eyes. Maybe she had plastic surgery so he wouldn't recognise her. That's the sort of thing women do.

He walks out into the cold, grey morning. Eyes narrowed. Heart beats fast. She hasn't noticed yet as she walks along the crowded road. Too many people.

Could he do it again? Only two days ago he was thinking he might be some sort of serial guy. Bible Buckminster, or Bible Basil, whatever his name was going to be. He was going to be the next thing, the next bloody murderer of any hue. And what had he done? Lost control and then staggered home to throw up, like a pathetic little child who couldn't take it. Staggered home, throwing up all the way, throwing up when he walked into the house; and still the thought of it turns his stomach.

Emma steps under the bus shelter and waits. Seven or eight other people there. He follows her and stands at the side. Glances over occasionally, but she doesn't look back. Suffers the churning in his stomach, feels sick every time he thinks of what he did. Could he do it again? This time she catches his eye and he recognises that look. Fear. Why were they all frightened of him? They didn't know what he was going to do. Maybe it wasn't fear. Maybe that's what he is looking for it to be. Maybe she's just got indigestion. So he smiles pleasantly and wonders which bus she is going to catch. He looks at his watch. He has to get to work, no point in arousing suspicion. There are too many people about anyway. This isn't a quiet street after dark. Morning rush hour is no time to make advances upon women, even when they ask for it. Gives her another look, which she avoids. Time to go to work.

He turns away from the bus stop, walks across the road and is nearly hit by a taxi. A horn blares.

10

Christmas Eve. Bloody awful morning. Had far too much to drink last night. Sat up until some time after three with Taylor, listening to all his marital difficulties. Wondered at first why he seemed reluctant to go home then, as the lager took over, he started telling me all about it, and I got what I had managed to avoid at the party on Monday night. The 'my wife's having an affair' speech. It comes to us all, and you hear it so often you become immune – until you're the poor sod in question.

Debbie's all right – not that I'd touch her with a stick – but she's a few years younger than him and that's always going to tell in the job. She's a teacher at Cathkin High, a recondite dump up on the hill above Cambuslang. I went there when it had just opened in the early seventies, all shiny new bunsen burners and gleaming gymnastic equipment. Now the only things that are shiny are the razors the pupils use to chop the drugs and she returns home every night with new horror stories of student brutality and didactic ineptitude. Combine that with similar tales of wretchedness from Taylor, and you can tell what fun nights they must have in. I kept thinking of the irony of him feeling guilty all year about his flingette with DS Murphy, when Debbie has spent most of that time impaled on the biggest dick in town.

So I arrive this morning, ten minutes after eight, feeling like shit, looking like the inside of a football boot. Sewer breath from Hell, totally forgotten about having to buy a present for Rebecca, and a night in with the station god-queen. Saw Alison on my way in – think it's going to be a regular feature – and she nearly wet herself laughing.

Cup of coffee to start the day, then a phone call downstairs. The thug brother had been released with the usual stipulations, and I was happy because it meant I could forget about it for a while. Ten minutes later we got a message from the hospital that brother number two had just unexpectedly died. Brain haemorrhage, as far as they could tell, but they weren't sure. So we have to go and get the first idiot and bring him back in. Up the charge to murder or manslaughter, whatever. Fortunately, that bit's out of my hands.

The clock has now ticked its way round to just after ten, and the office is in a state of ferment. Seventeen burglaries overnight, three reported rapes, a couple of major assaults, another ten or so minor ones, a shit load of other petty criminal activity, and in the middle of all that some guy walks in and says he saw Ann Keller not far from the cinema, sometime after eleven on Monday night. Several people are wetting themselves with excitement. Bloonsbury presumably, but it's hard to tell. He has looked this morning – if it's possible – worse than me.

I've been delegated one of the rape cases, just so a bad morning can get a little bit worse. Young Asian girl shafted by three teenagers on her way home from a party. White boys, of course. Father's going mental. Not at the three white boys – silent fury and a gun to the back of the head for them, should he ever find them – but at the mother for phoning us. There's no justice like you're own justice, and you keep yourselves to yourselves. Anyway, I got packed off with WPC Grant to start the ball rolling. Did our stuff, looked like we were investigating, and now the girl's downstairs making a statement to a couple of female officers, all us men being bastards and incapable of sympathy, such is the modern way of thinking. Fine by me, and now I'm back on the murder case, detailed to follow up various reported sightings of Ann Keller the previous evening. Most of them are futile – nearly half are downright impossible, given what we already know of her movements, and the rest are dubious. The only one to make any sort of sense was the bloke who came to the station. Everything he said tied in with what we already knew, and he came up with a good enough description of the guy we're looking for. Assuming, of course, that this bloke isn't him. These headcases move in mysterious ways. We got a photofit out of it anyway, and that'll be on the news all day. These things never actually look human, but sometimes they get results. Course, I've to spend the rest of the day following up all the other crank calls to see where it gets us, which will be nowhere.

On my way out, I bump into Sergeant Harrison. I hope I look human and experience has taught me to keep toothpaste in the desk drawer, so I'm no longer setting fire to everything upon which I breathe.

She's pinning something on the noticeboard about a police charity evening early in the New Year. I hate those things. Stand and watch her for a second, before realising I'm staring.

'Eileen,' I say.

She turns, smiles.

'Rough night last night, Dallas?' she says.

I ignore it. 'I need some advice.'

She sticks in the last drawing pin, checks it's straight, and steps back.

'Don't drink so much, and get to bed earlier.'

Everyone hates a comedienne.

'Very funny. What do you know about twelve year old girls?'

She smiles. I like Eileen Harrison. Not sure why. Maybe it's because I'm pretty sure there's no chance I'll ever get her into bed. Respect, you see.

'Well, I was one once, if that's any help.'

'I need an idea of what to get Rebecca for Christmas.'

'Your daughter?'

'Aye.'

She purses her lips.

'How much money are you spending?'

Not sure that I want to divulge that information to Detective Sergeant Harrison. Don't want to be judged.

'Fifty pounds,' I say anyway.

'She mature for her age?'

Feel like I'm under investigation. Imagine Sergeant Harrison viciously interrogating suspects.

'Not sure. I mean, you can't tell, can you? Who knows what she's like when I'm not there. She could be doing drugs and boys and all that stuff, for all I know.'

Purses her lips again, looks disapproving. 'You've been in the job too long, Dallas. Not all children are baby adults, doing dodgy deals and out for what they can get.'

'Aye, but some of them are.'

'Fine. Get her a piece of jewellery then. If she's older than her years that'll do her, and if she's not it'll make her feel mature, and show that you respect her. How's that?'

I look at her, she smiles and turns. Why is it that woman have so much more common sense than men? Must be genetic. We got testosterone, and they got common sense and all those orgasms.

'What kind of jewellery?' I say pathetically to Eileen Harrison's back.

She turns, still smiling. Pitying smile, this time.

'Use your imagination, Dallas, for fuck's sake, she's your daughter.' And off she goes to chew the bollocks of hardened criminals.

Suitably chastened, I make my way out of the station.

*

Three down, seven to go. This is going to be a long day. Sitting in the drab waiting area of a small lawyer's office in Tollcross as a result of a phone call from an Ian Healy, who says he saw our murder victim on Monday night. Sounds a little more plausible than the others, particularly the last one, a seventy-three year-old man who claimed to have seen her in Woolworths in Rutherglen at half past ten yesterday morning. Get a life, you sad bastard, I said to him, and walked out the door.

I didn't really say that.

I'm sitting under the watchful eye of a curious secretary, all ravenously curly hair and lipstick. Face like bread and butter pudding, the typical Glasgow polis sceptic. I want to arrest her for something, just to piss her off.

The door opens, out steps Mr Healy, preceded by a small man in tears, who looks suspiciously at me as he walks by.

'Don't worry,' says Healy to him, 'we'll get her back for you.'

The man half turns, gives a watery smile and is gone. There goes an interesting little story, the details of which I couldn't want to know less.

I stand up, take Healy's outstretched hand.

'Detective Sergeant Lumberyard,' I say. Firm grip, the guy's young and doesn't look like an idiot. We're a couple of goals to the good already.

'Come in, Sergeant,' he says, and ushers me past the secretary.

Walk in, simple enough office, sit down.

'Sorry about Mr McKay,' he says. 'Problems with his dog.'

'Ah,' I say. Don't give a shit, to be fair to the lad Dog.

'Very weird situation,' says Healy.

'I believe you might have seen Ann Keller on Monday evening?' I say, cutting to the business end.

He nods, looks serious, leans forward. 'Aye. Monday night, on my way home from the pub, you know. So it would have been some time not long after eleven.'

'Was she alone?'

He nods, looks even more serious. I hate lawyers. 'No, well, kind of, but there was a guy walking just behind her. I didn't pay that much attention, but I got the impression he was following her, hassling her, you know.'

'So why didn't you say anything? Give her some help?'

He swallows, looks guilty. The question wasn't fair – implied that the woman might not be dead if he'd done something. Doesn't do any harm to keep them on their toes, however.

'I don't know. You don't, do you? He wasn't speaking to her or anything. It was just an impression I got. I forgot about it until I saw the television last night.'

'Aye, fine.' Shuffle about in the pocket, produce a photofit picture, pass it across the desk.

He studies it, shakes his head. 'No, definitely not him.'

Good. That was a picture of Herrod, and the first two I showed it to already identified him as the killer. It'd be pretty funny if it was, but unfortunately he's got a hundred and fifty police witnesses as an alibi.

Pass over another picture. He looks at it, shakes his head again. Pass the third over, the real one this time. He studies it closely, then shakes his head again.

'No, not him either. At least I don't think so.'

I take it back off him, look at it, shove it back in my pocket. These bloody pictures are crap. It could be anybody. It could be this guy sitting across the desk.

'Do you think you'd be able to come down to the station later and make up one of these for the man you think you saw?'

Slight twitch, hesitation – just enough – then, 'Sure. Not for a couple of hours, but I could do it this afternoon.'

Don't betray your thought. 'That'd be great, thanks Mr Healy.' Wonder. You never know what these headcases are going to do. It takes a mad bastard to invite the police in when you've committed murder, but then it takes a mad bastard to knife a woman over a hundred times.

Five minutes later I'm walking down the stairs, staring at the photofit. It's not right, but it's not a million miles away. And our witness only got a brief look at him, so who knows how accurate the picture is in the first place? There was never enough there to suggest Healy's our man, just a suspicion, and if I'd still been hungover I would have missed it. There's a lot said for gut feelings, but I usually find they come to nought or make you look like an idiot. Sometimes, however, they pan out and then you look like a genius, so you have to go with them. Let the guy come into the station and then see what we can make of him. Won't be hard. Find out what pub he was in, who he was with, check it out. Could have asked him in there, but didn't want to give anything away. If the guy suddenly disappears and another fifty murders are committed, I'm going to feel terrible.

Another check of the list. Four down, three to go.

11

Two o'clock – the time I fixed for Healy to pay us a call – came and went without a sign of the guy. Gave him some time to be late and then we all leapt into action. I had communicated my doubts about him to Bloonsbury, so when he didn't show, Jonah pissed in his pants.

Taylor and I went round there. The office had been closed up, but then it is Christmas Eve. Went to his house and he wasn't there, went to the secretary's house, found her up to the armpits in

Christmas cooking and looking as miserable as ever. She told us that Healy had left the office not long after twelve for a lunch appointment and that as far as she knew he intended going to the station thereafter. Claimed ignorance as to where he was having lunch but the woman's his secretary for God's sake, she must have known. Taylor persuaded me not to employ thumbscrews and we left without any further information.

Now nearly five and I've got to get going. Pizza and presents with the children. Found five minutes to disappear into a jewelers this morning, in between interviewing suspects, and got Rebecca a gold chain. Good for women of all ages, according to the lassie in the shop. Bit nervous about what their mother is going to think of the diamond earrings. Shall see her briefly when I hand back the kids. Not as nervous as I am about what is to come later in the evening. Dinner with Charlotte Miller.

Walk into Taylor's office to say goodnight. We're all just out of the afternoon meeting, where we had the usual exchange of ideas. Things are moving forward. Plenty of calls from the public to follow up and now a juicy suspect has hoved into view. Pretty much decided that the boyfriend is off the hook. Doesn't have the right look about him, and the story about the necklace from the ex panned out. Checking out a few others from Ann Keller's roll-call of friends and relatives, but I still go for it being some psycho who hardly knew her.

Anyway, all we've got at the moment is our lawyer. However, once the initial gut feeling has passed, you have to be sceptical. It can't possibly be this simple. The guy wouldn't just present himself to us, no matter how much of a headcase he is. He probably hasn't turned up at the station because he's been knocked down by a bus, or he simply forgot. Anything. Hasn't stopped Bloonsbury breaking out into assholes and shitting himself with excitement, however.

Taylor looks up from his desk. Tired eyes, puffy face, the man needs a break. That and vast amounts of alcohol.

'I'm off, Jack. Got to go do the good father routine.'

He grunts. His desk is an unruly mass of paper. I've got a feeling that's the way he wants it, to keep him here well into the evening. Debbie must be out with her well-hung gymnastic instructor again. Feel huge pangs of sympathy for the man. Know what it's all about and all he has is his job.

'Exchange of presents?' he says, voice weary.

'Aye. God knows what they'll have bought me this year.'

He grunts out a laugh, face doesn't change.

'Right. I'm going to stay here for a while. Think Jonah's going to be working late. Two sad bastards together. See if I can help him save his career again.'

'He still ain't James Bond.'

Taylor stares into the morass of paper on his desk. Might be thinking about what I just said, might be thinking about a lot of things. Looks up eventually.

'Whatever. At least he seems to be going for this one. Mind in gear, cut back to one bottle of whisky a day. We'll see. Want me to let you know if we find your man?'

Hold up fingers in a sign of the cross. Not a chance.

'No way. I'm in at eight tomorrow. That'll do me.'

'Oh, aye. What are you doing after you've got rid of the children?'

Can't keep a bit of a smile off my face, but there's no way I'm telling him where I'm going. Shake my head.

'Things to do, Jack, things to do.'

He grunts again, no hint of a laugh this time.

'Shagging, eh?' he says, and it pains him to say the word. Can see him thinking of Debbie as he opens his mouth.

'Why don't you leave her, Jack?' I say, with accompanying instant regret. I don't have the time to get into this discussion at the moment, certainly don't have the inclination. Hold up my hand. 'Sorry, that was out of order. None of my business. Look, I've got to go. Will I see you tomorrow?'

Rubs his hand across his forehead. Tired, doesn't care, too much on his mind, even if it is only the one thing.

'Fuck knows, Sergeant. Don't know what I'm doing tomorrow. Don't know what she's doing tomorrow.' Looks pathetically up at me and shrugs. Poor bastard.

I nod, try an expression of compassion but don't know if it's anywhere near the mark. Shrug.

'Merry Christmas, Jack,' I say, and turn away.

'Ho fucking ho,' he says to my back.

Back to the desk. Herrod isn't in the immediate vicinity, which is good, because I can't be bothered with any smart arse remarks about bunking off early. Last look at all the paper. Hundreds of things to do but nothing which can't wait until tomorrow.

Jacket on, house keys, car keys, head for the door. Good nights to the few polis still lingering about the office, don't bother trying to kiss any of the women. Pass WPC Bathurst on the way out. Smile, wish her a merry Christmas, she sort of winces back at me. Fine. Piss off, then. Along the corridor to the top of the stairs. Look out the window to the dark of night. You can see the cold. Hear footsteps behind me and I turn, hoping it's not going to be work. Greeted by Bathurst, all rosy red lips and worried expression.

'Can I talk to you, Sergeant?' she says. Voice low.

'Sure. What do you want to talk about?' I say. She smells good up close, looks good, all that other stuff.

She glances over her shoulder, bites her lower lip. Can I help you with that, I almost say.

'Not here. Can I talk to you later? After work, maybe. Are you doing anything tonight?'

Tonight? Why tonight? My night is packed solid. The one night of the last three years when I don't have time for WPC Bathurst. Still, she does look as if she really wants to talk, which isn't what I'd be suggesting.

Shake the head and she looks disappointed.

'Sorry, Evelyn, tonight's the wrong night to ask.'

She bites the lip again, looks over her shoulder. I run through the course of the evening, wondering where I can make time. I could cut the kids short, I suppose, but hardly even consider being late for Miller. About to open my mouth but manage to stop myself. Bugger it, I see little enough of the children as it is.

'Really, I can't. Got two things on tonight. Christmas presents for the kids.' And I'm shagging the boss. At least, I presume I'm shagging the boss. Maybe she's just asking me out there because she wants to interview me for some Grand Lodge of the Knights Templar. Cover myself in tar and get to find out who's got the Holy Grail.

She smiles nervously and nods.

'All right. Maybe some other time,' she says.

'How about tomorrow?' I suggest. 'We could do lunch. No, not lunch, expect I'll be too busy. After work?'

'Aye,' she says after a hesitation. 'It's not urgent, I just need to talk to someone, that's all.'

'You don't have any plans for the evening? No parents or fifteen year-old strapping boyfriends to see?'

'Parents are in Inverness. I'm going up for New Year. I wasn't really planning to do anything other than watch *Jurassic Park* again.

'All right, I think I can save you from that.'

We stare at each other for a minute. Crosses my mind that she really is young enough to be my daughter, and almost feel paternal. Reminds me of my real daughter.

'Look, sorry, I've got to go. Pizza, you know.'

She smiles. 'I'll see you tomorrow. And I'm sorry about the other night. I was rude.'

Don't know what to say to that so I do the usual shrug.

'Right. See you,' I say, and turn out the door, the smell of her still with me. Along with that bloody nuisance, curiosity.

12

Standing on the doorstep of Miller's house. The doorbell has just rung with a comforting lack of affectation. I was expecting it be the *Hallelujah Chorus*, or something equally grandiose and pretentious, but instead it was a fairly close approximation of ding dong.

God, I'm talking pish. I have to relax. She's only a woman. Try not to wonder why I'm here. It would be nice to think it's because she finds me so attractive, but that seems difficult to imagine, whatever inflated opinion I usually have of myself.

Still in a mild state of excitement after the first meal of the evening. The kids were all over me, after ignoring my instructions and opening the presents there and then. They went down a bomb. I'll have to thank Harrison. Nearly fell out with Andy over the ridiculous fusty moustache he's attempting to grow, but then he's a teenager, and he'll do a lot more stupid things than that before he hits his twenties.

Anyway, their mother arrives, not just to pick them up, but to sit and have a drink. So there we were, the happy family. I hand over the gift to Peggy, she does the same opening it there in front of me routine, then nearly wets herself. You could tell the kids loved it. All the while I was wondering what Mr No Personality would make of it if he were to walk in but then the way the conversation went, I got the impression that he had taken his deficient character back to Paisley and was leaving my family alone.

They all ended up pleading with me to come and spend Christmas dinner, to which I agreed, leaving myself with the quandary of what to do about the delicious Bathurst. Almost asked if I could bring her along, but thought better of it. So I'll check out of work tomorrow at five, and rejoin the family mould; and if the merchant wanker has just walked out, it looks like I timed my expensive present to perfection. There are two things women never fail to fall for – diamonds and occasional displays of maturity. They work every time, and I managed to pull both off in the same day.

The door opens. Superintendent Charlotte Miller. I stand and stare at her. She leans against the door.

'Are you going to come in, Dallas, or are you going to stand out there all night. You look freezing.'

I'm no fashion freak – another plus to my character – so I don't know what you'd call what she's wearing. Sort of pyjamas and blue.

Walk tentatively into the house, not sure whether I'm going to find anyone else there. Had the sudden thought on the way down here that maybe she was inviting about twenty people from the station and we were all keeping it quiet thinking we'd been specially selected. Wander into a dining room, low lights, roaring fire, soft music, two place settings at the table, one very obvious bottle of champagne. Christmas tree in the corner.

'Can I take your jacket, get you a drink?'

I take my coat off, hand it to her. I've got that weird feeling in the throat you get sometimes when you know you're about to have sex.

'Vodka tonic, please.'

'All right,' she says, and shimmers out the room.

Bugger the questions as to why I'm here. They're still valid, but I can worry about them tomorrow. Plenty of time. Relax and enjoy yourself, Lumberyard.

I start looking at the pictures on the walls. Sailing ships and big seas mostly. I've heard tell she's a member of the Royal and Northern Yacht Club just around the corner. Doesn't sail, just goes there to hang out with the rest of the local money and to shag whatever big stick she can get her hands on. Very admirable.

The mind rambles on. If I had to guess I'd say the music was Mozart, but that's only because I saw *Amadeus* fifteen years ago.

She comes back into the room, rid of the jacket, and clutching a bucket of ice and a bottle of expensive looking French white. Pitches up at the drinks cabinet and sorts out my v&t. Pours herself some wine.

'No art can compete with life whose sun we cannot look upon,' she says, as I stare at a picture of some old sea battle. Stevenson, I presume, but I don't encourage her by asking her to explain what she's talking about.

She hands over the vodka, raises her glass.

'Merry Christmas,' she says.

Raise my glass in reply. 'Aye, right,' is all I can think to say. I'll have to do better than that.

She wanders over to the comfy seats by the fire, sits down. Her smell is intoxicating. I want to smother her in ice cream and spend hours licking it off. I want to rub chocolate sauce into her breasts and drink vodka from her belly button. I want to swathe her buttocks in pavlova and thrash them senseless. I want to pour syrup over her pubic hair and vagina, bury my head between her legs and emerge five hours later a sticky, gooey mess.

'Sit down, Dallas, for God's sake. And relax, you look like you're scared shitless. I'm not going to eat you.'

Damn.

I take the hint and sit down on the next available seat. Take a large draw from the vodka, which contains a comforting lack of tonic. Feel the warmth of it descend into my stomach; instantly relaxed.

I sort of smile at her and then stare into the fire. Hypnotic flame. Relaxed by it and by the smells in the air. Charlotte, burning wood, the real Christmas tree and it reminds me of being ten years-old and getting my first Scalextric set. Not that there was like, a gorgeous bit of tottie sitting next to me when I was ten and got my first Scalextric set.

Feel her looking at me, but keep staring into the fire. She asked me here, she can make the first move. Take another drink from the vodka and realise I've nearly finished it already. Better slow down or I'll be making a knob of myself.

'We don't talk much, do we?' she says.

I drag my eyes away from the flame. Her lips are moist, her nipples are obvious against the satin. I get that weird feeling at the back of my throat again.

'We're all too shit scared of you,' I say. Not sure about my candour, but it's out there.

She smiles. Sips her wine. Eyes shine in the light of the fire. 'It's good to get to know one's people a little better,' she says.

I nod. I want to smother her backside in honey, and drink champagne from her ears.

'I don't know what sort of things you'll have heard about me, Dallas. I'm sure I must have a reputation.'

I nod again. No idea what she wants me to say to that. Well, sweetums, we all think you're in it for the power, and you'll sleep with anyone who'll help you on your way.

'Well, it's all true,' she says. Finish off the vodka. 'Frank and I have an understanding.' She runs her hand through her hair as she says it. Smiles. Fuck.

'You sleep around and he doesn't mind?'

She laughs. 'That's about it, although it's not that one-sided. He's spending the night with some Malaysian tart in Gleneagles.'

The face betrays something as she says it.

'Sounds as if it bothers you.'

She shrugs.

'Why should it?' Then, 'Well, maybe you're right. It's funny. I do it often enough to him, but sometimes I think he's driven me to it.' Could be about to get the marriage history. Usually I'd take this opportunity to go to the toilet and hope they'd changed the subject by the time I got back; but this I want to hear. She disappoints.

'Sorry, I won't bore you with that.'

'I don't mind.' A sensitive, new man, me.

'Some other time, Dallas,' she says, shaking her head. 'I want to relax and enjoy myself tonight.'

The fire crackles, the music trundles along, all string quartets and harpsichords. There is a semi-uncomfortable silence between us. Want to break it, but I haven't the faintest idea what to say to her. Stare once again into the depths of the flames, because when I look at her I can't help gazing at her breasts. Stereotyped I know, but I have the same thing as every other man on planet earth.

'Get you another drink?'

I look up, she's standing in front of me, empty glass of wine in her hand. Beginning to realise that maybe she's as uncomfortable as I am. You get impressions of people and usually it's more extreme than the reality. We're all made from the same mould, that's the cliché I'm pointing to. Some guy might be an idiot but he probably won't be too much more of an idiot than you are yourself. It's just how he comes across. Same for every cool bastard, every comedian, every Neanderthal. Every foible, every personality trait is magnified under the eyes of the rest of humanity, when underneath we're not really that different. And so it might just be with Charlotte Miller. Strong, sometimes bruising exterior, all the better for climbing up the ladder, and putting men in their place; but underneath she's not that different from everyone else.

Here we go. Lumberyard, the classical fucking humanist.

We stare at each other, the back of my throat tingles and goes dry. Hand her the glass, our fingers touch. Feels like electricity stabs through me. Decide the signs are right, and to go for it. She's only human, same as the rest of us, and she hasn't asked me down here to discuss whether Thistle'll ever get back into the Premier League. Stand up, imagine myself as James Bond – before he got brainwashed by the Russians, or whatever it was that happened to him.

My head is about a foot away from hers, we stare at each other. My mouth waters. She smells glorious and I fight the urge for this to start in a frantic passion. I lean forward and kiss her soft lips – hardly any pressure – and taste the wine in her mouth. Gently with the tongue, and then I pull back. She opens her eyes, wanting.

'Got any ice cream?' I say, voice low. A second's curiosity, and then a slight smile. She comes forward, hands on my shoulders, presses against me.

'What flavour would you like?' she says, then our lips crash in a tangle of moist, alcohol flavoured flesh.

*

Five o'clock in the morning, Christmas Day. Driving back into Glasgow. Just spent my best night with a woman in a long time. Got a disgusting warm feeling, which points to me being moderately in love. That's usual, and it'll pass. No chance of blundering into marriage this time. The best I can hope for is a rematch but even that can't be sure. I'm fully aware that the next time I see her it'll be like it never happened, and I'm liable to get my face punched in for being crap at my job. But for the moment I'm content to bask in the glow of post-absolutely phenomenal sex. Body like a twenty year-old uberbabe, breasts you could lick ice cream off for weeks without getting fed up, a tongue on her like a knife and a technique honed over decades of experience. Spectacular.

Got a nice bit of dinner too. Chicken.

Drive through Glasgow, wishing the roads were always this quiet. Haven't given all the other things going on a thought all evening, and now they start to intrude. Bloody murderers, dinner with Peggy and the kids, what to do about Bathurst. Kicking myself for being so stupid as to double date on Christmas Day. Don't know what to do. Overnight Bathurst has dropped from the sexual wish list. Women of my own age or older from now on, and banish all thoughts of young constables twenty years my junior.

Pull up outside the flat just after five-fifteen. Tired, but feeling pretty cool. First night in a long while that I haven't drunk too much, although had I been stopped by a zealous young police constable in the last half hour I would still have been in trouble.

Up the stairs, let myself into the flat. Two and a half hours sleep and then a frantic fifteen minute rush to get to the station in the morning. At least the roads will be quiet. Wondering whether to tell Jack about my evening, but knowing I won't.

Walk into the bedroom, yawning. Don't turn on the light. The curtains are open and the street lights fill the room with dull orange light, dark shadows. Am in the process of undressing when I notice there's a woman lying on top of the bed. Fully clothed, but undoubtedly a woman.

13

Early Christmas morning. El Loono lies awake. Imagining he hears sleigh bells outside, can see the snow on the ground. Thinking of Christmases past and the presents he never got.

He opens his eyes and stares at the ceiling, a song about sleigh bells in his head, then that line about passing round the coffee and the pumpkin pie. He's never had pumpkin pie, doesn't like coffee. Wonders what sort of idiots write Christmas songs. Thinks they should all be locked in a room and made to listen to their own music for twenty hours a day. That'd stop them. Course, it's too late now as all of those bloody awful songs are out there.

Hum-fuckity-bug, and he starts to think of the ten worst Christmas songs of all time. Regrets it half way through, as tunes enter his head and refuse to leave.

Mary's Boy Child. Horrible, horrible. Who knew whose boy child he'd been? Then *Suzy Snowflake*, the one his aunt always used to sing to him when he was young. 'I want to be Suzy Snowflake', that's what he'd told the teacher once in class. They all laughed at him, but none of them knew what he meant.

Rocking Around the Christmas Tree. Sees Emma dancing naked around a tree, the red lights reflected in her pale skin. *Frosty the Snowman.* Sees Emma all in white, standing still, bobble hat, nipples erect with the cold. Frozen. *Santa Claus is Coming to Town.* In school again, arguing. Insisting that Santa is real, and everyone laughing. Sees himself as Santa, giving out presents to the children. An exploding something here, a bottle of anthrax to the next one. *Lonely This Christmas*, with the cheesy voice-over.

And, of course, *The Little Boy That Santa Claus Forgot.* Not only the worst Christmas song of all time, possibly just the plain worst song of all time, period. Doesn't recognise that, as well as the general awfulness of the song – even worse than the apocalyptically horrendous *I'll Be Home For Christmas* – it is because he was, and remains, the little boy that Santa forgot.

What else? What other songs had driven him to hatred through the years? *Stop the Cavalry.* Was that really a Christmas song? It's on all the compilation albums, but really it's a song about Winston Churchill, or something.

Happy Christmas (War is Over). No comment. Not as bad as *Wonderful Christmastime*, which is a shocker. He stares at the ceiling, his breathing coming faster, getting annoyed at nothing in particular, except his predicament, that he is alone on Christmas morning.

Lost count. One more, that'll do. *The Snowman.* Let the bastard melt! he always shouts when it plays. Piece of piss. And he closes his eyes and tries not to think about her. Christmas Day. God rest ye merry gentlemen.

14

Sitting in the lounge, small lamp burning dimly, coffee all round, the Christmas tree unlit and pathetic in the corner, one man's weak concession to seasonal spirit. On the settee Evelyn Bathurst sits, sleepy eyed, Nescafe gold blend, black, three sugars, in her hot little hand. Decided she needed to speak to me tonight, thought she'd come and wait for me, so let herself into the flat. Polis make the best criminals. I've hit the wall. Need sleep. I'm close on forty and massively unfit, not eighteen. I can't handle staying up all night shagging anymore. If she doesn't get to the point soon I'm going to fall asleep on her.

'I shouldn't be here. I'm sorry.' For the seventh time.

'Look, it's not a problem, Evelyn.' Another large draught of coffee, another cigarette; hope that they start kicking in. 'I don't mind. Just take your time, I'm not going anywhere. When you're ready.' Mr. Compassion, that's me. Course, I want to give her a shake and tell her to get on with it, but I can see when a young woman is troubled.

Glance at the watch. Almost six o'clock. Shit.

I look at her, the worry lines on her young face. At least this'll make it easier to get out of the thing tonight, assuming she actually talks to me in the next two hours. She looks like a wee lassie sitting there. About to tell her father that's she pregnant; or she's dropping out of university, to go and build water pumps for villagers in Burkina Faso. Can't believe I tried to get her into bed.

She drains her coffee. Looks at me. I recognise it. This is it. If she's about to tell me she's pregnant or that she's going to drop out of the polis to go and build water pumps for villagers in Burkina Faso, I'll be disappointed.

'You have to promise me that you won't tell anyone about this,' she starts.

Looks on the point of tears. Better sharpen up, take her seriously.

'Don't worry, Evelyn, I'm not about to tell anyone.'

'If this gets out at the station...,' and she doesn't finish the sentence. Lifts the mug to her mouth, finds it empty.

'I'll get you another cup. You get yourself together, and tell me about it when I get back in.'

She nods, wipes her eyes. I take the mug and head for the kitchen. Sounds serious.

Stare out the kitchen window at the cold and empty streets while the kettle boils. Wonder what she's going to say. Start to get a bad feeling, and for the first time think that maybe I don't want to know what she's just about to tell me. Sometimes ignorance is king.

Make the coffee, take it back in, hand it over, and sit down. This time there's no delay. Engages my eyes for a second, takes a deep breath, then she starts talking immediately. Words tumble out in a great rush, sentences tripping over each other.

And I'm right. I don't want to hear it.

15

Walking into the office, five to eight. Wide awake. Had a shower, still feel dirty. Brought Bathurst in with me and she's gone off to their locker room. She lifted the weight from her shoulders by transferring it to mine and came into work in a better frame of mind than she was in at my flat. Not that I can do anything for her, but I said the right things and she's made her confession. And now I'm stuck with the information.

The light is on in Taylor's office and I stick my head round the door. I'm glad that he wasn't part of what I've just heard about. Want to tell him, but know I can't.

'Morning, Jack.'

He looks up. Smiles, sort of.

'What were you up to last night then, you shagger? You were spotted three minutes ago promenading across the carpark with young Bathurst.'

Christ, you can't do anything, can you? I'm about to go on the defensive but decide against. They can think what they like.

Don't smile. Don't feel like it.

'Any news?'

He nods.

'Aye. While you were out shagging last night, some of us were working.'

'Spare me.'

'We got your Healy character. Picked him up at a pub in town, steaming out his face, about half ten.'

What was I doing at half past ten? I was deep in the arms of Charlotte Miller. Already seems a long time ago.

'And?'

'He sobered up pretty quick. Got him in a cell overnight. Jonah's coming in to talk to him this morning.'

'And is he going to be sober?' Almost spit the words out, knowing what I now know about Jonah Bloonsbury. If Taylor notices the tone, he doesn't comment.

'Is he ever? He'll have the run of CID today without the witch in, so who knows what he'll be like.'

Nearly spring to her defence, but manage to zip it.

'What do you think of our guy?' I say instead.

He leans back in his chair, tosses a pen onto the desk. Purses his lips. Shakes his head.

'Don't know, to be honest. I see what you mean about him, but I think he's just a stupid little shit.'

Implied criticism, I shouldn't have been getting everyone excited.

'Aye, right. I wasn't sure. Bloonsbury was the one frothing at the mouth over it. Just a gut feeling.'

He nods. 'Aye, well my gut feeling says it's not him, but Jonah's the one to make the decision. Anyway, we can get a blood sample, that should sort it out.' Another shake of the head. 'Why would a guy invite the polis in?'

'To give us a false description. Lead us astray.'

'Aye, well, maybe you're right. Fuck knows, eh?'

'Aye, right. Anything else?'

'Naw. Pretty quiet, so far. The usual shite after the pubs shut last night, but not much for us. That desk of yours looks pretty crowded. Maybe you'd like to see to some of it.'

'Yes, boss,' mock salute, and out the door.

Go to the kitchen to make a cup of coffee before I face the paperwork, most of which has been put off for several weeks. I could work non-stop on it for the next month and not clear it all away. Meet Alison in the kitchen, looking far more cheerful than I care for anyone to look today. She smiles at me, I do my best to respond.

'Merry Christmas,' she says, and gives me an almost lingering kiss on the lips.

'Merry Christmas,' I say back, and the words sound totally different.

She busies herself with the kettle.

'What's the matter with you, Dallas, you miserable bastard? It's Christmas.'

Deep sigh. 'It certainly doesn't feel like it. What are you doing up here, anyway?'

'Sink's blocked downstairs. They don't want us using the kitchen. And the bloody lift's broken.'

'Aye, I know.' Don't feel like making small talk, but I'm here now. No option. The woman did use to be my wife after all. 'So, you're not spending a cosy day with McGovern?'

'Cosy night,' she says. 'We both finish at four, then we're going down to the Creggans' in Strachur for the night. Tomorrow off. What about you?'

Have to think about it. Remember the wonderful family dinner coming up. Hope I'm more in the mood for it when it comes the time.

'Dinner with Peggy and the kids after work.'

She lets out a low whistle. 'Back in favour?'

Shake my head, wait for the kettle to boil.

'Who knows?' I say eventually.

She lets me go first, and I make the coffee as strong as possible. Plenty of sugar, turn to go.

'See you around. Have a nice time tonight,' I say.

‘You too. And Dallas,’ she says, making me turn back, ‘get some more sleep. You look fucking terrible.’

Thanks.

Back into the office, park my backside at the desk, stare at the mountain of paperwork. Not so much of a mountain, as I don’t have a noticeable in-tray, more of a sprawling landscape of hills and forests. Drink coffee, feel depressed. Try to think of Charlotte Miller and the wonderful evening, but thoughts of what Bathurst told me insist on intruding.

They, whoever they are, say that school days are the happiest days of your life, and I always thought that was total bollocks. But now, I’d give anything to be in the middle of three weeks holiday and be about to open up a barrel load of presents.

Think of Christmases past, and start the trawl through the paper. Good Christian men rejoice, with heart and soul and voice...

16

Here’s the story from Bathurst, and I’ve no particular reason to believe she’s making it up. No motive, your honour. It dates from just over a year ago, and the big murder case that temporarily saved Bloonsbury’s career.

At first I didn’t think it was going to amount to much. Another sordid tale of police corruption, no surprise to anyone, and just so long as the media don’t get wind of it, no one gives a shit.

Now Bloonsbury’s wasn’t the only career which was saved from the hangman with that case. There was also the matter of Detective Chief Inspector Gerry Evans, another drunken bastard who belonged at a 24/7 AA meeting. It was Bloonsbury’s case, but it was so high profile that it was all hands on deck and Evans got in on the act. It was sort of a joint credit thing, although Bloonsbury managed to whip more of the cream from the top. Evans escaped getting kicked into touch and when he did eventually take early retirement five months ago, it was with a good deal more honour than he would have had a year earlier; or than he deserved. The guy got out of jail.

A woman is found lying by the banks of the Clyde, not far from Carmyle. She's been assaulted, butchered with a sodding great knife and a packet of mini-Mars Bars, and left to die. Tells the usual story about a guy in a ski mask, and all sorts of ridiculously horrendous tales, then duly pegs it a couple of days later. The pathologists found a mini-Snickers bar surgically inserted in her abdomen, which the doctors had missed. It was all pretty gross. Whoever did it was very. very weird, you know what I'm saying? Still, from what we could gather from the victim, it appeared that it'd been an assault that had got a little out of hand.

So, it's not that the press get everything, of course, not until the trial, but suddenly every woman within fifteen miles shits her pants. They ignore it at first, but once she dies, the papers pile in there and make it the latest big thing; it being a slow month.

It's Bloonsbury's gig, and right from the start Evans is sniffing around in the background, breathing in Bloonsbury's alcohol fumes for extra sustenance.

Anyway, the press are a mile up their backside with how dangerous this comedian is, and how every woman in the city really ought to be living in fear. So, every woman in the city starts living in fear because they've been told to, and there's a public outcry about the lack of polis success.

Things are going badly, with none of us looking good. A lot of pressure, something needing to be done, and now, whoever it is that solves it is going to be a hero. It's at times like this that the odd polis will resort to fudging a little evidence. Give him some vague idea who he's after and he does the rest himself. It ain't right, but as long as you know you're gunning for the right guy, it ain't wrong either. Trouble is, they haven't a clue who the right guy is. None. They have hair samples and skin samples, and two and a half million guys in Scotland to choose from.

And in the middle of the feeding frenzy, when we're all looking like idiots and reputations are being exploded like bridges over the Rhine during the war, the guy nearly does it again. Same story, different outcome, still no more clues to his identity. This time the victim is some idiot who's out looking for the guy. Some stupid bitch who's been watching too many Steven Seagal movies and fancies a pop at the killer. Has been out on the prowl for him every night for two weeks, then finally finds him. Only, it isn't quite on her terms as she's anticipated. Comes from behind and raps her over the head with a brick before she has the chance to tell the guy she's a black belt in karate. Still, she's marginally more Buffy than Goofy, she manages to get him a good stiff crack in the gonads, and the two of them make a tactical retreat. Kind of a one-all draw, without going to extra time or penalties.

Course, the press don't give a shit that the woman's a bloody idiot. They love it, and it ends up being us who are queuing up to look stupid.

And then, out of the thick fog of this confusion, comes an arrest. Having done the usual thing when we're desperate of rounding up all the usual suspects, suddenly out of that lot, DCI Jonah Bloonsbury has his man, with Evans shuffling along in his wake taking as much of the credit as possible. The fun-size Mars Bar murderer is in custody, the streets are safe – these things are relative – and two careers have been saved. All out of nothing. There's a lot of suspicious looks cast between polis, but they've got the conviction, despite the guy denying it all the way. And more importantly, if it isn't him who did it, the real murder never strikes again.

And then.

This is where Bathurst comes in. She isn't long in the force at the time, determined to become Chief Constable of Strathclyde by the time she's thirty-five, all that crap. But not wet behind the ears, no way, like they used to be in my day when we joined. She knows what's going on, knows the sort of things that have to be done.

So, she's thrown into the middle of the investigation, and one night in the Whale she's approached by Bloonsbury, breathing mint and looking sinister. Everyone knows his story, the wife having just walked out, and now desperate for a breakthrough with the case.

He speaks in a hushed voice, gets all cosy and conspiratorial. Tells her that they have their man, but you know how it is, darlin', they just don't have enough to nick him. This is the first she's heard of it, but she's thinking, I'm just a constable, it's not likely that I'm going to know everything that's going on. So she buys it. They need her help, he says, but obviously there can't be too many who know about it. So keep it to herself. Lists the ones who were going to be in on it and no one else would know. A little evidence doctored, a few things placed where they shouldn't be, the odd clue left lying around, and they'd have their man. If she went along he would see that it benefited her greatly, and she doesn't need him to tell her that, because it's obvious.

So it doesn't take long, and three quarters of an hour and a couple of whisky soda's later, she's in. Along with Evans, naturally, Sergeant Herrod – no surprise – and young Edwards, who belongs to the *Hang 'Em High* brigade. Five in the gang, and off they ride into the sunset to fight for truth, justice and liberty.

I thought that was going to be the story, and I wasn't at all surprised. That's how these things go. I was beginning to wonder why she'd brought it to me now, because I've seen enough of these over the years to really not give a shit. Blind eye, and all that. Then she brings me up to date.

Monday night, Christmas party. Everyone getting pissed, the usual thing. It was the second one she'd been at, so she knew what to expect, i.e. a queue of drunken guys attempting to get inside that tight white dress of hers; me included. One of the pished Lotharios was Edwards of course, not long after he had stripped for the benefit of us all. Destined to get nowhere with her, but desperate all the same. He goes for it, giving her all the shite he can think of, subjecting her to a three-quarter hour rambling monologue. Starts talking about their great breakthrough case of the previous year, starts telling her things she never knew. She had been a bit drunk herself to start, but this kind of thing sobers you up quickly enough.

Bloonsbury and Evans had been in on it all along. Not just stitching up the guy, but the whole fucking thing. The murder, everything. The sick, demented bastard who committed the two attacks was Evans himself, with Bloonsbury's full knowledge. He carried out the first assault in an intended series, but of course got a bit carried away with himself, probably because he'd found his true vocation in life, and murdered the girl. Then they let the hysteria build up, feeding morsels to the scavengers every day to sustain and cultivate the frenzy, then timed the second attack to perfection, so that when things were at their most wild, when the heat was at its fiercest, they stepped in and picked up their man.

Christ, no wonder he protested his innocence. The guy didn't have a clue, but they must have had their eye on him right from the start. I don't know how they did it, but they knew they had a guy who wouldn't have an alibi for either of the two nights. They must have been planning it for months. All right, they had taken the guy from the list of usual suspects, so it wasn't as if they got a complete innocent. Justice is justice, however.

Stitching guys up, when you know you're doing it to the right person, that's all right. Doing it to someone when you're not sure, but you need a break, well, you can understand it. Pretty stupid, and it can backfire, but we've all done it. But this was way beyond that. Committing the crime, so you can solve it and take the credit.

Surprised? No way. Evans was a sick man, and Bloonsbury was just pathetic and desperate. Don't know what Herrod or Edwards were up to, but then Edwards told her there was a bit of infighting after the first assault turned to murder.

So that's the story, and as she was telling me all this my mind wasn't working particularly quickly. I took it at face value, still vaguely curious as to why she thought she had to tell me everything. Then she dumps it on me, the thought that had occurred to her, the seed that had been sown and which was growing into a monster of a beanstalk.

She was sickened on Monday night, and went home questioning herself and what she had allowed herself to get drawn into. Then Tuesday morning dawns in a wail of frantic activity. She gets down to it, the same as the rest of us. Then sometime during the day it hits her, a massive punch to the face. Maybe it's a repeat performance. Maybe it's another set up. Bloonsbury was getting himself drunk in front of us all, but who knows what Evans is doing these days? Hitting the bottle in the backwoods, certainly, but it's not as if we can account for his movements. So, maybe he's committed the crime in cahoots with Bloonsbury, and after another murder or two they're going to go through their tried and trusted stitching up routine.

So, that's the story. All true, except the last bit which is speculation. The first lot is bad enough, and I'm clinging to the hope that the second lot is Bathurst's overactive imagination. I think I managed to persuade her as such, but it's got me thinking. Can't get a fix on a logical, clear argument. Not surprising. There are too many questions. What would be in it for Evans? Maybe it's nothing to do with Evans, and Bloonsbury's got someone else to do the dirty work this time. But what could Jonah Bloonsbury give anyone as payment for that kind of thing? All his money is in alcohol. Herrod, Edwards, they couldn't possibly condone this? The first was an assault that went wrong. What happened on Monday night was some miles beyond that.

I don't know. I need to get away from it all, think clearly. I need to persuade myself that they had nothing to do with Monday night. The knowledge of the previous case is bad enough, without being lumbered with all this. I want to talk to Taylor and I'll need to if they're involved with this murder. But if they're not – and there's no reason to assume they commit every crime around here for their own ends – then I know Taylor won't want to know about it. I certainly don't.

I need vodka and tonic, and lots of it.

And fuck the tonic.

17

Made a decision. Going to go up to Arocher and speak to Evans. Haven't the faintest idea what I'm going to say to him, but I know if I don't follow this up it's just going to eat away at me. After that, I don't know. Depends a lot on what he says, although I'm not sure how I'll raise the subject. Try and drop it casually into the conversation: 'Hey! Gerry, how's it going, mate? Jammed a Snickers Bar up someone's arse lately?' Just have to wing it. Leave it until tomorrow, however. Tonight I've got dinner with my happy family and I'm not going to let it get in the way of that. A problem put off to another day, is a problem solved, that's my motto.

Lunchtime, sitting in Taylor's office chewing the fat. I mean that literally, having purchased a ham sandwich from the canteen. Taylor's preoccupied, presumably thinking of that wife of his.

'Ever hear of Evans?' I say to him.

He looks up.

'Drunken Gerry?' Shakes his head, distasteful look on his face, as we all have when we think of Evans. 'Naw, and I don't want to either. Think Jonah went to see him last month, or something. Said his place was a shit-tip.'

I nod, make another bite into the rubber of my sandwich, another swig of coffee to mask the taste – something like building a petrochemical plant to obscure a rubbish dump.

'Why do you ask?' he says.

Can tell from the tone of voice that he doesn't care, making the question easier to avoid.

'Just wondered.'

Taylor grunts and resumes his morose reflections. Decide to plunge into the middle of them myself.

'So, what you doing tonight?'

He looks round, shrugs. 'Cosy Christmas dinner at home with the wife and the in-laws. Mum, dad, sister Betty, her bulbous husband Anthony and all fifteen fucking children, or however many it is they have.'

'You going to make it?'

'Don't know. They're waiting 'til six and if I'm not in, they'll get on with dinner. And you can see how busy I am, so I'm not sure. Might just be held up at the station.' He puts his hands behind his head and stares at the ceiling.

I nod. Sound thinking. I've never met Anthony and the children but I've heard enough about them.

I'd been on the verge of asking for an update on his marital status, but decide against. It's Christmas Day and I've already got enough on my mind without being burdened with all his troubles. Very Christian of me, don't you think?

Another foray into the midst of the sandwich, followed by instant regret. Catch a whiff of alcohol in the air, look up to see Detective Chief Inspector Jonah Bloonsbury standing in the doorway. His nose glows effervescently red in the midst of a dour face. Fresh from interviewing our prime suspect.

'Good work, Dallas,' he says, 'but it's not him. I see what you were thinking, though.'

Aye, right. Don't care, having already had the thought myself. Gut instinct goes wrong again. Might have to do something about that, but not sure how you improve your guts. Bisodol, maybe.

'You let him go?' says Taylor, a man who still possesses guts of steel.

'Aye,' says Bloonsbury. 'It just wasn't right, you know. And it turned out the bastard was up to his neck in alibis.'

Look up. No way.

'You're kidding?' I say.

Shakes his head. 'Produced a couple of names, checked out. Think he was taking the piss when he was talking to you, stupid bastard. Last thing he did was threaten to sue, so I pointed out to him that that might not be a very good idea. Think he got my meaning.'

'Blood test?' says Taylor. Tone of voice that says he couldn't care less.

Bloonsbury shakes his head.

'No point,' he says. 'He's not our man, and if I start drawing blood from the bastard then we will get a law suit. You know what these lawyers are like. Anyway, says he was serious about the description he gave us, so we'll check it out. He's doing a photofit just now. Probably be totally different from the other one we've got. Maybe we should pick up that first bastard who came in.'

'You can't go arresting everyone who tries to help us, Jonah,' says Taylor. 'Bad for business.'

Bloonsbury grunts, get a whiff of J&B.

'Aye, whatever. I'm going to get something to eat. Any of you want anything?'

I hold up the worst sandwich on planet earth and Taylor shakes his head. Bloonsbury grunts again and wanders off. Glad he didn't stay much longer.

Plunge into the sandwich again, come up with meat.

'Seems a bit odd,' I say, 'don't you think? The lawyer suddenly coming up with alibis, I mean.'

'Fuck, who knows? Lawyers, they'll do what they want. If it makes the police look stupid, they don't care.'

'But to spend a night in a cell for nothing.'

'Probably got his reasons. Trying to get away from his girlfriend. Anything. More likely, fully intending to sue. And if that's the case, I'll bet he won't be put off by an idle threat from Jonah. Fucking lawyers. Not much business, so they go looking for it themselves.'

'Still got a bad smell to it.'

'That was Jonah's breath. Forget it, Dallas.'

Nod the head. What am I doing worrying about it, anyway? It seems moderately suspicious but on a scale of one to ten it's about a half, so it's nothing to be getting excited about.

Briefly wonder where this leaves the tentative theory about Bloonsbury being behind the whole thing. The further I get from the conversation with Bathurst, the more disinclined I am to believe it.

'Where now?' I say to Taylor.

He sighs big and leans even further back in his seat.

'Fuck knows,' he says.

*

Four-fifteen, daily roundup. The investigation has almost ground to a halt. All those of whom we were suspicious check out. The boyfriend, ex-boyfriend, anyone who has volunteered information, the family, the neighbours. We've got a hold of everyone that ever so much as kissed her, and come up empty. A brick wall. And that's one of the problems with this job. We could at some point have spoken to the guy who wielded the knife, but you never know.

Bloonsbury looks depressed. I'm trying to remember what he was like during the last murder case, because if Bathurst is right, then he knew all along that he was going to solve the crime. Any worry or exasperation on his part would have been feigned. All I can remember is the guy holding off the drink, and making us all suffer with him. Seen to be not drinking would be part of the plan, the anguish it caused him a genuine consequence.

This time, however, you can tell the difference. You can smell it on his breath, on his clothes and his skin, you can see it in his face – the man has not decided to hold off from the booze. Jonah Fucking Bloonsbury; legend. Not even good for an Elvis impersonation at the Christmas night out anymore. And that's what he's become. Elvis. Wasted, bloated, permanently smashed out of his face. Clinging to the songs of the past, but become a bitter caricature. In years to come people are going to be doing Jonah Bloonsbury impersonations around here. But at the moment, he's the one doing it.

But what should I care? I've never been impressed with him, and now I know he's as much of a criminal as the scum we've been hauling in here all these years. He deserves what's coming to him. I have a vision of him in three years time – or three months – sitting on Argyll Street under the rail bridge into Central Station. A scab on his nose from where he drunkenly fell into the gutter, a dirty beard and wearing the same clothes he now wears; hat on the ground, growling at passers-by to give him some money for methylated spirits or brake fluid, or whatever it is that the jakes are drinking these days.

He's standing with his back to us, looking at the pictures of Ann Keller which still adorn the walls, and which will continue to do so until we catch our man, or until they are pushed aside by new photographs of new victims – the real fear and possibility. He turns, looking bloody awful, slumps against the edge of the desk. A liquid lunch.

'Sgt Harrison, give us what we've got,' he says.

Herrod's got the day off, ho, ho, ho. Hanging out with Bernadette, the kids, and most of her family. Wonderful

Christmastime. Bet he's just itching to come into work, but she won't let him.

Wonder how Miller is getting on with her dull husband in Braemar. The thought of her gives me a warm feeling – hardened cop turns to mush over woman in authority – as it has most of the day. Love's sweet music.

Mind on the job. Sgt Harrison.

'We don't have much, sir. All avenues of enquiry have so far led to a dead end. We've had a big response from the public. Several people saw her at the cinema, and we can be pretty sure she was alone. We've had two sightings of her walking along the street, post-cinema, two descriptions of a man either talking to her or walking close behind. The descriptions don't match however.'

'Conclusion?' says Bloonsbury, butting in. The voice displays no interest.

Harrison shrugs. Here's a woman who enjoys her job but would rather be somewhere else.

'It was dark, too brief a passing glance. Somebody passes you by in the street, you've no reason to remember them, the mind is not going to have very good recall.'

Bloonsbury grunts. He was hoping for some illumination on whether one of them was lying, preferably the first one since he's already decided our lawyer friend is innocent. Harrison is right, however. These things are a joke at the best of times.

'So,' says Harrison, 'we're struggling with any witnesses from Monday night. We've spoken to her boyfriend, with whom she had a fight on Monday during the day, and to seventeen ex-boyfriends or lovers.' Seventeen? Hey, my kind of woman. 'Everyone checks out. Small family, but they all seem genuinely upset. There's nothing there to suggest a motive from any of them.'

'Again, conclusion?' says Bloonsbury. Wonder if he's even listening to her.

She thinks about this.

'Either her killer was someone who barely knew her, or did not know her at all,' she says eventually. 'Or, we've missed something in all our interviews,' she adds, not a concept to bet against.

Bloonsbury nods his head, sort of mumbles to himself – increasing the impression that the man is losing it. A low mutter, the words indistinguishable. Perhaps considering the possibility that he was the one to miss something. A drunk faced with his own fallibility – what else should he do but mutter? Or perhaps he curses the rest of us.

'Right, then. That seems to be about it, eh? Any of the rest of you lot got anything to say?' he says, looks around. 'Lumberyard?' Bastard.

Shake the head, but decide to volunteer comment.

'Who knows? He carries a grudge, beyond rational thought, either against her or someone who looks like her. If it's the latter, we're in deep shit, because he's going to be bloody hard to find. Who knows how much Ann Keller looked like the object of his hate? It could be any guy out there. Any fucking guy.'

Bloonsbury grunts. 'A bit of profile, no clues, no substance. That's all we've got.' He's right, and it doesn't amount to anything. 'Anyone else?'

Most of us stare at the floor. There's nothing else to say. Christmas Day and we're sitting here with those pictures looking down upon is, if the cadaver with no eyes can look. None of us want to be here.

Bloonsbury sighs, heavy breath, you can small the drink. Even at the back where I'm sitting with Taylor – a silent, preoccupied Taylor, other things on his mind.

'Right, folks, bugger off. Away home and enjoy your Christmas if you can,' and the words sound especially bitter from Bloonsbury's mouth, as we all know he has no home, no family, to which to go. 'We're going to have to start afresh tomorrow. Go over all the family and boyfriends again, see if we can come up with anything. If it was one of them, I want to know about it. If it wasn't...,' and the words trail off.

If it's just some guy who chanced upon her and went about his business, then we're in trouble. Another clue might not come our way until the next auburn haired woman he chances upon ends up mutilated in a ditch.

18

The imitation log fire flames away in the middle of the room; the tree sparkles in the corner, green and red; the lights are low, dark shadows haunting the warm colours; candles flicker, glinting in Peggy's diamond earrings; Nat King Cole sings Mel Torme; there's a scent of spices, and in the air there's a feeling of Christmas. Large dinner, safely washed away with a bottle of 1987 South African red. We're sitting on the floor, backs against the sofa, staring into the fire. Holding hands. Warning shots are being fired, but they're obscured by the Christmas haze.

Arrived only a little late, and was immediately swamped by ex-wife and children, still glowing from yesterday's feel-good dinner experience. Spent an hour looking at all the different presents, noticing that there was nothing from the suit from Paisley, or from any other possible suitor. Let it pass without comment, however. Masses of food, all good-natured, and a damn sight better atmosphere than we managed most of the Christmases we were still together. I may have detected a concerted family plan to win back their daddy, but I'm not sure. Never jump to conclusions where women are concerned.

Stevenson must have written that one, somewhere.

And so we come to the crux of the evening. The kids are packed off to their rooms, quite happily for once, to play with computers and all that other modern crap that we didn't have when I was young, while Peggy and I sit with our backs to the sofa watching the flames. I think I know where this might be leading, but sometimes these things do not always end there. She squeezes my fingers and I decide it's time to ask the question which has remained unasked these last couple of days.

'Out with it,' is how I broach the subject.

She looks at me and smiles.

'I love it when you talk to me as if I was a suspect.' Kisses me on the cheek. 'What are you talking about?'

'Brian.' The merchant wanker was called Brian.

'Oh.' The smile disappears and she looks vaguely detached.

Chews her lip, which I know means she's about to tell me something she would rather have kept to herself. Wonder if she's murdered Brian, and his body rots underneath us in the cellar.

'He left me for some twenty year-old hairdresser.'

I don't quite manage to hold in the laugh, at the tone of voice as much as at the fact of it. She tries to look serious, but starts laughing as well. I always loved that laugh. The first thing that attracted me to her, and led me away from the acidic arms of Jean Fryar.

'What's the story?'

She sighs. 'That tells it all, doesn't it? It would be nice to have always intended to invite you for dinner, but this time last week I still thought it would be me and Brian.'

'He dropped you the week before Christmas?'

She gives me a look. 'Must you say drop? You make me sound like a footballer.'

'Who was she?'

'Don't know, don't care. Can honestly say I've had bigger disappointments in my life.' Another squeeze of the hand. 'It really was a lot nicer having you round, and the kids were a lot happier too.'

Well, of course. The kids would have been happier having their dentist round than Brian.

'Don't know what you saw in him in the first place.'

The answer is on her lips, and I know what it is, but she bites it back. Not the time or the place. It wasn't as if she immediately married someone else when we split, the way one idiotic half of the partnership did.

'What about you?' she says, neatly changing the course of the discussion, 'married any constables lately, or are you just slowly working your way through the station in a deliberate passage of sexual frenzy?'

Very funny. The tone is such that I let her away with the marriage jibe. The question has me thinking of Charlotte Miller, however. Decide that I'll refrain from telling Peggy about her, but don't acknowledge to myself the consequences of it. If she had been some casual shag I would have told her, but it was more than that. Or at least that's how I've blown it up in my head.

'Nothing much. Struck out with a twenty year-old constable at the party on Monday night.'

'Twenty? You like them older these days?'

'Piss off, Peggy.'

She laughs again, grabs the nearest wine bottle and fills up the glasses. She leans against me, her head rests on my shoulder. I look at her, can see down her blouse to the full sweep of her breasts, safely tucked away in a BHS 36C. Spectacular. Think of Charlotte Miller's breasts, but try and keep my mind on the job.

'But, I mean, there's no one special at the moment? It's so long since I've seen you.'

Someone special. Well, I've decided the Superintendent is special. Why do you ask?

'Jack, he's special,' I say. Hide behind crap humour, the male way to deal with awkward questions.

'You know what I mean,' she says.

Think about it. Am almost on the point on owning up to these new feelings for the boss, but decide not to be an idiot. She's met Charlotte Miller, so she'll pish herself laughing if I tell her what I'm thinking. It would also be goodbye to the night's entertainment.

'No, no one special,' I say.

Feel her head burrow a little further into my shoulder.

'The kids have missed you,' she says, lets the words fall out into the warm Christmas atmosphere.

What is she saying? It's obvious what she's saying and wasn't this what I wanted? Massively expensive Christmas present, remember? That was before last night.

Forget last night, you moron.

'A week ago you were snuggling up to Brian.'

Her hand rests on my stomach. A finger finds its way through my shirt, starts drawing circles on my skin.

'I know. I can't describe it. It's not like I miss him. I mean, the guy was, I don't know, something.'

'Boring as fuck?'

'Aye, I suppose you're right,' she says, laughing. 'Boring as fuck.' Another long pause. 'It's just been really nice having you around these last couple of days.'

She looks up at me, and I don't even hesitate before the inevitable happens. Lean down and kiss her warmly on the lips, feel her tongue immediately in my mouth. She always kissed like a goddess, Peggy, and three years of kissing a sea-anemone hasn't dulled her abilities.

Finally manage to expunge the thoughts of last night and give in to the moment. Let her dominate which was always what she liked to do. And when it begins, it's at a hundred miles an hour, and just keeps getting faster.

19

There's no snow, it's not even cold. Christmas Day, grey and mild, given way to dark and bleak evening, moisture in the air, relentless drizzle threatening. And what a night for Emma to be out. Why should she be out on her own on Christmas Day?

He had caught her eye in the bar. She smiled and didn't flinch, so chances are she's as strange as he is. Must be some explanation. On her own at a table, reading Lobey Dosser. Auburn hair, big eyes, pleasant smile. Not at all like Emma really, but there was something similar. He wanted to go and speak to her, but couldn't bring himself. Nervous around women, he had to admit it.

She had finished her drink, and now was walking slowly towards the bus stop. Won't find many buses today.

He walks ten paces behind, wondering whether he should make his move. What does he have in mind? He's not sure and whenever he thinks of Emma under his bloody knife, he winces. How many times would he have to kill her for it to make a difference?

In an occasional moment of clarity he knows that not all women with auburn hair are Emma, but the moments pass.

The woman stops ahead of him and turns. She looks at him, he slows his pace, stops five yards away.

'Well, are you just going to follow us all night, or are you actually going to talk to us?'

He stares. This isn't Emma. The mouth is too big, the eyes too wide, the voice is different – wrong accent. Sweet Emma. Doesn't really know what to say. Much easier to talk with a sharp instrument.

'What's your name then, pal?'

Should he tell her the truth?

'Jack,' he says, with hesitation.

'So, you do speak?' she says. 'Is that your real name?'

He feels intimidated. Maybe this is Emma. It's like he has this giant ball of sludge or fudge or mud or something in the middle of his brain, preventing him from thinking clearly. 'No, no, it's not,' he says eventually.

She nods at the door into the old tenement beside which she stands. A dirty grey building, damp and depressing under the orange glow of the street lights. The door has a voice entry system but the lock is broken.

'You want to come up?' she says.

She's inviting him in! He doesn't say anything, can't, and follows her into the close.

Up the stairs. She smiles to herself, and wonders how much money he will have in his pocket. She imagines she recognises the type. Rip them off and they're too embarrassed to come back and trouble you about it. You can always tell the quiet, pathetic, easy ones a mile away.

'You don't say much,' she says, opening the door.

He straps on his mental boots and decides he better stop thinking like a wee boy. This could be the real thing.

'You didn't ask me up here to talk,' he says with a good deal more confidence than he feels.

The doorway leads straight into a large sitting room, sparsely furnished. Old TV in the corner, a settee and matching seat, picture of Wallace and Gromit on the wall.

'Would you like a drink?' she says.

‘What’s your name?’ he asks.

‘Margaret,’ she replies, but he hears Emma. Because of the sludge in his head. His eyes flash, she notices and has the first pang of doubt. No messing around, slip him the powder, take his money and bundle him out.

‘A drink?’ she repeats.

‘Just water,’ he says, and watches her walk through to the small kitchen.

‘Take your jacket off,’ she says, and he wonders what to do with the knife in the inside pocket. He decides he doesn’t need it yet, and leaves the jacket on a chair by the door. Maybe he shouldn’t use the knife at all. Relax, enjoy himself. The woman wants sex, give her what she’s after.

She comes back into the room. She has removed her coat, and is holding a glass of water in one hand, white wine in the other. She hands him the water, while he stares at her breasts. He’s all man.

‘Like what you see?’ she asks, taking a drink of wine. It has been open too long, cheap to start with – an overtly fruity Spanish white, with hints of creosote and Salvadore Dali, excellent upper body but a bit flabby around the buttocks with a tendency towards persistent pernicious haemorrhoidal activity. But she swallows it anyway.

He holds the water, but doesn’t drink it, which is bad. He is mesmerised by her chest, and she straightens her back to emphasise it. She reaches forward, holds his hand – which is a little too slug-like for her liking – brings it up to her right breast and leaves it there. His fingers take a grip, tentatively squeeze. She suddenly feels horrible, and wants him out of her house. Is beginning to recognise the personality type she has attracted tonight. How can she be so wrong when reading these men? When she brought them back to her place, she had to be certain she had the quiet, pathetic ones. The ones who wouldn’t cause trouble. Not the loonies. Sees it in his eyes.

He presses on her breast. The sludge is moving around inside his head like dough inside a bread machine, churning slowly, galumphing round in a doughy, watery, yeasty munge, humming quietly. He needs time to think.

‘Sorry,’ he says, voice measured, surgically detaching his hand from her breast. ‘I’ll have to go to the bathroom.’

‘Oh, aye, right.’ Thank God for that, she thinks. ‘Through that door there,’ she says, ‘first on your left.’

He starts to walk away, thinks about the knife, but there’s nothing he can do that would not be obvious. He gives her a strange look, then walks from the room.

This is a weird guy, she decides to not waste time thinking about it. There is a jacket to be searched. She picks it up, is about to put her hand into the outside pocket, when she notices what rests in the inside. Just the butt of the knife, that’s all she sees, but it is enough. She drops the jacket back onto the chair. There are two reasons for carrying a knife in your pocket when you go out for the night in Glasgow, and she doubts that he’s about to start cutting up onions to put in the curry. She stands up, no time to think, and makes her decision.

Our cowboy stands in the bathroom, looking at himself in the mirror. Trying to imagine he’s someone he’s not – well, doesn’t everyone, even the ones who aren’t insane – but can’t decide if he wants to be Valentino or Hannibal Lecter. Or Fabrizio Ravanelli.

He’ll have to wing it. He could stand there all night and never arrive at an answer. He is everybody that’s ever been, and he’s not going to arrive at the definitive man inside by standing here looking in the mirror.

He heads back out into the hall. Expecting her to still be standing in the sitting room, but she is gone.

‘Margaret?’ he calls out. The front door is closed, her wine lies on the small table beside the glass of water. ‘Margaret?’ again. No reply.

He checks the kitchen. Has the thought that perhaps she has gone into the bedroom and awaits him, naked, prostrate, ready and beckoning. Like one of those bags of pre-washed salad you get in the supermarket.

He walks over to his jacket and picks it up, realising as he does so that it was not as neatly hung as he’d left it. He finds the knife, searches the other pockets for his wallet. Nothing has been taken, but if she went through his jacket, she knows about the knife. Shit.

He looks round.

'Emma?' he shouts. 'Where are you?'

He lifts the knife and runs into the bedroom. He flicks the switch, the unclean room is bathed in harsh light. He notices the giant poster of Batfink on the wall, but Emma is not there. Runs back out into the hall, then goes through every room in the house, every possible hiding place. It is a small flat, it doesn't take him long.

She's gone.

He seethes. This has tipped the balance between all those personalities raging inside. He stands in the middle of the lounge, and pointlessly looks at his watch. He must have been in the bathroom for at least three or four minutes. How far could she have gone? Far enough.

There is no possibility that he can wait for her to return. She could have gone for the evening, and in his rage he kicks at one of the seats. Picks up a vase and throws it at Wallace and Gromit. Catches Gromit on the ear, the poor little bugger. He picks up the small table and breaks the legs of it on the floor.

Suddenly he explodes in an orgy of violent rage, room to room, breaking and smashing. Massive destruction. He swears as he does it, curses Emma for bringing him to this. Sees her face when he looks in the mirror, smashes his fist into the glass. His hand comes away bloody, but he doesn't notice the pain. Picks up a lamp in both hands, the clay breaks beneath his grip, such is his wrath. Attacks the mattress with the knife, stabbing violently, eyes closed, furious slashing.

There is a knock at the door.

He stops. A piece of glass tinkles to the ground, a light, friendly sound. A sound like Christmas. He stands in the still of the bedroom, breathing heavily, sweat on his face. It is near dark, the lights having yielded to his fury, the flat dimly illuminated by the street lamps outside.

Gentle tapping at the door again. Insistent. He is curious. It is not the knock of an angry neighbour. It insinuates itself into the room. Still he does not move, listening to the beating of his heart, pondering what to do.

The quiet knock at the door continues, his curiosity triumphs over trepidation. He walks back through the hall and sitting room to the door. Is the visitor still on the other side? Imagines he can sense them, feel them breathe. It is a man. Some other lover of Emma's perhaps.

He turns the handle, the lock clicks, the door opens. He looks out into the dark, surprise registering on his face. He knows this man, doesn't understand. Backs off, but leaves the door open. His visitor smiles, walks into the room. Closes the door behind him; the click of the lock the only sound.

20

It's a typical Boxing Day. Grey, cloudy skies, the threat of rain, mild and miserable, not even a chill in the air. A day with nothing to recommend it, the barrenness of it made all the more stark by the night before, the second consecutive night of glorious passion.

Driving along the Loch Lomond road on the way to Arocher. The loch looks bleak and humourless, the surrounding hills lost in the low cloud. In the winter it is unutterably depressing, and in the summer, when it looks good, half a million people swarm out of Glasgow to check it out. There's usually about one day in late March when it's worthwhile.

Other things on my mind. Spectacular sex with Peggy. Then we sat up in bed for three hours, reading the Calvin & Hobbes. A perfect evening, which finished up with the expected result – she asked me back. Not in a direct, unsubtle, come on back Dallas, kind of a way, but the suggestion is out there, hanging, waiting for me to pluck it out of the air. And I'm at a loss.

Two days ago I would have jumped at it. Now, because of a night with Charlotte Miller – another man's wife, a woman completely out of my league – I hesitate. I'm being an idiot but I can't do anything about it. I know I'm not about to lure Charlotte away from her boring suit of a husband, but there exists the possibility of more nights of luxurious passion. Go back into the bosom of the family, and that door is closed.

I was nervous going into work this morning. Waiting to see what her reaction would be towards me, waiting for a sign. As it was, she never showed up. Things were pretty quiet, and at shortly after ten I made my excuses and set out for the unclean hole that will be Evans' abode.

So, general confusion on the women-front – no change there – and I try to think about what to say to Evans. But I can't. No idea how to confront him.

Drive into Tarbet, dull and empty, and up the hill past the Black Sheep. Its doors optimistically open, two sad cars parked out front.

Know I can't just come down here for a chat, that I have to force something from Evans. Also know that he will be a reluctant interrogatee. Why should he be anything else? If Edwards was telling Bathurst the truth, Evans isn't going to go volunteering the information to a member of the force who wasn't part of their gang. Have also considered the possibility that Edwards was bullshitting, in the mistaken hope that he would impress Bathurst – he was drunk, after all, and desperate. Consequently, I know I can't barge in there and start smacking Evans about.

Down the hill, turn the corner, past the hotel and into the village, such as it is. Loch Long looks as grey and depressing as Lomond, the mountains on the other side completely obscured above a few hundred feet. Keep wondering what I'm going to do with any information I come up with; keep wondering how I'm going to tell Peggy that I'm not coming back; wonder if I should go back anyway, or what part Charlotte Miller will play in the decision. I don't know, and I should stop thinking about it.

Round the head of the loch, up a small side street, pull up in front of the house. Mind on the job, but I can smell Charlotte Miller. Taste her.

Evans' old Vauxhall is parked outside, still in need of massive bodywork repair. There's a spit of rain in the air as I stand and look at the house. Feels colder down here, underneath the hills. Pull my jacket in and go to the door, ring the bell. Can hear the faint sound of a television. Creaking floorboard, then a second later the door opens.

Evans stands before me. He breathes, I nearly choke on the fumes. He never went in for spirits. Beer man, and a bottle of wine if he felt like it. His face is a disaster site, and he looks like every jake you ever passed in the centre of town.

The smell from the house isn't too fine, and I'm not sure that I want to get invited in. Wonder how long his pension will keep him in this, before he gets kicked out of the house and ends up where he belongs.

'Lumberyard?' he says, unpleasantly. 'What do you want?'

'Thought I might have a word, Chief Inspector.' Show respect, even though I can think of no one less deserving.

'Jonah sent you on an errand?' he grumbles. 'Let you in on the secret. Herrod told him to piss off, I expect. Need someone to do their dirty work after last month. Well you can tell him to fuck off.'

I shake my head, as he begins to close the door.

'This has nothing to do with Jonah. I don't know what you're talking about.'

He stops. A half-truth – I haven't the faintest idea what that was all about. I can worry about it later.

'What is it, then?'

'Christmas. Thought I'd just come and see you, see how you're getting on.' Absolute pants. Serves me right for not giving it more thought on the way down here.

He steps back from the door, ushers me in.

'Fucking shite, Lumberyard, but you might as well come in since you're here.'

He walks down the short hall and into the room with the TV playing. I close the front door behind me.

The room is a tip. Empty wine bottles, beer cans, dinner plates, microwave oven ready meal containers. Evans' wife left him ten years ago, taking all four of the kids with her. He moved into this place just after that, and some of this stuff looks as if it's been here since then.

He slumps into his favourite chair – the one surrounded by the greatest amount of detritus – and stares at the television. A *Morcambe and Wise* re-run. At least, you have to assume it's a re-run. The bloody BBC will do anything these days to try and get an audience.

'Have a seat,' he says, and gestures to an old settee. I sit on the edge, clearing junk out of the way.

'Here,' he says, and tosses me an unopened can of warm McEwan's.

'Thanks.' Rather drink my own urine, but I try not offend. Open it, take the merest sip and put it on the coffee table with all the other litter.

I really don't know what to say – beginning to feel stupid – so sit and watch the TV. Eric and Ernie are in bed together. By Christ, the 70's were innocent times.

'Well, what is it Lumberyard?' he says. 'You didn't come down here to drink my fucking Export, did you?' He's got that right. 'So what is it?'

Consider subtlety, but that's not really an option. It would have required some prior thought. Have no option but to be straightforward. Not completely straightforward, however. I have learned the odd thing about interviewing suspects in the last twenty years.

'Heard a rumour,' I say.

He looks at me. Can tell he's interested.

'What kind?' he says.

'About you and Bloonsbury stitching up your man over the murder trial last year.'

He nods his head, takes a loud slurp from the can.

'What about it?'

What about it? I don't know.

'Did you do it?'

'Did I do what?'

'Plant evidence? Incriminate him, because you didn't have enough to put him away?'

He looks me full in the eye. Contempt.

'What is this, Lumberyard? You working for some polis commission? You on some fucking crusade against injustice?

Fighting on behalf of the wrongfully imprisoned Fucking Headcase Killer Bastard One?'

'What did you mean about Bloonsbury needing someone to do his dirty work after last month?'

He barks out a laugh, chokes on a swallow of McEwan's, washes it away with another loud slurp from the can. Shakes his head.

'Listen, Wee Man, why don't you just fuck off, eh? You obviously don't know what you're talking about, so take a fucking hike. You're out you're depth, Wee Man, out you're fucking depth.'

Stand up to go. This is getting me nowhere and I'm not going to tell him everything I know. And what difference does it make if he did murder that women? I'm not some crusader for truth and justice; I'm not about to flush my career down the toilet by rocking the polis boat.

One last question, because I don't care what he thinks about me asking it.

'You have anything to do with that woman getting murdered the other night?'

He looks up at me, but there's nothing in those eyes. No give away, no hint.

'What the fuck are you talking about, Wee Man?'

Calls me Wee Man once more and I'm going to have a swing at him.

'Ann Keller. She was murdered in Cambuslang on Monday night.'

He shakes his head, rolls his eyes. Plenty of drink, no acting. Nothing to do with it. Gut instinct.

'Wee Man, the only times I've left this seat in the last five months is to go for a shite, and to open the door to you. Now fuck off. And excuse me if I don't see you out.'

Look down at him. Had enough. The stench, everything is leaving a bad taste in my mouth. And I hate getting called Wee Man, particularly by drunken old farts who're about a foot shorter than me.

I see myself to the front door, step out into the rain. It feels clean and cold, and the grey day seems a lot fresher than it was ten minutes ago.

21

Walk back into the office just after lunch, having helped myself to a Little Chef all day breakfast on my way home. Can tell something's happened. Herrod's in, talking agitatedly to someone on the phone. There are a few more constables about the station than should be on Boxing Day, and they all look as if they've got something to do. One of them calls over that Taylor wants to see me, then scurries off. The door to Miller's office is open and I can hear her speaking to what is obviously an inferior. Know the tone. All connects with the press hanging around outside the front door. The place is in a state of controlled excitement. Wonder if we've got our man, and where General Bloonsbury is amidst the turmoil.

Herrod slams down the phone as I walk past.

'Where the fuck have you been, Lumberyard?' he growls at me, and I've a good mind to tell him what I was doing, and that if he ever talks to me like that again I'll get him thrown in jail. Ignore him. He gets up, and walks quickly out the office, grumbling as he goes. Urgent work to be done, presumably. Doesn't mean he's not an idiot.

Another constable buzzes past. Catch the faint trace of alcohol in the air. Called in unexpectedly over Christmas – what do you expect? Walk into Taylor's office, expecting to find him feverishly arresting criminals. He's leaning back in his chair, feet up on his desk, a cup of tea in his hand. Looks as if he's just enjoyed a nice bit of lunch. An oasis of calm. Pull up the seat across the desk but don't go so far as to put my feet up.

'Can I take it I missed something?'

He takes a drink from his tea, places the cup back on the desk, puts his hands behind his head.

'Where've you been, Sergeant?'

'Pursuing an independent line of inquiry,' I say.

He nods. Trusts me enough to know he'll find out about it when I'm ready to tell him. Although, in this case, who knows when that's going to be.

'We think our man had another go last night. Followed a woman back to her flat in Rutherglen, she asked him in,' raises his eyebrows as he says it, and he's right. Don't these people read the papers? 'She starts thinking there's something a bit weird about him. He goes to the toilet, she looks in his jacket, discovers a knife. Usual thick bitch with her head in the sand, doesn't know anything about the murder on Monday night. But she does know she's got some heid-the-ba' in her bathroom, so she gets out. Goes to a friend's house. The friend is a bit more switched on, shows her our first photofit in the paper, and she thinks it's him. Waits until this morning...'

'What?'

He shrugs. 'That's the helpful public for you. Anyway, she gets a polis to go back to her flat with her, just in case he's lying in wait. Long gone of course, but not before he's ripped the shit out the joint. Stupid bitch is still downstairs peeing her pants.'

'Fuck,' shake the head.

'Anyway, we've got a bit of a better description out of it, but who knows? It's a distinct third photo we've got now, anyway, rather than an evolution of the first or second. These people are just fucking useless. The lot of them.'

Takes his feet down, drums his fingers on the desk. 'Useless,' he repeats. 'Still, he blew it, and we should be a step closer.'

'So, how come you're sitting here with your feet up, if everyone else is in ferment?'

'Thinking. Got to think in this job, Lumberyard, I've told you before. That's why you're still a sergeant.'

One of the many reasons.

'Where's Bloonsbury?'

'Still down there. Got the crew going house to house and the SOCO's going over the flat. Jonah's in charge, and bloody miserable that the guy got away. Has this theory that now he's blown one, the guy'll back off and disappear and we'll never get him.'

'What do you think?'

'I think he'll show his hand. These headcases can't keep their knives to themselves. Bloonsbury's too busy wallowing in J&B to be positive about anything. Had a pickled napper for the last ten years. Still don't know how the fuck he solved that murder case last year.'

Used to wonder about that myself. Now might just be time to tell Taylor, but I hold back. I have to know more and I haven't the faintest idea how I'm going to find it. CID just doesn't train you well enough in investigation.

Change the subject.

'How'd you get on last night?' I ask.

He snorts, shakes his head.

'Awful. Just awful. Those arseholes were as bad as usual, then Debbie gets a call about half nine and was on the phone for God knows how long.'

'King Dong?'

That one hurt, hold my hand up in apology.

'Aye,' he says eventually. 'Bastard. I ended up coming in here, didn't go home until about three.'

'Get anything done?'

'Worked like a dog. Took my mind off it.' Indicates the desk, and there's a lot less shite lying on it than usual. 'You should try it some time.'

Ignore that remark. 'What you going to do?'

'About Debbie?' he says, shrugging. 'No idea. Don't know why she doesn't just leave.'

'Maybe he doesn't want to take her in.'

'Aye, maybe.' Nods his head, purses his lips. Looks resigned and miserable. 'Suppose that's what she's doing. Trying to get me to leave, so she can have the place to herself.'

'Why don't you talk to her about it?'

Shakes his head and I realise I'm out of my depth with this. I'm no counsellor. I've always just accepted my marriage break-ups with a Calvinistic resignation.

'We haven't talked in years, Dallas,' he says.

He looks terrible and I wish I hadn't reminded him of it. We'd been doing fine, and the juxtaposition of that with my own Christmas Day – my marriage going in the opposite direction, if I want it to – makes me feel guilty.

Change the subject again.

'So what have you been thinking?'

He sits back, toys with his tea. Think I've got his mind on to it just in time.

'Just wondering if we could flush him out.'

'How you going to do that?'

'Bait. This one last night saw him in a pub. He didn't speak to her there, but followed her when she left. Follows the pattern of Monday, where we think he followed her out of the cinema.'

'Don't know that for sure.'

'But it's possible. Anyway, the guy is going for auburn haired birds, he's working in our area. We've already checked out the pub from last night, spoken to the staff that were on, a few of the regulars. No one can remember him. Not a known face around town.'

Light up a cigarette. Tastes good – always does for an hour after food. 'But we have to know the public places he's likely to frequent.'

'Fuck,' says Taylor, 'we're talking about Rutherglen and Cambuslang, not New York. There ain't that many pubs. We've got to think about the way he's worked so far, decide which are his likeliest haunts, see if we can set a trap. So that's what I was doing. Thinking.'

Very commendable. More than Bloonsbury will have been doing. More than me too, with my preoccupation with Charlotte Miller and the relationship of that to the possibility of reopening hostilities with Peggy.

'How many auburn polis have we got?' I say.

'Three, maybe another couple who could pass. I'm sure we could manage to get wigs from somewhere, however,' he says, voice condescending. I deserve it. Of course we could get wigs. It's time I switched the personal stuff off and actually thought about this. It's the usual flawed bunch riding into the sunset for justice and liberty: Bloonsbury soiled with alcohol; Herrod drunk with the desire to arrest anyone – in this case probably everybody in Glasgow over the age of twelve with a penis; the cuckolded Taylor, consumed by doubt and depression by the actions of his wife; and me, just consumed by doubt. Someone's got to be doing some clear thinking and I can't leave it all to Jack.

'We could even get a few of you young constables and sergeants dressed up as women,' he says, smiling. Bastard. 'I see you in red,' he says, 'or pink maybe. Pink stretch cycling shorts, wonderbra and a hair net.'

'Very funny. I see you with a boot up your arse.'

Smell the perfume first, then look up. Charlotte Miller stands in the doorway, arms folded, looking down on us both. Wonder how long she's been there, because Taylor wouldn't automatically have deferred to her.

'Interrupt a serious debate, did I, gentlemen?'

I shrug. Taylor looks at her as if he doesn't care.

'What can we do for you?' he says.

'Some work would be nice, or do you think you can do your jobs without ever getting up off your backside?'

'The job's getting done,' is all he says. Cool, better than I would be if I was here on my own.

'See that it does,' she says, and the voice is just the way you'd expect it to be. Sharper than a pint of freshly squeezed lemon juice. 'Nice of you to come in, Sergeant. Where have you been all morning?'

'Something to follow up,' I say.

'You want to share it with me?'

Aw, Christ. She makes me feel like I'm at school. She doesn't usually keep track of my movements. I knew it. It's started already. I slept with her, and now she's going to treat me like dirt for the rest of my life.

'It's a little awkward,' is all I can say.

She gives me the look she gives dog shit when she steps on it in the street.

'Perhaps then you'd like to come into my office and explain it to me,' and before the words are out of her mouth, she's turned on her heels and gone. I look at Taylor, he smiles at me, then laughs.

'What'd you do to deserve that?' he asks.

Shake my head. I'm not about to tell him that either. I stand up – better not keep my executioner waiting.

'So where were you this morning?' he says.

Breathe heavily. 'Tell you later,' I lie, and walk out.

Walking through the office I start to wonder if she's asking me in there so she can jump me across the desk.

Get to her office, step through the open door, close it behind me. She's sitting at her desk, reading a file. I can feel the dryness at the back of my throat, that strange sensation of arousal. I can smell her and it makes me nervous. Wish I could feel more in control.

She lifts her head. The eyes tell it. I'm not in here on any romantic expedition.

'Now, Sergeant, where you were this morning?'

Curse silently to myself.

'I was pursuing an independent line of inquiry,' I say. Sounds lame.

'And are you going to keep this independent line of inquiry to yourself?' She says the words 'independent line of inquiry' in a mocking tone.

I stare at her. No idea what to say, no intention of telling her what I was doing. I'm not protecting anyone – maybe Bathurst – because I don't care about most of these bastards. I just can't go mouthing off about this when I don't know yet whether any of it's true. There is also the possibility that Charlotte Miller already knows all that there is to know.

'Could it possibly be related to our ongoing murder inquiry?'

'I don't know.' Found the voice, at last. 'Might be.' Although, I don't think Evans had anything to do with Monday night. Gut feeling. 'However, I don't think it is,' I add, under the weight of the stare.

'Very well, Sergeant, if you must keep these things to yourself. However, can I remind you that this is a very public inquiry and everyone is demanding quick results. The Chief Constable more than anyone. We work under enough tight constraints as is it, without being able to afford the time for senior Detective Sergeants to swan off for four hours on a whim. Do we understand each other?'

I nod. Nothing to say. She has most definitely managed to dampen my ardour.

'That will be all then, Sergeant,' she says, and I know when I've been dismissed. Turn to go. Get a quick look of a picture of her in uniform on the wall. Looks severe. Seductive as fuck, but severe.

'Dallas?' she says to my back. Almost at the door, I turn round. Harsh, then the sudden use of the first name. The usual management technique.

There's a smile on her face – of sorts – which I naturally can't read.

'I hope we can be mature enough to keep these things separate from our private life.'

Our private life? I shrug. Still feeling like a wean with a skelped arse.

'Sure.' Don't say anything else – lost, you see.

She hesitates, as if she's not sure. Shyness in someone else, you might think.

'Frank's away to Italy at the weekend,' she says. Missing another game at Ibrox. What kind of fan is he? 'I was wondering if we could do something?'

I nod. Stay calm. 'Sure,' I say again, and manage what I hope is a smile. Be cool and calm, and I quickly make my exit, before I betray myself.

Stand outside her door and ward off the curious looks from one or two constables and non-uniform staff in the office. Immediately excited at the prospect of spending more time with her, immediately guilty at what Peggy and the kids would think if they knew. Due to phone her this evening, and I know they'll want to see me at the weekend.

Already thinking about my excuses as I make my way back to my desk. Crack open a fresh packet of Marlboro's and proceed to smoke most of them in the next hour.

22

Nearly nine o'clock, still in the office. As always when there's some big murder inquiry on, there's even more crime than usual. I got farmed off to deal with an aggravated assault and an attempted bank robbery. Suspects were apprehended in both instances. In the first case it was a wife turning on her husband – after fifteen years of abuse, she says, and there was a time when you would have believed her. Now, you just can't tell anymore.

The bank robbery was a joke. Amateurs. Even so, they would probably have still managed to get away with it if they'd remembered to fill the getaway car with petrol.

Found time for a brief word with Bathurst. Curious about that remark of Evans' when I first arrived. Bumped into her downstairs, on her way home at the end of her day. I was wondering if she had told me everything there was to tell. People very rarely do.

'Went to see Evans this morning,' I said to her.

She looked frightened straight off. Saw it in the eyes, heard it in the voice. Bit her lower lip.

'What did you say? You didn't mention me?'

'No, don't worry.'

'Why did you tell him you were there?'

Didn't know what to say to that and I wasn't going to admit to being so clumsy.

'Just asked him a few questions. Suppose he might have worked it out, but his brain must be so pickled it's hard to tell whether he's capable of any clear thinking. Look, I really don't think he or Bloonsbury had anything to do with Monday night. Don't worry about that, all this is nothing to do with what happened last year.' She nodded slowly – unconvinced. 'There was something else he said. About having had dealings with Bloonsbury and Herrod last month. You know about that?'

She looked even more worried. Puzzled.

'He assumed at first that was why I was there,' I said.

Kept shaking her head. Bit at a nail. Not at all happy.

'Look, I don't know,' I said. 'I'll dig around, but I have to be careful. Don't want people getting suspicious.' Then I suggested a way out for us both. It would need a lot of courage from her and nothing from me, but it wasn't me that created the situation in the first place. 'You could go to Miller, tell her everything. You're going to look bad, but if it's bothering you that much...'

The thought of that scared the shit out of her.

'I can't,' she said.

'She's not as bad as she seems,' I said. Personal experience – get her in bed and she's a kitten. 'If this is going to bug you, if it's going to make you not want to be in the polis, then you've got to let it out.'

'It'll be the end of my career,' she said.

I wondered if I could deny it, but I couldn't. If she wasn't kicked out for her part in it, what polis would want to work with her after she'd done this?

'Depends how much you want your career. Cause if you do, you're just going to have to forget it, get on with your life. It was a year and a half ago – you've done all right so far. You'll have to let it go. Believe me, Monday night had nothing to do with those guys, so you've either got to accept what you were part of and forget about it, or get it out and face the consequences.'

She kept shaking her head. It was a big discussion and warranted a hell of a lot more time, but I didn't have it.

'Look, Evelyn, I've got to go. Think about what I've said. Don't do anything yet and we'll talk at the weekend.'

She smiled weakly at that, and nodded. Not sure, of course, if I'll have the time to see her.

That was it, and we went our ways. We're both in work tomorrow, and we can take it from there. A right bloody shambles.

Had a brief interview with Charlotte as she disappeared for the evening. Wants to go away tomorrow evening, spend the night in some hotel somewhere. Said she had a place in mind. I didn't fight it and as I stood in her office having the brief discussion on the subject, I just wanted to leap over the desk and rip her clothes off.

Not long after that the expected phone call from Peggy came

through. Juggled enough women in my time to sound cool about it. Even so, like a complete idiot, I couldn't bring myself to say definitely no about tomorrow night. Put it off until tomorrow.

So, just after nine on a Friday night, up to my eyes in paperwork, and I can't concentrate on a single line of it. Charlotte, Peggy and Evelyn Bathurst keep intruding into the thought process. Mostly Charlotte.

As far as I know, she's spending the evening alone. Very tempted to go down there when I've finished at the office. Utterly succumbing to infatuation and there's only one road to go down once you start feeling like this; there's only one thing that's going to happen. You're going to make an idiot of yourself.

I'm thirty-nine for God's sake, it's not as if I haven't had plenty of women; and yet for the first time in years, I'm getting carried away. Right smack in the middle of the biggest murder inquiry we've ever had in this patch.

The quicker I fall flat on my face and screw everything up – get dumped by Miller and screw up with Peggy, end up with no one but two-bit scrubbers picked up in the pub on a Saturday night – the quicker I can get on with things. So if I go to see her tonight I'll either get put in my place, not before time and just what I'm needing, or else I'll get into her bed for the night and plummet deeper into the abyss of infatuation.

First, however, I've got to get this work done. Christ, who joins the polis to do paperwork?

Finish off the cup of tea at my right hand, sit back in the seat, stare at the ceiling. Begin contemplating getting out of here, doing all the crap tomorrow. Ponder what my reception will be in Helensburgh.

*

Of course – because it's the way of things for there to be copious amounts of crap dropped on me from an enormous height – however shit I imagine I might end up feeling when I get there, it doesn't even begin to wipe the backside of how shit I actually end up feeling. Not a bloody patch.

Lumberyard dives further into the toilet of confusion.

23

Evelyn Bathurst looks not unlike Emma.

She parks the car on the road at the bottom of the garden of the large house in Helensburgh, steps out into the rain. Stares at the lights in the house fifty yards away along the driveway, wonders about what she is doing. Shivers, pulls her jacket closer around her.

She locks the car door. Her own car under repair – faulty brakes – she has borrowed the car from Constable Hodson, on duty through the night. Hodson believes that she may repay the favour sometime.

She will not get the chance.

She swings back the gate, feels the beating of her heart. Looks at her watch, wonders if the Superintendent will be at home. A Friday night, not long after ten o'clock. Whatever it is that Miller does, she will find this an unwelcome interruption, with unwelcome information.

Takes a deep breath, tries to calm herself; begins the long walk up the driveway.

Should she have listened to Dallas Lumberyard? But it wasn't Lumberyard talking, it was her conscience. She had been meaning to do the same thing for the past year. Slowly the desire had worn off. The months will do that to you. But now it was back, born of fear, guilt and self-loathing for what she had been a part of. There was no need to confide in Lumberyard any further. What he had said earlier in the station had been all that she was needing to hear.

Her ponderous steps take her nearer to the house, her stomach crawls with nerves. She wonders if she is about to be dismissed, in the manner she has heard Miller dismiss so many officers in the past. Not as bad as she seems, Lumberyard had said, and she hopes it is true.

She has automatically rung the bell, without a clear thought in her head; moves back from the second step so that she is outwith the meagre protection of the front of the house. The rain soaks her head. She shivers again in the cold. Throat dry, nervous fingers.

The door opens, catching her unaware. She stares into the dim light of the house, feels the rush of warmth from the house. Charlotte Miller stands in front of her. Doesn't recognise Bathurst at first. Miller wears a long, blue silk pyjama top, her legs are bare. Bathurst looks at her skin, smooth and gold in the dim light from behind.

'Constable Bathurst?' she says, surprise in her voice coming with sudden recognition.

Bathurst nods, says nothing. No words. They stare at each other for a few seconds, before either awakes to the other. Miller shakes her head, feels the cold, summons her inside and closes the door behind her.

Bathurst stands in the hall, looking around. Unaware of what her husband does for a living, she wonders what Miller earns as a superintendent to afford such opulence.

'I'm sorry to bother you on a Friday night,' she begins, but Miller stops her with a shake of the head.

'Don't be silly. Take your coat off and I'll get a towel. How long were you standing out there?'

Bathurst thinks about when she stepped out of the car, seems like an hour ago. Doesn't answer, removes her coat, Miller ushers her into the sitting room.

'I've just got a quick phone call to make, then I'll get the towel,' she says. Disappears.

Bathurst stands in the middle of the room, suddenly warm, aware of the dampness of her hair. The remnants of a single place setting linger on the dinner table, a fire crackles in the hearth, the warm Christmas tree glints in the corner. Beside the large chair next to the fire is a brandy glass almost empty and a strewn pile of papers. She has interrupted her working on her Friday night.

A minute and Miller walks back into the room, hands Bathurst a towel. They smile awkwardly and Bathurst begins rubbing her head. Smells the perfume from the towel, her eye catches sight of Miller's legs. Stares, then comes out of it; looks at Miller and smiles, hopes she doesn't know what she was thinking. Miller watches her. Already knows why Bathurst would come to see her at her home, late on a Friday night; it is a call she has been expecting for the past year.

'Can I get you something to drink, Evelyn?'

Bathurst hands back the towel. Looks at the brandy glass, laughs nervously, smiles.

'I'll have one of those,' she says.

Miller nods, hangs the towel over the back of a chair, goes to the cavernous drinks cabinet. Pours the brandy. Bathurst watches her, staring at her back, the smooth curve of her legs. Shivers again despite the warmth.

Turning back, Miller notices the death end of the shiver, holds out the drink to her.

'I don't make you nervous, do I?' she says.

Bathurst laughs awkwardly, does her best to smile, and takes a sip from the glass. Doesn't recognise the quality of the taste.

'No, I'm fine,' she says, adding hurriedly, 'it's why I'm here that's making me nervous.'

Miller nods. Time to play the game. She isn't the first constable who has come to her with tales of police corruption, although perhaps this one is a tale on a grander scale. It still comes down to the same thing, however. Work out the best way to shut them up.

'Come and sit down, Evelyn,' she says, beckoning Bathurst beside her onto the settee. She follows her, takes her seat, looks into Miller's eyes. She swallows, allows her eyes to drift. Miller sits back in the sofa; her thighs are naked, Bathurst catches a glimpse of pubic hair, quickly looks away.

You don't have thoughts like this about your boss.

This close, Miller can smell her. Closes her eyes, and it reminds her of a woman twenty-five years before. Long summer afternoons on the outskirts of the city, where the hills rose gently up to the blue skies, the days were warm, and she first discovered love with another woman. Feels the tingle, the shiver. Opens her eyes.

'You must be warm, Evelyn, why don't you take your jumper off?'

Is she warm? She nods, realises that she is and it's not just her nerves. Sits forward, pulls the jumper up. As it comes off, with her arms raised, her breasts are displayed beautifully, obvious under the thin white top she wears beneath. Miller watches every movement, has the briefest moment of doubt. Is this calculating, or is it real? Would she make love to Evelyn Bathurst, even if she didn't have a secret she wanted her to keep?

Bathurst drops the jumper on the floor, sips self-consciously at her brandy, places it on the table next to the settee. Is aware that Miller is studying her, feels her nipples harden at the touch of her eyes on her breasts. She nervously lifts the glass again, looks up when Miller rests her fingers on her knee. Swallows.

'I know why you're here, Evelyn,' she says, 'I know it's about the Addison case from last year.'

The surprise shows in her face.

'You know?' she says. Almost a high-pitched ejaculation.

Miller squeezes her knee, smiles.

'They're not the first officers to fabricate information. When you know you've got your man, sometimes it's the only way.'

Bathurst looks into her eyes, wants to believe, wants to be convinced, but she realises that if Miller does know about it, it can only be half the story.

'I know it's difficult, these situations always are. But it generally doesn't do much good to try and bring them out. The only person who wins then is the criminal.' – Bloonsbury and Evans are the bloody criminals! – 'They broke the law, but only in a way that plenty of others have done before. I've done it, and you were part of it at the time. You know it makes sense.'

Bathurst gazes into her eyes, can feel herself begin to cry. Wants to scream. No! Miller doesn't know. She thinks she does, but she doesn't know the full horror of what they did. Maybe she could ignore fabricating evidence, but not murder. You can't ignore murder.

Miller puts her hand to Bathurst's face, wipes the first tear delicately away from under her eye. Is surprised with herself that she feels genuine affection for the constable.

'Don't worry about it, Evelyn. We can talk tomorrow or Monday. Give yourself some more time to think about what you want to say.' Hesitates, allows her fingers to stroke the soft skin of her face. 'Relax.'

Bathurst closes her eyes, trying to forget. But how do you forget about what they've done? Miller's fingers gently run down and along her neck, then back up over her cheek. Her thumb crosses Bathurst's lips and automatically she kisses. Breathes in deeply, smells her, recognises the perfume, the faint trace.

The fingers continue to run across her face and neck, she leaves her eyes closed and slowly begins to give in to the hypnotic effect, the tormenting touch, and soon the grey deeds of others are far from her mind.

Then Miller's lips are on her cheek, a delicate touch, taunting, tantalising. Her fingers play in her hair and Bathurst moves her head round so that their lips meet. At first just a gentle, lingering kiss...

*

Half past five in the morning. The rain still falls in a steady drizzle, as Constable Bathurst steps out of the large house and walks slowly up the garden path. Her legs ache, thigh muscles tortured, her body covered with bite marks and tiny flesh wounds and bruises. Her senses still tingle, every nerve is still taut, the wrongdoing of DCI's Bloonsbury and Evans the farthest thing from her mind.

She turns at the garden gate and looks behind her, but the door has already been closed to the cold, Miller already on her way back to bed. She steps out into the street and slowly gets into the car of Constable Hodson. As she drives off she turns on the cassette player, is adequately prepared at five-thirty in the morning to listen to Simply Red, settles in for the drive along abandoned roads back home.

*

Constable Bathurst arrives at the station, leaving Hodson's Peugeot in the car park, the keys in the exhaust. He will be off duty in a couple of hours. From there she will walk home, a ten minute promenade through wet, deserted streets in the middle of the night.

As she steps out onto the street and rounds the first corner, someone sees her, sees her auburn hair dully reflect the orange street lamps, but she does not see him. She walks on, the dull ache in her leg muscles heightened from sitting in the car for half an hour.

She thinks about Charlotte Miller, has vague thoughts of Dallas Lumberyard, but thinks not of the problems with which she stepped out that evening. Wonders whether to have coffee when she gets home, or whether she should go straight to bed.

She will, however, never get to choose.

24

Having a weird dream where Peggy and Charlotte are naked together on a huge front lawn somewhere, singing Aerosmith – *Crazy* – when the phone rings. It plagues the dream for a while, before I'm plucked from the fantasy into the cold early morning. Still dark outside, cold in the bed. First thing I think of is driving down to see Charlotte last night, and getting my rude awakening. Constable Hodson's Peugeot 305 sitting outside her front gate. Hodson, fuck. So I sat there feeling like a total idiot, before turning around and heading back home. Resisted the pull of the vodka bottle, went straight to bed. I cannot believe she went for Hodson. Course, I can't believe she went for me either, but at least I'm not some spotty constable for whom shaving is a distant dream.

Look at the clock while my hand makes its tortuous way out from under the covers, on the long journey to the phone. Not yet seven o'clock.

'Yeah?' I mutter down the phone.

'Lumberyard? It's Ramsey. You'd better get in here.'

*

Dawn's grey light begins to show behind the tenement buildings. The rain has stopped, the cold does not seem so cold. The small area at the bottom of the park where the body was found is log-jammed with polis; the entire park is cordoned off from the public. The Saturday between Christmas and New Year, and not too many people have crawled out of bed. A few anoraks who've brought their dogs out to let them dump on the park, stand around and watch the police activity, such as it is. What are they expecting to see?

And what are any of us doing, these too many chiefs and too many Indians? The SOCO's are doing their business, while the remainder of us stand around in monstrous misery and anger.

The body of Evelyn Bathurst has already been removed.

The first polis at the scene did not recognise her, her face having been dealt with in the same manner as Anne Keller five days ago. Multiple stab wounds, so that she was utterly disfigured. The body was identified by the ID card in her inside pocket. Strangely, it wasn't until then that the constable on duty had to throw up.

The gang's all here, each and every one of us looking sick. What makes it worse? That she was one of us? That she was so attractive? Or is it just that it's happened again, the killer has struck once more?

Bloonsbury is still drunk from last night. Very fetching he looks in his abject misery and inebriation. Taylor at least has managed to sober up, just looks hungover – the same as that idiot Herrod. And Charlotte Miller stands alone. Even saw her shed a tear. Haven't seen her at the scene of a crime since she got here, but this is different. This is a combination of all our worst nightmares.

Tried speaking to her a few minutes ago, got nowhere. She looks in shock. That hard bitch act is exactly that, but you would have to be built of granite to not be moved by this.

'And when he was home, there lay his uncle smitten on the head, and his father pierced through the heart, and his mother cloven through the midst.'

That was what she said, those her only words. Her voice was small, and like all intellectuals who cannot speak the truth of their emotions, she hid behind some inappropriate literary reference. The usual source, I presume, but I don't know. Don't care. She does, at least, look genuinely distraught.

Hodson walked past her not long after and they didn't even look at each other. And what were they up to no more than a few hours ago? Why would a Superintendent have a constable back to her house? There can be only one reason, and it's the same one that took me there on Christmas Eve. Makes me wonder why she's asked me away for Saturday night.

Tonight in a hotel looks extremely unlikely and if I don't spend the entire evening at the station, I can be glad of the fact that I did not dismiss Peggy's invitation. These, however, are trivial considerations at the moment. They would be, even if this latest murder had not been one us, and a popular member of the force at that.

I've got my back to a tree, the tenth smoke of the day in my hand, my mind all over the place. I'm going to have to talk to Taylor, no doubt. Who is there for me to betray, now that the only one of the gang of five whom I would have protected has been killed?

Sequence of events. Monday night – Anne Keller is murdered, and at the same time Edwards is mouthing off to Bathurst about the great conspiracy of last year. Two days later Bathurst fills me in on the full story. Doesn't want me to tell anyone else, so I have to presume she hasn't. I go to see Evans, he looks dumb about Monday night – and gut instinct says he's telling the truth – although there is something about Herrod and Bloonsbury, as if the conspiracy is still active in some way. Our killer tries to strike again, this time unsuccessfully, and the potential victim gets a good look at him. Bit of a vague description of course, since all these people are idiots, but it certainly isn't anything like Evans. The guts continue to say that he had nothing to do with the murder. I speak to Bathurst, advise her to go to Miller, and the next episode in the story is the one where she gets murdered.

So was she killed by the same man who did Keller – the same m.o. as far as anyone can tell at this stage – or was she murdered in copycat to keep her quiet, in which case, how did they know she was about to play the whistleblower? Could I have alerted them by my pointless trip to see Evans? That is the thing which consumes me the most. Was I to blame for her death?

Jesus, it's a horrible thought. But the gut feeling says that Bathurst was just another victim in the line. Auburn hair, walking alone through the streets in the middle of the night, she fits the mould of the victims.

But then there's that other gut feeling, the one which says there is no such thing as coincidence. If she's dead now, it's because of her knowledge of what happened last year. And if somehow they know that she told me...

Get the shivers, feels like a hand at my neck. Light another cigarette as the cold morning continues its painful appearance. Another media crew pull up and I wonder how Bloonsbury's going to handle them in his state.

Taylor appears, looking hellish, much the same as the rest of us.

'You all right, Sergeant?' he says.

Cigarette in the mouth, I nod. Why is he asking me?

'I mean,' he says, 'you two, you had something going, did you not?'

Aye, right enough. He thought I spent the night with her leading into Christmas Day.

'Nothing but another in a long line of rejections for me, Jack,' I say, and the cigarette tastes awful. Serves me right for smoking more than a half packet before breakfast.

'Oh,' he says, and looks disinterested. Doesn't believe me, which is fine.

'This is a fucking mess,' he says, looking around at the commotion. And a hell of a bigger mess than he supposes.

'Telling me,' I say. Crush the cigarette under foot, determine not to have another until I've eaten something. 'Look, I need to talk to you, Jack.'

'Aye, sure, whenever. Not now, though. Someone's going to have to talk to the press. Jonah's in no fit state.'

'Still pissed from last night.'

'Still pissed from Monday night,' says Jack – in one of our old jokes – and mumbles off to talk to the gathering herd of TV, hungry for the story for the morning news. Nothing people like better with their Cornflakes than a bloody mutilation.

Cornflakes. I could eat a bowl of them, right now.

*

Been a long day. Our battered husband woke up and wants to press charges. Had to go and speak to him, and having found the wife unlikeable and hard to believe, he was just as bad. Perfect for each other, except that one of them is a brutal, lying bastard. Or perhaps, as occurred to me at some point during the day, they're both brutal bastards and they're both telling the truth about the other's brutality. Got a feeling it's going to be like Michael Douglas and Kathleen Turner in *War of the Roses* and they'd save us all a lot of trouble if they just went off somewhere and fell from a chandelier together.

The shit has hit the fan, of course. Masses of the stuff, in great sodding dollops. The Chief Constable showed up, acting like he owned the place – I missed him fortunately, the guy's a moron – dragged back from his 'winter retreat' – that's what he called it, the fucking idiot – and not too happy about it. As it is the need of authority to dump on the next most senior in the firing line, Miller got it in the neck and everyone expected her to come firing thereafter. Didn't happen, however. She got them all together – missed this as well, at the hospital – and gave them some concerned talk, considerate, subdued, about the need for a quick result, not only for the benefit of the public, but for our own good. Stressed the need for good, honest work, to do the job well and not try anything that could backfire. Good polis chat, but not at all like Charlotte. Usually she's in amongst us like a lunatic with a chainsaw. Never been around her when she's lost one of her people before, so you don't know what she'll be like.

Mirrors the entire mood of the station. Everyone's the same – subdued, miserable, determined. We've got to get the guy, there's going to be no messing about and every other crime that gets committed along the way is even more of an irritant than usual.

At some point in the afternoon Mrs Bathurst showed up from Inverness, all tears and anger. Never wanted her daughter to be in the polis in the first place. Once she'd got her anger off her chest she broke down, and Charlotte spent a lot of time with her. Another surprise.

Got a message to phone Peggy but I haven't got around to it

yet. About tonight, there's just no way. It's going to be a long evening and I'm just not in the mood for any happy families. She's got to realise it, though, and if she doesn't then we're no further forward than we were two years ago.

Into Taylor's office, finally, at some time after six. Been wanting to talk to him all day and been growing more frustrated at the delays which have piled up, at the rubbish which keeps getting in my way. Had hoped to make the late afternoon brief, but missed that as well, thanks to another aggravated assault in Rutherglen Main Street. Don't know what's happening down there.

Find Taylor staring at the wall, his usual position. Thinking. Shut the door behind me, pull up a seat across the desk, light up a Marlboro. Started tasting good again around three o'clock.

'Got some bad news for you, Dallas,' he says.

What now? Taylor looks bloody terrible. Hope the bad news isn't going to be about him, that really it's bad news for him, not me.

'What?'

'Thistle lost two-one at Raith.'

'Fuck off.'

'Ayr won, so did Ross, so you're down to ninth.'

'Fuck.'

'Winning one-nil, let in two goals the last five minutes.'

'Aw, fuck.' Bloody Thistle, bloody useless. Should start supporting one of those pish wee teams in the third division; you know the ones who draw a crowd of six and get pumped every week.

'I don't care anymore,' I say, in a voice that suggests otherwise. 'I'm an East Stirling fan these days.'

'They got beat, 'n all.'

'Very funny.'

He laughs, but it's not a day for laughing and it dies on his face.

Time for work. Got a small knot in my stomach.

'What have I missed?'

He lets out a long breath, runs a hand through his hair. Christ, he looks tired. He needs a break and when I think about it, I can't remember the last time he had more than a day off.

'Same m.o. as before,' he begins. 'Exactly. Almost the same number of stab wounds, 'cept a hundred and twenty-seven this time. Got some skin samples and they've already checked out. It's the same guy. Strangled her first, but didn't kill her, then laid into her with the knife.' Feel sick, try to be dispassionate about it but this is Evelyn Bathurst. 'Mostly to the face and abdomen again, and some around the crotch.' Lets out another long breath. 'Only other thing, and I don't know what to make of this, they found evidence of her having had a sexual encounter with a woman. Small bite marks and bruises. Least, they presumed it was sexual.' Looks at me for the first time since he started talking. 'Did you know that about her?'

Shake my head. Have that instant egotistical thought – this explains why she rejected my advances. Feel guilty for having thought it.

'No one seems to know what she did last night. You any ideas?'

Already been asked, of course. Shake my head again.

'So, who knows where she was? Time of death was around six. Couldn't have been dead longer than about ten minutes when she was discovered. Night watchman on his way home from work. Apart from that, fuck knows. Aye, and one of those spotty little constables – Hodson, I think – gave her a loan of his car, but he says he's no idea where she went with it. He was on duty all night and she brought it back and left it. You all right?'

Stare at him. Try to keep my mouth closed. Fuck! Aw, Jesus Fuck. Feel that hand on my guts, squeezing, twisting.

What does it mean? Look away from Taylor, stare at the floor, fumble with the pack of cigarettes, try to gather my thoughts. Bloody Jesus. It was her that was with Miller last night, not Hodson. She went down there to tell her about the gang of five, and then what? They had sex? That doesn't make sense. And after she tells her, she gets killed. Coincidence again? It can't be. Too many coincidences. So, what? Miller is in on it and she followed Bathurst back up here and took care of her? No way. The same killer as the last time. A man, definitely a man. Maybe she phoned Evans, got him to do it.

'Sergeant, you want to share this with me?' he says, and I

suppose I owe it to him. But I can't tell him about Miller, not yet.

Where do we go from here? Evans, it leads back to Evans. The guy reeks of more than just alcohol. He was the one who murdered the woman last year, he is the one capable of the crime. Ignore the gut feeling, because there's definitely something going on with him and Bloonsbury, something more recent.

'Where's Jonah?'

'What?'

He looks at me funny. He's right. My thoughts are all over the place. What is Bloonsbury in all this? He's been too drunk all week to know any better. During the last murder case he was off the drink, you could tell he meant it, he had an eye for the crime – even though I didn't know how much of an eye at the time – but now he doesn't have a clue what's going on. He's lost it.

Evans was slime, you could see him doing this to someone, a fellow officer, anyone. But Bloonsbury is just a lush. A sad, pathetic bastard on a downward spiral.

'Jonah?' I repeat.

'Think he's gone to talk to some friends of Bathurst's. Not on the force. Ain't going to help, but he's desperate. Word is, and it's got to be coming, Miller's about to kick him off the case. Don't know though.'

Then what? Us, probably.

'Want to go for a drive?' I say.

'Where?'

'Arocher. See Evans.'

Leans forward onto the desk. Looks sharper.

'Evans? What the fuck has Evans got to do with any of this?'

Stand up, stub out the cigarette.

'Come on, I'll tell you on the way.'

25

Driving along the dreich banks of Loch Lomond by the time I finish telling Taylor of the last few days. Nothing excluded, except the bit about me turning up in Helensburgh last night and seeing Hodson's car parked outside Miller's house. That, and me shagging her.

He's listened carefully, asked the occasional question, knuckles growing gradually whiter as we've gone on. When we got into the car we had to listen to the Beatles, as usual, but they got hoofed pretty quickly.

Just past Luss when I wrap up. He breathes deeply, shakes his head. I've finished with me telling Bathurst yesterday evening that she should go and see Miller, and left it at that. First thing he says:

'We need to know where Bathurst went last night. You sure you've no idea?'

I've watched enough people lying to know how easy it is to get caught out. Shake my head, say 'no' in as positive a voice as I can manage.

'Well, if it was something to do with this conspiracy of yours, then why would she need the car? Not for Jonah. She could get a train easy enough. Herrod's a bit further away, but the same applies. That leaves Evans or Miller.'

Hadn't really thought this through, because I already know what she did. Didn't think about how easily he might be able to come to the conclusion.

'She could have got a train to see Miller. It's only Evans lives off a rail route.'

'Aye,' he says, 'but you said she was scared the other day. If she really thinks Evans is the murderer, would she go charging down there on a Friday night?'

Fair point – it was the last place she would have gone.

'But Miller, that's far more likely. And if she went quite late, then she would know the trains might well be off by the time she got back. And...'

He moves to the right and steams past a slow moving truck, the car groaning all the way. I'm not thinking straight, but I should know what he's about to say.

'And what?'

He raises his eyebrows.

'Baird said she thought Bathurst had had lesbian sex.'

It's where he's going, so I might as well go along with it. Not look like an idiot.

'And we know Miller has a certain reputation.'

'Exactamundo,' he says. 'Fuck's sake. Is there anyone in that station she hasn't shagged other than you and me?'

Almost leave too long a gap, almost damned by silence.

'She couldn't have shagged Jonah surely?' I say.

He smiles ruefully.

'You're kidding me?' I say, a little revolted. 'She shagged Jonah? He can still get a hard on?'

He laughs. 'I doubt it. It was years ago, when Miller was a young detective constable, and Jonah Bloonsbury was Jonah Bloonsbury. Still wallowing in all the shite that came after the Dixie Klondyke business. At the time he helped her along the way.'

Stuck in slow moving traffic, little chance of getting past. Where are all these comedians going on a dreich Saturday night?

'Anyway,' he says, and the laugh is gone, 'it doesn't make sense. Bathurst goes down there to reveal some great police conspiracy and Miller gets her into bed. And Christ, it couldn't have been Miller who killed her afterwards.'

'Maybe it wasn't Miller she slept with,' I say, and I can feel the words choke in my throat – lying to the boss. 'Maybe she borrowed the car to go and see some girlfriend, something like that.'

He nods. 'Aye, maybe. Certainly makes more sense. But if that was it, it was someone she kept quiet about, cause no one at the station knows anything about it.'

'Wouldn't you?'

Lets out a long sigh, says, 'Aye', and descends into silence.

We approach Tarbet, glad to see all the slow traffic continue along the Lomond road, while we turn off.

'Did you know already?' I ask as we pass the Black Sheep, the ubiquitous two cars sitting out front.

'Know what?'

'What I just told you. That they stitched the guy up, not the bit about Evans.'

'Not the specifics. Same as you, same as the rest of us. I knew they'd stitched him, but I didn't know exactly how and I assumed they still had the right guy. Not the rest of it, though.' Thank God for that.

'And what about this? You think Evans is the killer?'

'Don't know. Is he capable of it? Aye, course he is. But any identification we've had of the guy this week, none of it's indicated Evans. And you said yourself, about the way he acted when you went to see him. He'd no idea why you were there. And the one thing about Evans was there was no artifice to him. The man was an open fucking book.'

'What about Jonah?'

Down into Arocher, a few lights dotted around the head of Loch Long.

Shakes his head again. 'Just don't see it, Sergeant. The guy's a lush. This week, he's no idea what he's doing. His career is disappearing down the toilet. He's about to get presented with his cheque and a pension, and in three months time it'll all be gone. We'll see him hanging out on the streets of Glasgow.' Slows down as we come to Evans' house. 'He ain't pulling any rabbits out the hat this time.'

He turns off the engine and we step out into the wet, dark of evening. The house looks deserted, no sound from within, no lights. That old car of his has gone. We stand and look at the house, feel the light drizzle in my hair. Taylor leads the way up the garden path, says:

'Think we've missed him.'

He rings the bell and we stand out in the cold and wait. Look out over the loch, dark and dead in the night, a few lights away along its banks. Can hear the water lapping quietly on the shore, fifty yards away. Shiver.

Taylor rings the bell again, shouts in through the letterbox.

‘Gerry! You in there Gerry?’

Nothing. He tries the door handle, but it’s locked.

‘How’s your shoulder, sergeant?’ he says.

My shoulder’s fine, thank you. I’ll use the soul of my right boot if you don’t mind. He steps back. I’m about to kick at the lock when the door of the adjoining house opens up. Old guy appears, looking suspicious, annoyed about his Saturday night being disturbed.

He stares at us, doesn’t look happy. Taylor produces his badge, but it’s dark and from the way the guy is squinting, he could have brought out a parking ticket and he wouldn’t have noticed the difference.

‘Detective Chief Inspector Taylor, this is Detective Sergeant Lumberyard. We’re looking for Gerry Evans,’ he says.

The old man stares warily, grunts after a while.

‘What kind of fuck name is Lumberyard?’ he says.

I get that a lot. I stopped arresting people for it a long time ago, though. Too much paperwork.

‘We’re looking for Evans,’ Taylor repeats, ignoring the old geezer’s remark.

‘Well, youse’ll no find him,’ he says.

‘Why not?’ says Taylor, taking a step closer.

‘He’s pissed off.’ – A voice comes from within: ‘Would you close the fucking door, it’s freezing in here!’ – ‘Called me up, says he was going away for a few days, asked me to look after the place. Cheeky bastard. Look at it.’

‘When was this?’

‘Close the fucking door, ya eejit!’

‘When was what?’ says the old guy.

‘When did he call you?’

‘I don’t know, do I? Fuck’s sake, you think I log every one of my fucking telephone calls?’

Taylor continues, patient, understanding. I admire that in him. I would have arrested the guy by now. Bad hair in a residential area after the hours of darkness.

‘Well, was it this morning, yesterday? When?’

The old guy looks over his shoulder, sees something on the

television.

'Look, I'm going to have to go. I think it was this morning, all right?'

'And did you see him go?'

'Naw, naw. I told you, he phoned. Now, are you finished?'

Taylor nods, the old guy turns away.

'He didn't leave you a key, did he?' he asks as the door begins to close, and gets the negative reply as it slams shut.

He turns and looks at me.

'Don't you just love the public sometimes?' he says.

'Think we should arrest him?' I say.

'Bad hair?'

'Aye.'

He smiles. Too bad it's not part of the law anymore.

'Right you, the door,' he says.

Haven't had to do this in a while. Usually there's some strapping young constable not long out of Kicking the Door Down School on hand to do the job for you.

Boot to the door, as high up and close to the lock as possible. First kick and the whole thing creaks, and suddenly I'm not surprised because I remember what a shit-tip the entire house is. Second kick and the door smashes open, the lock flying backwards up the hall.

'Feet of steel, or rotting door frame?' he says.

'Very funny.'

He leads the way – no need for subterfuge – and puts on the hall light. You can smell the alcohol, the decay, and we split up and go room to room, through everything.

There are no surprises. The house looks much as it had done the previous day, certainly smells the same. Empty beer cans or wine bottles in every room. Liked his cheap German shite by the looks of things. The walls are bare and sad. Some of the drawers in the bedroom have been left open, a few clothes scattered about. Either someone else has been here searching – an incomplete search – or, more likely, Evans hurriedly packed a bag and grabbed a few stinking clothes before he went. Although it might be that he lived with drawers open and clothes strewn about his bedroom in any case.

Don't bother to count but find approximately two hundred porn magazines under his mattress. That's really sad. That's where you keep them when you still live with your parents, but when you're a middle-aged man living on your own? Why not just have them lying out on the bedside cabinet? Habit, presumably. He's kept them under his mattress for forty years. There were a couple of them off-the-shelf from the newsagent, but most of them were a lot more disgusting. Sick Scandinavian things, with animals and all sorts of kitchen utensils that even Nigella Lawson doesn't know exist; the more we search his house, the sicker we realise he was.

In a cabinet in another room, Taylor finds the wholly expected and utterly massive video collection. Most of them are in unmarked boxes but we don't bother to check them out. He must have picked up most of this stuff from polis hauls. We have warehouses jumping with this kind of crap, as well as a variety of other illegal products, and there are plenty of polis who'll use these places like a supermarket.

It's not a big house; half an hour and it's done. I need a shower, feel disgusting. We stand in the middle of the sitting room. Depressed. Morbid. This guy was one of us.

'You surprised?' says Taylor.

'No, but it's horrible. Jesus, the man's a slime. If he ever comes back and he's not the one committing murder, I want to get him for something. Weird porn, whatever.'

Taylor nods his head, looks around, thinking.

'He isn't coming back though, is he?'

Rhetorical question. There's no way he's coming back. Shake the head.

'You're right.'

'So, what do you think?' he says, and he starts moving towards the front door as he says it. 'What does this make Evans? A murderer?'

I nod my head as we step out into the cold darkness of night – the breeze off the loch feels refreshing, after the sleaze and stench of the house – and I close the door behind me. It shuts, but only just.

'Aye, I think this makes him an anything.'

We get into the car and sit and stare into the darkness. The windscreen is smeared with rain and it's like the fuzz in front of us stopping us from getting a clear view of the situation.

'What now?' I say.

He shakes his head.

'Not sure. But I think we should just keep this to ourselves. Fuck, I don't know. If Evans killed Bathurst, does that mean Jonah was in on it?'

'He must be. There were things done to the body that the press never got hold of from the first murder.'

He nods again, then shakes his head. 'This is bad. Fucking Jonah. But then, maybe not him. Maybe it was Miller. We don't know she wasn't in on the Addison case. Or maybe, Evans had nothing whatsoever to do with Bathurst dying. Maybe he's just gone off somewhere. The guy's retired, he can go where the fuck he wants. Maybe he went to see some of those bloody awful children of his,' he says, then shakes his head again. 'All right, no way he did that, but who knows? All the evidence points to last night's killer being the same as Monday night's killer, and all the other evidence points to that not having been Evans.'

Take a deep breath. A neat summation and basically we haven't a clue where to go next.

'Either way,' he says, 'we keep this to ourselves at the moment. Hope no fourteen year-old delinquents decide to break into the place and find all that crap.'

He starts the engine, gets the heater going full blast then turns the car round, and heads back towards Loch Lomond.

*

Arrive back at the station some time just before ten. The thought of spending a night in a hotel with Miller has long since vanished. Is suddenly reactivated by finding a note asking me to ring her at home. Heart immediately starts to thump faster, for different reasons this time.

There's a light on in Bloonsbury's office, Taylor goes in to speak to him. The great man is head down on the desk, grunting in his sleep. An empty bottle of White & McKay sits openly at his right arm.

Taylor lifts it, places it in the bin, then turns out the light as he closes the door behind him.

26

On the doorstep in Helensburgh, where I was three nights ago. Made a brief call to Miller and she asked me down. Don't know what the hell I'm doing here. Half expecting to find Evans waiting behind the door with a knife. Was tempted to tell Taylor before I left, but I couldn't. Kept my mouth shut, like a bloody idiot. Walking into the lair, completely defenceless. It's the sort of thing you watch people do in the movies, and you think, what are you doing, you idiot? Get some back up!

But I could hardly come screaming down here with back up, could I? The demon's lair? It could just be that I'm the biggest and stupidest jessie on the planet. So what if Bathurst and Miller had sex? Under other circumstances I'd have been watching the video.

The door opens and Miller invites me into the den. Dressed similarly to the other night, but a different colour scheme. She smiles, doesn't say anything, looks nervous. Closes the door behind me and ushers me into the sitting room. The Christmas tree still burns, but it looks incongruous now.

Half waiting for the appearance of Evans but my guts are telling me it won't happen. Stand by the warmth of the fire, wonder where Frank is, but don't really care. Remember Italy as I hear her pouring drinks behind, then she is beside me and I've got a vodka tonic in my hand.

We stare into the fire. Think I'm going to let her do most of the talking. Need a cigarette.

'Mind if I smoke?' I say.

She shakes her head. Produce the packet, shake one loose and light up. Feels good tonight, probably because I haven't smoked many in the last couple of hours.

'We are all busy in this world building Towers of Babel; and the child of our imaginations is always a changeling when it comes from nurse.'

That's all she says. I've heard that one before; we all have. It's her favourite line, and she gives it to all the new recruits. Can't imagine that it means much to most of them, but it sounds good, and I know what she's thinking. She would have said those words to Evelyn Bathurst, and what Towers of Babel can she build now?

'Did you know her well?' she says.

Stare deep into the fire. It's the first time I've slowed down all day. Take a longer drink from the glass than I intended. Feels as good as the cigarette, the alcohol burns its way down, the chill hits my stomach.

After the shock of the start of the day, it's been turned into just another murder. You have to stay focused on these things, can't let them get to you, but it doesn't mean your brain doesn't occasionally kick into overdrive. A warm fire, vodka tonic in your hand and a woman who might be implicated in the murder standing next to you.

Your back was turned. The glass could be poisoned!

Control your fevered imagination, Lumberyard, you fucking idiot.

'No, not really. Not any better than the rest of us.'

'No,' she says, and the voice is small.

'When was the last time you spoke to her?' she says, after another long silence in the crackle of the fire.

Take another large swallow of the vodka, nearly drain the glass. Does she know that I told Bathurst to come and talk to her? Does she know what I know and that I know it? Christ, I could run rings round myself. I have to trust her, because why else am I here?

'Last night, about five. She was just on her way out.'

'How did she seem to you?' she asks quickly.

How did she seem?

'I don't know. Like normal, I suppose.'

I may have decided to trust her, but I'm not telling her a thing.

'She didn't say anything about what she was doing last night?' The eyes flicker at me, I wonder if she knows that I'm in possession of the facts. But how could she?

Shake my head, drain the glass.

'No, she didn't. Said she was going out some place, but nothing specific.'

She doesn't say anything. Out of sight her hand slips into mine, her fingers squeeze. Her touch electrifies and terrifies at the same time. Lift my glass without thinking, the ice cubes clink down to my mouth, with the dregs of tonic. I need another one.

When she speaks again the voice is even smaller than before, the words stab out.

'I heard you went into work together on Christmas Day,' she says. How the hell did she hear that? 'How was that, Dallas? You spent the night with me.'

I can almost feel my flesh crawl. She sounds like a spurned lover, a little girl lost in the deep fathoms of a relationship which she doesn't understand. But this is Charlotte Miller, I can't believe she's hurt.

I look at her, and the first tear has started to trickle down her face. Jesus. Can't be real. Try to think rationally. Which is new for me.

Her head rests on my shoulder, a tear drops onto the back of my hand. She's either toying with me or getting genuinely emotional. Either way, I'm out of my depth.

Instant decision.

'Look, Charlotte, I think I'd better go.'

The hand squeezes a little tighter, something approaching a sob escapes her lips. This is the woman who rules the station with an iron hand in an iron glove.

'Stay with me, tonight,' she says, her voice cracking as she speaks, and it feels like a hand squeezing my stomach. Why does she need me to stay the night?

Christ, she's not going to kill me in her bed. Get a grip you stupid loony.

I don't reply but I know the answer. She looks up at me and her face is streaked with tears, her eyes red. I'm getting sucked in and if she's playing me, I'm falling into the game. Blinded by her air of vulnerability, the sexuality of it – which may be as much blinded by deception, no matter how aware I think myself to be.

She stretches a little, I lower my head, and our lips meet. I can taste the tears, I can feel her tongue gently probe into my mouth.

We kiss for a long time in front of the fire, until her tears have dried, than we go to her bedroom and this time the lovemaking is more tender and infinitely more intimate than before.

27

It is a cold morning, winter finally seeming to have arrived, after an eternal autumn of mild and wet weather. The clouds are low, the threat of snow in the air. The night before has been busy, the usual Saturday fracas, enhanced by the time of year. Assaults, knifings, burglary, a guy dressing up as a packet of Rice Krispies. The station buzzes, more crime to be dealt with than anyone has time for. In the middle of two murder enquiries, Detective Sergeant Herrod is landed with an assault from the night before; all the while he ponders the state of his Chief Inspector. The night asleep at his desk, bundled into a taxi and sent home a couple of hours before. A man to inspire loathing and the distant memory of respect.

Herrod hates every minute of the work that he does, loves it at the same time. The perfect conduit for his rampant ill-humour, the perfect outlet for his paranoia, a brilliant excuse to escape his home and his wife.

Nearly noon and he wonders about Lumberyard – yet to appear this morning. A Sunday perhaps, but this is no time for a day of rest. Taylor is at his desk, thinking as usual, but no Lumberyard, and he hopes he is not out investigating a lead. Hates the idea that it might be Taylor and Lumberyard who solve the murders.

Has had a vague thought as to why Evelyn Bathurst might have been killed, but refuses to believe it, refuses to think about it. Sometimes he is aware of his own paranoia. There is always another reason.

The phone rings as he is in the middle of putting together his report on the attempted assault, and he scowls at the ring. *If this is some other piece of shite...*

'Herrod,' he growls down the phone, imagining it sounds hard. Sees himself as the tough cop.

There is a slight hesitation, a small voice.

'Sergeant Herrod?' says a woman. Doesn't recognise the voice. Sounds like a call box. Still disinterested.

'Aye, I said that already.'

More hesitation. Bloody women. If this is another one about to report some pointless piece of shite, he'll tell her to go get a life and hang up.

'What is it, Hen, I'm busy?'

'I was told to speak to you. It's about these murders,' she blurts out.

Herrod's eyebrows raise a fraction. Could be something, could be some stupid sad woman who wants a bit of attention. She does sound nervous, however.

'All right, Hen. Take your time. Now, what's your name?'

She doesn't answer, doesn't want to tell him. He controls the desire to shout down the phone at her. Something he's used to doing with the public.

'I can't help you if you don't tell me you're name, Hen,' he says.

'I'm scared,' she replies.

He tries to lower his voice and sound compassionate, although he knows it's beyond him.

'Where are you phoning from?'

'Not Glasgow,' she says, after a few seconds. 'I don't really want to say.'

Herrod rolls his eyes, and thinks: bloody hell, here we go. No name, no address. Are you on Planet Earth, he wants to ask.

'All right, you don't have to tell me that either, just tell me why you're phoning.' On the verge of hanging up.

‘I went out with a man in Glasgow. A few months ago. Just a few times.’ She stops, he wonders if she might be crying. ‘Nothing really happened. We went to the pictures, once, you know.’

Herrod holds the phone in front of his face and looks at it. Oh my God. She’s phoning up to complain about a movie. *Jurassic Park III* was cack, can you go and arrest Speilberg, or whoever the Hell was responsible?

‘Yes?’ says Herrod, tentatively. This is almost laughable, and he has that weird sense of humour that kicks in briefly before he completely loses the head.

‘It was one of those retro showings, you know. A retrospective,’ she adds.

‘I know what a retro is,’ says Herrod, slowly, although he’d actually thought she meant retromingent – the ability to urinate backwards.

She doesn’t saying anything else, not immediately. More money gets put into the machine. Herrod taps his fingers on the desk. Lightening up. What the Hell, might as well spend day on the phone to some delinquent loony.

‘You want to tell me what you went to see?’ he asks after a while, and almost curious as to what it’s going to be. One of those films about Jesus, maybe.

‘Well,’ she says quickly and anxiously, ‘he was always a fan of the show, you know. The film came out a few years ago, and he just didn’t want to know. Avoided it, totally, that’s what he said. Then, we were going out on this date, and he’d talked about it the first time we met, so I persuaded him to go along and see the film. They were showing it in one of those wee theatres in town.’

‘I understand. What,’ says Herrod, very slowly, stretching out every syllable, ‘film?’

‘*The Avengers*,’ she says, almost annoyed, as if he should have guessed.

Herrod holds the phone away from him and stares at it again. Gives it a withering look and brings it back in.

‘Aye,’ he says, knowing for sure now that this woman is from another dimension, ‘I heard it was rubbish.’

‘Oh,’ she says, ‘it was terrible. Really terrible.’

‘Marvellous,’ he says. ‘What about *Sinbad And The Eye Of The Tiger*, did you like that one?’

Laughs to himself at his own sarcasm.

‘What?’ she says. ‘No, no, it’s about *The Avengers*.’

Herrod shakes his head. ‘Go on,’ he says. I could die while having this conversation, he thinks.

‘He was obsessed with the TV show, you know. The woman. Emma Peel. Obsessed with her.’

‘Aye,’ says Herrod. It takes all sorts of freeking weirdoes to make a world.

‘Well, it sounds ridiculous, I know, but he was totally weirded out by the film. Traumatised.’

Herrod doesn’t say anything.

‘No, really,’ she says.

‘And your point is, caller?’ asks Herrod. Feels like he’s Alan Green on Radio 5, taking some endless call where the caller refuses to ever get to the point.

‘He wanted me to start looking like she looked in that film, you know, long auburn hair. I dyed my hair, combed it out straight, you know, at first, before I realised. But it all started getting too weird. The guy was totally weirded out. Totally bizarre. It was scary.’

Herrod nods. And back on Earth...

‘And you point is, caller?’ he says again.

Wishes that Lumberyard was there to listen to the cutting edge of his sarcasm.

‘I dumped him. It was just too freakish. He started hassling me and stuff, but I lost him. Moved away. But he’d threatened to kill me before I left, it was that bad.’

‘Because he didn’t like the *Avengers* movie?’ says Herrod, still with that cruel smile on his lips.

‘It was really awful,’ she says.

‘All righty,’ says Herrod. ‘And so, did he kill you at all?’

‘Not me,’ she says, stating the obvious, really, and missing the continued sarcasm of his tone.

‘Who then?’

‘Well, you know, these two murders that have taken place. The women. They both had auburn hair, and the one who got away as well.'

Herrod is still disinterested. He nods his head, looking sagely at the phone.

'You think this guy is killing women because he didn't like the Avengers movie?'

'Aye,' she says. 'I do. One of the photofit pictures you showed of the man, there was just something about it. Didn't really look like him, but, God, I don't know.'

'All right,' says Herrod. From nowhere, he has a flicker of interest; not yet a flame. 'Has he got a name?'

It would be cool, he thinks, if this was the breakthrough, no matter how stupid it sounds. Every case has one. And he's the one on the phone – Bloonsbury is asleep, Lumberyard's out somewhere doing God knows what, Taylor is staring at the ceiling.

'I don't want him to find out I phoned. You promise?'

He nods down the phone. 'Don't worry, Hen, it'll never get back to you. You'll be quite safe.'

Another long hesitation. He hears her swallow, imagines her chewing her lower lip.

'Healy,' she says. 'His name was Ian Healy. He was a lawyer in Tollcross or somewhere like that.'

Herrod closes his eyes. Oh my God! Out of the blue. She has got to be kidding? This can't be for real. His fists clench. He looks around the office – it's busy with people going about their business. No one knows what he knows.

'Ian Healy?' he says, voice lower, 'you're sure about that?'

'Yes.'

Herrod could kiss her. The lawyer Lumberyard had brought in, and whom he and Taylor and Bloonsbury had all been happy to dismiss. Bloonsbury had even spoken to the guy for about an hour, and come up with nothing. The man had to be permanently pickled. Ian Healy. He would go round and get him now. No reason for the guy to be suspicious, and it will be him that has the collar.

Life is sweet.

'Now, we can bring this man in, but you have to give me your name and a telephone number where I can reach you,' he says. He keeps his voice low, tries to sound reassuring, tries not to betray his excitement.

'Can I not call you back?' she says, and Herrod shakes his head. But it doesn't matter.

'It'd be better if you gave me the number,' he says.

'I'm sorry,' she says, 'I'm frightened. I'll call you tomorrow,' and the phone clicks off.

'Stupid arse,' says Herrod, but there is a smile on his face, and he taps his hands happily on the desk. Absurd, totally absurd, but sometimes these things are.

Taylor appears from his office and looks at him.

'Just found out someone else you don't like has died, Herrod?' he says.

Herrod shakes his head, and mumbles. Taylor can go and sing *Dixie*, he thinks.

'Where's Jonah, you know?' asks Taylor

'No idea,' says Herrod, lying. I'm not telling you he's home in bed, still drunk out of his face from last night.

Taylor mumbles something himself, and walks back into his office. Herrod smiles. He hadn't got her details, but she'd call again. He had the feeling. Now, however, there were more important things to do. He would go and seek an interview with Ian Healy, then bring the guy in.

He knows he should not go alone, but that's the way he prefers to work. Particularly on something as big as this, where all the credit would be his. Sees his name in lights.

As he lifts his jacket, an earlier thought – how did the woman know to ask for him? – slips his mind.

'Got a few calls to make,' he shouts through the open office door at Taylor, who mutters, 'You don't have to tell me what you're doing, you miserable bastard,' in reply. Then Herrod is gone.

28

Christ. Woke up at almost twelve o'clock. Not hungover for once, which left me disorientated for a start, compounded by being in someone else's bed. The curtains were open, the grey light of another dull day filled the room. Got up and stumbled around – wasn't until I looked out the window at the leaden Firth of Clyde that I remembered I was in Helensburgh. Charlotte was gone, to work presumably. So, I had a wander round. Took my time. Kept expecting to bump into a butler or a maid or something, but it never happened.

Should have been in the office all day, of course, given the circumstances, but since I was already late, I thought I might as well make the most of it. Had a shower, made myself some bacon and eggs and a strong cup of coffee, left just after one.

As I was walking down the drive to my car, who should walk in but Frank. Strangely, I had a moment's guilt about the fact that I hadn't washed up after breakfast, rather than the fact that I'd knobbed his wife. We nodded at each other. The guy must have known why I was there.

'Charlotte at home?' he said.

I looked over my shoulder, then back to him.

'Nope,' I said. 'Work, I presume.'

You could see him thinking, hear the question in his head. Well what the fuck are you doing here then?

'Well, good day, Sergeant,' was all he said.

'Frank,' I said, nodding, and we passed each other by.

And so it is that I arrive in the station at not much before two. Herrod's nowhere to be seen and there's the usual scurrying activity from spotty constables. The door to Charlotte's office is closed, which means she's in town.

Been awake for two hours and have so far managed to keep my mind completely clear of everything that's been going on; that way leads to confusion and worry. Did suddenly remember at one point – crossing the Erskine bridge, I think – that I should have called Peggy last night. Back in the dog house, and maybe it's where I want to be.

Walk into Taylor's office. For once he's attending to paperwork. Looks up, isn't impressed.

'God's sake, Lumberyard, one of our number was murdered yesterday. Where the fuck have you been?'

Immediately feel like an idiot. Shrug. Can't even be bothered lying, so I just don't answer.

'Right, got something for you to do. Seems Bathurst was a bit if a writer. Letters, diary, that kind of thing.' He gestures to a cardboard box on the seat next to him. It's large and it's full. 'Journals, letters from friends, whatever. I want you to read it all see if there's anything there. Anything about Evans, you know, and the other thing.'

Obviously I don't look impressed.

'And you can take that fucking look off your face. If you hadn't been so late you'd be finished by now.'

'Aye, all right, all right.'

Go and lift the box, start to walk back to the desk.

'And if you find anything, you know, compromising, about her or anyone else at the station, forget it.'

I nod, stop in the doorway, turn back.

'Where are the great crime fighting duo?' I ask 'How come Herrod hasn't got hold of these?' Herrod would love this.

He shakes his head.

'Haven't a clue where Jonah is. Might be out there somewhere, but I suspect he's at home and not answering his phone because he's in his usual position.'

'And these?' I say, holding them up.

'Fortunately I got hold of them first. You've got them because we know what Herrod would be like with those in his hands. The bastard would be making photocopies.'

Ain't that the truth? I nod, and plod back to my desk.

And so it is that I spend the next five hours in the private world of Evelyn Bathurst. One of the standards of detective work – spending hours at a time going over the mundane, hoping to find one small fact which might help you along. At first I thought it might be quite interesting, but inevitably it proved otherwise.

Turned out to be a collection of dull letters about Barney's cartilage operation, and Meadowbank the Dog's psychological problems. Someone, somewhere taught me to be thorough, however, so I find myself reading every word. Got quite interested in the end in the relationship between Aunt Sophie and the gardener; entangled in the innocent and small plots of Bathurst's family life.

The main thing, of course, was going to be the diary. From the time of the Addison case and from this past week. The first one was disappointing; she didn't mention it at all. Must have been pretty scared but a very wise move. It never does to write things down when you're committing a crime. Asking for trouble.

She finally mentioned it in the past week. There were only a couple of entries after Monday night and both times she talked about the past in vague terms. Expressed a few of her fears, but nothing that would have had meaning to anyone else. Didn't learn anything new. And the last entry was made on Christmas Day, so there was nothing about going to see Miller on Friday night.

So what do I have after five hours in her world? A better understanding of the girl, and a weighty depression. I liked what I read. I liked Bathurst anyway, and now it's all the more painful what's happened to her. Want to go out there, find whoever did it, and kick fuck out the guy.

By the time I'm done it's long been dark outside, well past seven o'clock. There's been a change of shift, but there's still the same crap going on. Charlotte emerged about three and walked on by. Acknowledged my presence and that was it. She looked tired, and I don't think it's only because of what we did last night. Still haven't phoned Peggy, although I've been meaning to most of the day.

Walk back into Taylor's office. He's been gone most of the afternoon, only came back about half an hour ago. Spent the time since staring at the ceiling.

Plant myself in the seat, uninvited. Light up. He looks at me, eyebrows raised in question. Shake my head.

'Nothing,' I say.

'Shit,' he says.

Lies his head back, lets out a heavy sigh.

'There has to be something, Sergeant. There has to be something we're not getting. The same person killed Ann Keller and Evelyn Bathurst. So which is it? Was Bathurst's murder coincidental with her involvement with the Addison case – or was it connected, in which case Keller's murder must also be connected.'

'I.e. Evans,' I say.

'Exactamundo.'

And maybe Charlotte, but that I keep to myself.

'I wish I could think straight,' he says. He's not alone.

'What'd you do this afternoon?' I ask.

Shakes his head, stares at the floor.

'Went home, went round to Jonah's place.'

'And?'

His eyes are glued to a piece of dirt on the carpet, his mind glued to something else. About to get further revelations on his marriage, I suspect. Brace myself, but I should be willing to hear them. Lets out a long sigh.

'I could do without all this shit at the moment.'

'What's happened?'

'Jonah's just a fucking mess. Jesus.'

'You go in? Share a bottle of Teachers?'

'Wouldn't let me in. Opened the door after I'd been ringing the bell for about five minutes, just stood there breathing fumes over me. Jesus. This is it for him, Sergeant. There're going to be no sudden revelations this time, no great victory from the jaws of defeat.'

'Unless he's behind it all like last time.'

Shakes his head, laughs bitterly.

'Not a chance. Look at the guy. I've always admired him and he did use to be the star that everyone took him for. I know he was past it by the time you met him, but the guy was up there. But it's been at least ten years now since he did any good work, at least that. And if all that about the Addison case is true, well the guy's just sold his soul to fucking Hell. The quicker he gets there the better.'

'If he keeps on drinking...'

'You think? I know for a fact that he was told by his doctor three years ago that if he didn't cut out the whisky altogether, not just cut down, he was dead in six months. Well, it's been a long six months.'

He's right. The guy is dead.

'So do you think you'll get landed with it?' I ask.

He lets out a low whistle.

'Well, that's what I thought, but...'

'But what?'

Raises his eyebrows.

'Heard a rumour,' he says.

'Aye?'

'Miller's thinking of taking over the investigation herself.'

'You're kidding?'

Shrugs his shoulders.

'Just what I heard. I think Jonah's out, but the word is that she's hacked off at the lack of progress and wants to take charge.'

'She can't!'

'It's her station. She can do what she wants. She can clean the fucking toilets if she chooses.'

That wasn't what I meant, but he didn't know that. I know she has the authority, but Christ! she had sex with Bathurst a couple of hours before the girl was murdered. She could be involved, for God's sake, how can she lead the investigation?

Cover up. Pretty obvious really. So it seems.

'Fuck,' is all I say, shaking my head.

'Fuck, indeed,' says Taylor. 'And Debbie left me,' he adds as an afterthought.

'What?'

'She left. Confounded all the critics by moving in with her young man. So, I'm a middle-aged bachelor again.'

'Jesus! You all right?'

He stares at the floor, puffs out his cheeks, lets the air out slowly.

'Don't know,' he says.

‘Want to go for a drink?’

He nods.

‘Love to,’ he says, and gets out of his chair. Takes a look at some of the papers on his desk, murmurs something under his breath and heads towards the door, putting the light off as he goes.

‘Any idea where Herrod went? He’s been away all afternoon,’ I say, following in his wake.

‘No idea,’ he says. ‘Lying dead in a ditch somewhere, if we’re lucky.’

*

But Herrod does not lie dead in a ditch. He hangs dead on a wall, impaled by an ornamental sword through the lower chest cavity, his feet dangling three inches off the ground. The drip of blood from his mouth has long ago stopped, the pool on the floor disturbed by the scurrying feet of rats.

29

There is no solace but the solace of pain.

The pain of hurt; the pain of rejection; the pain of humiliation. The pain of defeat.

Can’t stop thinking about Emma. Consumes his thoughts. Bloody Emma. Face tortured, agonizing smile. Cool haircut, terrible accent.

Wants to take himself somewhere, somewhere within his imagination. A city; big, brassy, loud; where the action is. Just him and Emma hitting the clubs, hitting the night spots. Drinking, gambling, dancing. And getting in adventures. Him and Emma battling it out with all sorts of weird scientists and splinter groups and secret societies. Big adventures, with good direction and a solid script.

But it never works out like that. From the prison of his mind, he can’t sort out the fantasy. Can’t construct it. Like a sixties tower block, it looks good for five seconds, then begins to crumble and crack.

He'll never see Emma again and, if he does, she won't be interested. Not bloody Emma. Emma with her knee-length boots, Emma with her knowing smile. And his fantasies disintegrate into a sordid mess; him and Emma alone in a dark stinking room, getting nowhere, doing nothing.

Eventually he will be purged. Eventually she will understand. She will be at one with him, and the hurt she inflicted upon him. Maybe then she will smile at him and they will be one. She will love him.

30

Another day, another hangover. Four hours in the pub with Taylor, by the end of which I had persuaded him that he really didn't want to be married to Debbie anymore anyway. Did my bit for his peace of mind, although whether he'll still be happy about it this morning I don't know. He looked bloody awful when I saw him, but he wasn't in long before he left again. Away to speak to a couple of friends of Ann Keller's. A great believer in re-covering old ground. You always learn something new.

Bloonsbury is in his office, doing God knows what. Door closed, hitting the sauce more than likely. Miller called for him about half an hour ago, dismissed him ten minutes later. He came out looking like an angry man, but then he always looks like an angry man.

Herrod has disappeared. Took a call yesterday morning and went out, no one knows where. May be dead in a ditch after all. The station is certainly a more pleasant place to be without him, however. Maybe he's accepted an expensive transfer offer from another station. Haven't seen a paper this morning; it could be on the back page – *Herrod in Shock £20M Deal With Old Trafford.*

As usual I've been landed with the detritus of the weekend – muggings, rape, robbery. It's all showing how desperately undermanned we are. Dire straits. There's just far too much going on, and when we could do with all hands on deck for the murder enquiries, officers are continually getting pulled away on more mundane crime.

Writing up the report on a break-in at a newsagents at the bottom end of Cambuslang Main Street when Miller appears from her office. Approaches, looking around her as she does so.

'I'll need everything you've got on the Keller and Bathurst cases, Sergeant. Everything. Notes, random thoughts, vague ideas.' She stares at me, and I suppose I must be giving her a look. 'I've taken over from Chief Inspector Bloonsbury. I'll be leading the investigation. I want everything you've got as soon as possible.'

She can't do this. Say nothing.

'Where's Taylor?' she asks.

'Speaking to a friend of Anne Keller's, I think.'

'And Herrod?'

Shake my head. I'm not his bloody keeper.

'Tell them both I want to see them when they get in.'

She stares at me for a second, then turns away. She stops as she passes the closed door to Bloonsbury's office, perhaps considers going in. Walks on, back to her own office. Closes the door behind her.

Well, Jesus, Taylor was right. The criminals have taken over the asylum; the suspect has taken over the investigation. Except, she's nobody's suspect except mine.

Head in palm of my hand, eyes open. Not really aware of the noise of the office going on around me. Certainly no bloody thought for this stupid newsagents. Criminals got away with several thousand cigarettes and a bunch of pornos. Christ, maybe this was Evans as well.

Forget Evans. What am I going to do about Charlotte Miller? She's the last person to have seen Bathurst, she slept with her; then maybe an hour later, she's dead. And Charlotte Miller isn't telling anyone about it.

But do I really believe she had something to do with it? If she didn't, then is there anything wrong with her leading the bloody thing? If the two of them were intimate, then maybe she'll be switched on to it – certainly a damn sight more switched on than Jonah.

I stand up, decision made, even though I've no idea where it's come from. She can't do it. She's got thirty officers trying to discover where Evelyn Bathurst was on the night she died, and whose bed it was that she lay in.

Knock on the door, don't wait to be invited in. Walk in, head up, full of aggression. She stares at me and I immediately wilt at the knees, and want to make a retreat. Can't think of the right words, so I just come out with the first ones that are there.

'What the fuck are you doing?'

Christ, good start Lumberyard. Suddenly have the image of me sitting on an inter-city train; first class ticket, eating one of these brie and black grape sandwiches, ice-cold v&t, on my way up north for a bit of a holiday.

'Sergeant?'

One word, but what a voice. A coiled snake. You can hear it in those two syllables, the anger just waiting to explode. No one talks to Detective Superintendent Miller like that. I'm going to just have to go for it. All guns.

'You slept with Evelyn on Friday night.' Good opener.

Her shoulders straighten. Face tightens.

'What?' is all she says. The anger's gone, she no longer sounds as if she's about to machine gun me.

'You slept with Evelyn. Half the fucking force is trying to find who her lover was on Friday night, and it's you.'

Shut up, let the words sink in. She just stares at me, nothing to say – or doesn't know what to say.

'Christ, you're involved. How can you be in charge?'

She starts shaking her head, staring at the desk.

'How long have you known?' she says. 'How do you know?'

'I've known all along,' I say. Not true, but it's all I'm saying.

Looks up at me; scared. Bloody marvellous. They've all got their vulnerable side, these high-powered uberchicks. Particularly when they've been caught with their pants down.

'You've not told anyone?'

Shake my head. Not yet.

She swallows, stares me down. Seems to regain herself; climbing slowly back into the saddle. No way she can get back to the stage of whipping me, however. At least, I don't think so.

'What are you going to do?' she asks.

Christ, I don't know. I didn't come in here to talk sense, did I? I'm just here to mouth off.

What should I do? I should tell Taylor; I should tell anyone who wants to listen. Maybe it doesn't mean she had anything to do with the murder, but it's certainly pertinent to the investigation.

I stand there like a lemon, looking stupid. Have lost all that sparkling fire I had when I first got in here, sixty-five seconds ago. Which one of us is vulnerable?

Show some balls, Lumberyard, for God's sake.

'You should put Taylor in charge.'

She doesn't answer. Looks up from behind the swathe of paperwork. Her mind is working and it's disconcerting to know that it's a hell of a lot sharper than mine. Have a fleeting thought that maybe I should demand that I get put in charge, but that might be pushing it a little. *Useless DS on Slow Track To Nowhere Put in Charge Of Scotland's Biggest Ever Murder Hunt!* The Sunday Post would have a field day.

'And if I don't?'

I was hoping she wasn't going to ask that.

'Just do it, Charlotte. I don't know what the fuck was going on between you and Evelyn, but you're too close. And if it ever gets out, you're fucked, especially if you take over the investigation. It's just going to look like you've got something to hide.'

Bites her lower lip. God, I love it when she does that.

'And what do you think? Do you think I've got something to hide?'

'Jesus, I don't know.'

She nods, breathes deeply.

'Do you know why Evelyn came to see me?'

Get swallowed up by those eyes. Try to stay calm, think clearly.

What's this about? Wants to know how much I know about these bastards and what went on last year? I'm lost. Big time denial, that's the only option.

'No idea.'

A long pause. I wish I knew what was going on in there.

'Did you know she was coming before she came?'

She's fishing. I'm such an idiot that if I let her fish, she'll catch something before too long.

'How, when, it doesn't matter. I know, that's all. Are you going to put Jack on it, or not?'

'If I do, what will you tell him? What if he instructs you to spend all your time looking for Bathurst's female lover? What then?'

She gives me the shivers, for a hundred different reasons. Time to go.

'I don't fucking know, Charlotte. Just do it.'

Give her my best look of steel. Try to be hard. Turn on my heels and walk out before she can see through it – although I'm probably about five minutes too late for that.

Close the door behind me, feel the relief. Have no idea what I'm going to do if she decides to go for a test of wills by completely ignoring me. All I can do is hope she pays attention and lets Taylor get on with it. Otherwise...

As I cross the office, the legendary Jonah Bloonsbury emerges from his office. Looks awful, but that's no surprise. Facing up to the fact that his career has finally disappeared round the u-bend. Some guys look good on the back of four or five days stubble – like me for instance – and some guys just look terrible.

He stops to talk to me as our paths cross. Looks broken. Shoulders hunched; clothes pretty much the same ones he's been wearing for the past week; eyes bloody red, might have been pierced with a knife; ruddy face, bulbous nose of the alcoholic, combined with the hollow cheeks of someone who hasn't eaten anything for months; thinning hair, matted, dirty. We get druggies in here who look better than he does.

'The bitch tell you what she's done?' he says. Words trip over each other on their way out of his mouth. Can smell the whisky.

Stale and fresh at the same time.

'Aye,' I say.

He slumps against a desk. Herrod's desk, as it happens. Head collapses onto the top of his chest, and then he appears to notice that Herrod isn't there.

'Any idea where this bastard is?' he asks.

'If we're lucky he's been transferred,' I say.

'Who'd have him?'

Aye, well, right enough.

'Got a smoke, Lumberyard?'

Go to my desk and dig out the packet of Marlboro's. Remove two, light up, and then hand him the other and the lighter. It shakes pathetically in his hand, flame flickering, and he takes several seconds to find the end of the cigarette. Wish I'd done it for him.

'What you going to do now?' I ask.

He doesn't answer immediately; starts coughing up a variety of revolting substances from his lungs the second the smoke hits the net. A young WPC I don't recognise walks by, looks at Jonah as if he's scum. Perhaps assuming he's on the other side of the great law and order fence. Which he probably is.

'The bitch wants us to resign.'

'And?'

Coughs some more as he tries again with the cigarette.

'No chance. I'm here 'til they get rid of me. She can go fuck herself.'

He looks up at me, points the cigarette.

'I fucked that bitch before, you know. Long time ago, you know, but I did it.'

Aye, I know. Back in the glory days, when Jonah Bloonsbury was worth it.

'Now look at her. She's the bitch fucking me.'

Don't know what to say to him. You're not the only one, big man.

He stands up, attempts to straighten his shoulders.

'Well, they can all piss off. I'm not resigning for any bastard. Especially not her. Hasn't heard the last of Jonah fucking

Bloonsbury.'

The phone rings behind me, just as he starts to walk off. Saves me from further discourse – not that I was going to say anything else to him anyway.

'If that's for me, tell them I'm away getting pissed,' he says, and stumbles out of the office, bumping into PC Hodson as he goes.

If it's for you, they'll already know you're getting pissed.

Lift the phone. 'Lumberyard.'

'Dallas?'

Peggy. Bugger. Had to happen sometime. Couldn't keep avoiding her for the rest of my life. Especially not if I want to marry her again.

'Peggy, how are you?'

'I'm all right, Dallas. I tried to get you all weekend. What were you doing?'

Sounds annoyed. Here we go again. The same old story. Except, this time she's got a point.

'Look, I'm sorry, Peggy, but you must have seen the news. Saturday morning...'

'Aye, of course.'

'It's been bedlam all weekend. I'm on the case, and I keep getting landed with all the other crap that's going.'

'I understand, but you weren't there all Saturday night, were you? Or Sunday morning? What were you doing Dallas? You must have slept. You could have slept here. You could have called.'

It's a sixth sense thing. She's got me by the balls. Peggy's not one of those high strung neurotic types who disappears up the backside of insecurity as soon as you mention another woman's name or appear home fifteen seconds late for your dinner. The only reason she's annoyed at me for not showing on Saturday night is because she knows. I can feel it. So I'm going to have to put a lot more effort into my lying.

'Look, Jack's been sending me out on a whole bunch of shite. Just haven't stopped.'

'He didn't know where you were on Sunday morning. Thought

you were with me.'

Shit. Backed up against a wall. Gun at my head.

'The children were looking forward to it, Dallas. You could have called.'

She pauses, but I've no idea what to say. She knows nothing, and yet I feel as if I've been well and truly caught with my pants down.

'Look, I know we're not back together or anything,' she says, 'but Christmas Day...you know. I just thought... well, if there's someone else you could at least tell me.'

Stand fast. Lie big time.

'No, honestly, there's not. I was following up all sorts of shite that even Jack doesn't know about. This whole murder thing's getting freaky.' That's not a lie. Can't believe I used the word 'honestly'. A sure give-away. 'Can I see you tonight, I'll tell you all about it. Promise.'

'Is there any point?'

'Honestly, there's a lot going on, Peggy.' Stop saying fucking honestly, you moron. 'I'll come over tonight when I can get away. Tell you all about it.'

She hesitates, but I've got her.

'All right,' she says. 'I'll wait up.'

'Good. I'll try not to be late.'

'Like I said, I'll wait up.'

Right. The phone goes dead. Put the receiver back down. Feel like I've just got out of jail, but that I'll probably be going back in later on tonight. If I ever get there.

Start going into my feelings on the whole thing. It was her who left me for another man. She divorced me. We had sex for a night, and then wham, I'm under obligation again.

Suppose she's right. It was me that coughed up the diamond earrings. A few days ago I thought I was still in love with her. One infatuation later, and what? I don't know. I should be still in love with her, but I may be too much of a heid the ba' for that.

Bloonsbury reappears. Smell him before I see him. He stumbles past the desk, leaning on anything he can.

'Can't believe I forgot my fucking booze,' he says, heading

back towards his office.

31

Two hours later and just about finished that report on the newsagents. Paperwork. It's not that I'm sitting on it; I keep getting interrupted. The usual shite of any given Monday. I've had enough. Need a holiday from all this. Murder, pointless little criminal investigations, Peggy, Charlotte. I need a break from it all. Except Charlotte.

Taylor arrives. Appears to be slightly more awake than usual. Look of curiosity on his face. Walks past me, sits down at Herrod's desk. Leans over in a conspiratorial manner. Looks like the big man might have something. Low voice so the rest of those idiots who inhabit this place can't hear.

'You got something?' I ask. 'Ann Keller's friends?'

He shakes his head, doesn't immediately answer. A wee smile appears on his face. Hard to tell.

'That got me nowhere,' he says. 'What can you expect? Just thought I'd give it a try.'

'So why are you looking like a smug bastard, then?'

I suppose you shouldn't really speak to your boss like that, but no one has any respect these days.

His voice drops another notch.

'Sergeant Harrison just asked me out for dinner.'

No fucking way! My jaw drops.

'Eileen?'

He nods.

'I thought she was, you know...'

'So did I,' he says.

'Bloody hell. Eileen Harrison.'

'Exactly.'

Bit of a shock that.

Pathetic, isn't it? Two grown men, and the minute a woman is mentioned we start acting like twelve year-olds.

'So do you think she's just doing it because she's heard about Debbie and she feels sorry for you?' I ask.

'Thanks, Lumberyard.'

Don't mention it. Look mildly embarrassed. Kick a man when he's down, why don't you?

'Maybe she's been wanting to do it for years. Now she's got the chance,' I say. Good recovery.

He stares at the floor, thinks about it.

'Nice thought. But I doubt it. We're talking about Eileen Harrison here.'

We both shut up and sit there. Thinking about Eileen Harrison. Do we know for a fact that she's a lesbian or is it just one of those things that we've always assumed? Try to remember if there's any definite proof.

Charlotte Miller appears in front of us, just as Taylor and I are at the height of inactivity.

'Gentlemen.'

We snap out of it. The usual thing. I look like I've been caught sleeping with a fourteen year-old; Taylor looks as if he couldn't give a shit. Charlotte looks pretty impressive standing there in that power suit.

'I'd like to see you in my office, Chief Inspector,' she says to him, and turns on her heals.

Taylor looks at me, waiting until she's out of earshot.

'Maybe she wants to ask me out to dinner as well,' he says as he gets up.

'Don't get carried away Jack,' I say. 'You're still an ugly bastard.'

'Fuck off,' he says.

Bit of banter.

The phone goes and, in common with everyone else, I look at the thing as if I want it to explode. Odd that, because sometimes when the phone rings, it's good.

'Lumberyard?'

'Ramsey here,' says the detached voice. Bloody Hell, just what

I need. Another theft of Winnie The Pooh masks in Rutherglen.

'What is it, Stuart?'

'Got a woman down here wants to talk to Herrod.'

'Aye?'

So what? Tell her he's not here and get her to come back in three years time.

'It's about the Keller and Bathurst murders. Said she spoke to Herrod on the phone yesterday morning.'

Instant wake up call. They said that Herrod disappeared after taking a call.

'Can you show her to one of the rooms, Stuart. I'll be down in a minute.'

'Aye, no bother,' he says and is gone.

Put the phone down, drum my fingers on the table. Got a weird tingle. It's a polis thing. Gut instinct. About to get a breakthrough. Won't go leaping into the midst of the Taylor-Miller conflab just yet. Wait and see if my guts are in order for a change. Don't want to interrupt them if she is asking him out to dinner.

Bloody well better not be.

Get up and start walking downstairs, with the horrible thought that I'm becoming possessive about the woman.

Get a grip on yourself, you sodding idiot.

32

Breakthrough.

Just had a visit from Maretta Johnson. Twenty-six, dirty blonde hair, bit of a looker. Something of the Uma Thurman about her. Bit of a goofy face, but smouldering sexuality – you know the thing. Anyway, her sexuality really doesn't have anything to do with it; that's just me playing to the big male stereotype.

She called Herrod yesterday because she thought an ex-boyfriend of hers might be our murdering headcase. Didn't give

Herrod her name or a number cause she was scared. Tried to call him again today, couldn't get him. Something made her come in and cough up the beans.

Started rambling on about how she saw this guy for a while, and the whole thing was a bit weird. Got some story about the *Avengers*, and I was beginning to think that she should be talking to one of our shrinks, rather than a hardened, cynical-type like me.

She saw the description of the guy – the photofit was a bit off the mark – but speculation that his victims might be a substitute for the object of his wrath, did it for her. She called the idiot Herrod. And then finally – and this was after a good twenty minutes – she dropped the name. Ian Healy.

Well, for goodness sake, it all sounded like a complete load of pants. I mean, I know *The Avengers* was an ugly, ugly movie, but you don't go murdering women that look like Emma Peel just because of it. Unless, of course, you're an unbalanced heid the ba', and this tips you over the edge. In which case... There are a lot of strange people out there, and frankly, nowadays, I'm prepared to believe anything.

So I left her sitting there with a cup of tea and a WPC for company, grabbed Taylor and made big feet for Healy's office. Taylor had just emerged from Charlotte Miller looking moderately apprehensive. Just been put in charge of the whole murder inquiry, you see. Big relief.

We could have come out like the fucking cavalry. Guns, back-up, the whole bit. But it's not Taylor's way. Doesn't want to go tramping all over town if we're going to look stupid. There's no such thing as coincidence in crime – apart from when it happens. Ian Healy might be our man; he might not.

Now we're on the road between Healy's office and his home, having come up empty. His secretary sat there looking like a dozey little clown. Said she had no idea where he was, and if she knew and wasn't saying or if she didn't know and she was worried, she hid it perfectly. Polis resentment to a tee.

Short drive to Healy's place somewhere in Parkhead. If I was him I wouldn't live so close to my business, but the guy obviously isn't rational. Not by a long way.

Taylor hits the London road. Not too much traffic – no need for any flashing blue lights. Briefly reaches ninety-five in the outside lane. He's pissed off.

'How long did Jonah interview this bastard?' he says.

'Don't know,' I reply. 'An hour, maybe more. Not sure.'

'Christ. I mean, what the fuck was the man doing? He's supposed to be a fucking polis. How can you interview a murderer for half the fucking day and then decide he's not your guy? Christ, you fingered him after two seconds in his office. Fucking Jonah spends all morning talking to the bastard and doesn't even bother getting a blood sample.'

'Come on. I let it pass. You said yourself you didn't think this was it.'

'Fuck that,' he says angrily. 'I spoke to the bloke for three minutes. Jonah practically moved in with him.'

'What do you expect, Jack? Bloonsbury's dead. He couldn't pick the murderer out of a line-up of four nuns and a blood-covered guy with a chainsaw. He's finished.'

'Dead right he's finished. Dead right.'

Another nail in Bloonsbury's coffin. Haven't even been thinking about nails in Herrod's coffin. Healy might be our man so there's a chance Herrod's dead. And for all that he's an open sore on the backside of humanity, you never want to see this happen to one of your own.

Up into a side street, then we're parked in front of Healy's tenement. No messing about. Up the stairs, third floor. Start to slow down as we reach the top. Walk more quietly as we near the door. Green paint, slowly peeling.

We stand at the door. Deep breath. Look at each other. Nervous. This could be it, this could be nothing. Wish we'd brought guns. Taylor rings the bell and we stand and wait.

'We should be armed,' I say to him.

'Don't be a jessie, Lumberyard.'

Tries the doorbell again, gives in to the inevitable.

'Right then, John Wayne,' he says. John Wayne? 'Do your sergeant thing and kick the door in.'

Marvellous. Nearly twenty years on the force and it's all I'm good for. Decide to have a go at something I saw in a movie once. Try the door handle.

With a genteel click, the door opens. Nice and easy. Give Taylor a look of superiority, and he scowls.

Swing the door open, step inside. Taylor in front. Immediately feel it. The darkness, the silence. The curtains are drawn. Not a sound. Not even the faint hum of a fridge or central heating. Scary.

Taylor hits the light switch. Nothing. The electrics are out or the light bulb's gone. Either way, we're walking into a darkened house with every possibility of a psychotic killer hiding behind a door.

'We should've brought guns,' I say to him, voice low. He ignores me, starts walking slowly into the flat.

Leave the door open to let in some light. As we take the first few tentative steps, begin to notice the smell. Off milk. Not some rancid pungent stench. Just a hint of it.

The hairs start to spring up on the back of my neck. On my arms. Feel the shiver. A tightness in the chest. I hate this. Walking into the unknown. Who knows what kind of man Healy really is? If he leaps out brandishing a knife, fine, you get into a fight. Take care of it. It's the creeping around in the dark that's the problem. That's the fear. Waiting. For the shock.

I follow Taylor into a room. In the pale light from the door I can see the settee, the TV in the corner. Light behind the curtains. Taylor walks over and opens them and the grey light of another bloody cold and miserable Glasgow afternoon comes flooding in.

Look around the room, quickly behind the door; half expecting Healy to be there with an axe. Got to get a grip.

It's a sad depressing little room. Horrible 70's furniture; 15" portable TV; drab wall paper, drab paintings; brown carpet; bin overflowing with rubbish; chipped coffee table, covered with magazines and photographs.

We go to look at them at the same time. Porn mags, photography mags – which pretty much look the same from the cover – newspaper supplements. They each have a picture of a woman with auburn hair on the cover.

We look at each other. It's coming together. We have our killer. No doubt. I can feel it. If only we'd had the sense to break the door down when we first came to check on the guy.

Back out into the hall. Look into the bathroom, try the switch again, still nothing. We can see it fine, however, in the light from the other room. A nasty little room, unpleasant aroma. Move on.

Skin crawls! Feel it stretch and strangle; a noise from another room. Feint but distinct. A slight movement and then there's silence again. We are not alone.

Look at each other, walk slowly back out into the hall. Muscles tense. Every sense heightened. That smell getting stronger. Waiting for the attack. Small flat, only two rooms left. Kitchen and bedroom. Kitchen first, glance in. Can barely make it out in the dark. Large room, but plain. The fridge door is open, emits no light. A bottle of milk lies smashed on the floor. So much for the smell.

Bedroom. This is it. No light from the other room penetrates in here. We stand unsure in the doorway.

'Anyone there?' says Taylor. Silence. 'Healy?'

We wait. Nothing. Look at each other, barely make the expression out in the dark.

'Aw, bugger this,' he says after a few seconds. Walks quickly into the room, me behind. Straight to the curtains, starts to drag them open. Something scampers from underneath the bed, past our feet. Fuck! Heart jumps. Fists clenched. Realise it's a fucking cat. Look to the door as the curtains open and light pours in. No cat. It's a rat. Big and grey and ugly. Bloody huge thing. Small dog.

Finally see it out the corner of my eye. Turn round. Big rat to keep my attention off this. Taylor is already staring at it. Hard to miss. On the wall above the bed. Bloody; pale; dead. Detective Sergeant Herrod impaled through the stomach with an ornamental sword; suspended on the wall. The blood has long since stopped dripping. His mouth is open, blood congealed on his lips; his eyes stare blankly back at us. The weapon missed the tie, a subdued silk Woolworths job he must have got for Christmas. It hangs free, some of the blood from his mouth having dripped upon it. Squares of beige and blue, black marks streaked across. A new design.

Shoes are gone. Herrod's feet in dirty white socks.

We stand and stare for some time. Drinking it in. One of our own, impaled on a bedroom wall. Try to get a grip on my train of thought. What it means for the murder inquiry. What it means for the station. The second polis down in two days. Think of Bernadette; bitter; she'll enjoy it in a perverse way. We stand and stare, as if expecting something to happen.

'Keep waiting for him to tell us to fuck off and mind our own business,' says Taylor.

33

Monday afternoon roundup. A bit later than usual as a result of the day's events. First one with Taylor in charge. Bloonsbury's back in the office having heard about Herrod, but he's staying out of our way. Sitting silently in his room with a bottle at his right hand. Don't know why Charlotte doesn't just send him on his way. The guy is on duty and embarrassing himself and everyone who has to come into contact with him.

Beginning to think Miller might be as far off the rails as he is. She's losing it. Two of her officers have been killed in the last couple of days, she's got a murder inquiry exploding out of her control, and she's lost. Saw her for a few seconds on her way to talk to the press. Pale, shocked, almost broken. Still not returned, which is perhaps why she hasn't got hold of Jonah yet.

The door closes, the gang's all here. Taylor stands in front, done this loads of times. Never this big, though. Never for the killer of two of our own. Hard to fathom the feeling in the room. It wasn't as if any of us liked Herrod, the man was too personality-deficient for that, but a colleague's a colleague. If nothing else, it could have been one of us. Selfish, but that's how the mind works.

We've put an alert out for the guy. Picture in every paper, on every noticeboard. The first part of any murder inquiry is out of the way. We know who did it. Now we just have to catch the guy. Bloody frustrating that we had him here; locked in a cell too. And Jonah Bloonsbury decided to let him go. Don't know who to blame. Bloonsbury himself; Miller for putting him in charge in the first place; or me and Taylor for leaving him to it.

Taylor starts up.

'Right people, here it is. I know this is hard, but we've got to think straight, be professional. There's a nutcase out there and we have to get him off the streets. We can be mad, we can be outraged, we can be depressed, we can feel guilty, whatever. But it can all wait. First off we have to be clear headed and we have to get our man.' He hesitates. 'And on that point – we all know we had him here and it was decided to let him go. If the press get hold of that we're going to look like fucking idiots. So we keep our mouths shut. No one, all right? Not even wives and husbands and mothers or whatever. Mouths shut.'

A few heads nod, most of us stare blankly at him or at the floor. No one's going to tell anyone anything. We all feel too stupid. Maybe if he doesn't go, Bloonsbury'll get his head panned in.

'So, what have we got? Herrod took a call from Maretta Johnson yesterday morning, putting him on to Ian Healy. Went round there on his own. Given what happened, he was a bloody idiot.' Pauses, takes a deep breath. No friends of Herrod here to offend. 'Whatever the exact turn of events, it ended with the sergeant dead. Healy, realising we're onto him, disappears. From hair samples in the flat, forensics have confirmed that it was Healy who killed Ann Keller and WPC Bathurst. Some of us may wonder about why Evelyn was killed, but it looks as if she was just in the wrong place at the wrong time.'

Looks around the room. Was that last comment directed solely at me? Might have been. He's right, anyway. Forget about Evans and some great conspiracy. Bathurst goes to see Miller to give her confession; for whatever reason they end up in bed, as you do; on her way home in the middle of the night, Bathurst is stumbled upon by Healy, and that seals her fate. Shouldn't have been walking alone through the streets in the middle of the night when there was a killer loose. No conspiracy.

‘Now Herrod. Three murders, and our killer has gone to ground. We know he’s our man, we need to know where he is. We need to speak to everybody that’s ever met the guy. Family, friends, clients, whoever. Lumberyard, you just been down to his office?’

‘Aye. Brought back everything we could find. Just about to go and look through it all, see what we can get. The secretary’s downstairs, trying to be stoic.’

‘I know. I’ll speak to her when we’re done. But she won’t tell us anything. Nothing to tell.’

He stops, looks around the room again. Not one for speeches our Jack. My mind strays again to Miller, as he starts dividing up the areas of responsibility. Who’s to look where, talk to whom. I know what I’ve got for the next few hours. Looking through bloody file after file of Ian Healy’s confidential papers. Landed with Morrow to help. Still be a long job. Look at the watch – almost seven o’clock already. Think of Peggy for the first time since this morning. Have to cancel again. She should understand. If she doesn’t, then there just isn’t any point, is there?

Too much is happening. Two women; a murder inquiry, which quickly consumes two colleagues; an old polis conspiracy involving who knows how many idiots at the station. Too much crap going on at once. I just need a few hours to step back from it, assess the whole lot. Make some decisions, discard some of the garbage. But I’m not getting the chance. Every ten minutes there’s something new. A revelation, a demand, whatever. At least today has simplified it a little. We’re looking for Ian Healy, period. What I also need is for one of the women to tell me to take a hike – or both of them for that matter – and then things would be even simpler.

Switch back on for the wrap up.

‘Right people. You all know what you’re doing. We need this sorted out quickly, so get out there and get on with it. And no fucking about.’

Taylor walks from the room and the meeting breaks up. Trail out near the back, no one saying anything. There’s a job to be done, have to get on with it. Get back to my desk, Morrow comes trotting up.

‘Right, Tom. Might as well sit at Herrod’s desk. Seat should be cold by now.’

Raises his eyebrows, doesn’t look too impressed. A dead man’s seat. I push a box of papers over to him.

‘What are we looking for?’ he says.

‘No idea, Constable,’ I say. ‘Let me know when you find it.’

Lift the phone. Get the call to Peggy out of the way before I start. One ring and she lifts straight away.

‘Hello?’

‘Hi, it’s me.’

‘Oh Christ, Dallas,’ she says. Sounds relieved. ‘Are you all right? I heard about Herrod.’

‘Aye, I’m fine. He’s not doing so well though.’

‘What’s going on there, for Christ’s sake?’

‘Everything’s cool. Herrod was just stupid.’ I’m all sympathy. Peggy didn’t like him any more than I did.

‘Well, just you be careful.’

‘Aye, I will. Look, I’m not going to be able to make it over tonight. This just keeps getting worse and worse.’

‘Oh, please, Dallas. I’m worried. I want to see you.’ Start to object, she doesn’t give me the chance. ‘I’m not going anywhere. It doesn’t matter when you come, I’ll be in bed whatever time it is. Just come over and join me.’

What the hell, it doesn’t make any difference. Might as well sleep at their place as my own. Although, what happens if I’ve somewhere else to go tomorrow night.

‘Aye, all right then. But really, don’t wait up.’

‘I won’t.’

‘OK. And as long as you’re not going to be annoyed if I crawl in at half-five.’

‘It won’t matter.’

‘Right then, I’ll be there.’

‘Thanks, Dallas. The children’ll be delighted to see you in the morning.’

All part of the plan.

‘Aye, it’ll be good.’

Say our goodbyes, hang up. Morrow’s got his head buried in his pile of paper, good lad. If Herrod had still been there he would have been listening avidly to every word and not attempting to hide the fact.

Phone goes again as soon as I hang up. Internal. If this is Ramsey with some apology for a crime, I'm going to give the bastard a doing.

'Lumberyard.'

'Dallas.' It's Charlotte.

Shit. Look up. Her office door is closed. She must have come back while we were in the meeting. I was wanting things simplified.

'Hi.'

I bet Morrow would want to listen to this if he knew who was on the phone.

'You'll be working late?' she says.

'No question.'

'I understand. Of course. But I was wondering if you could come over later?'

Aw, naw. Come on. I don't need this. What, I'm supposed to go charging down to Helensburgh at three o'clock in the morning, or whenever it'll be I get finished? And I can't. Not tonight. Can't stand up Peggy again.

She is aware of my hesitation. Sounds anxious.

'Not Helensburgh. I've got a flat. Kelvinside.' Of course. 'You could just come over there when you've finished.'

She sounds like a normal human being. Alone. Vulnerable. Breathe deeply. You promised your ex-wife, your possibly soon to be next wife.

'Things are just getting a little out of hand,' she says. 'I need to talk, that's all.'

Aw, bugger. Why now? Why tonight? Why can't she want to talk tomorrow night? Where's the idiot Frank when you need him?

'All right,' I say. Fingers rubbing at my forehead. Dallas Lumberyard – the dunderheid who can't say no.

'Thanks,' she says. Immediately sounds more assured. 'I'll be here late as well. I'll speak to you before I go.'

'Aye.'

She hangs up. Put the phone down. Stare at it. Wait for it to ring again with some other demand on my time for the middle of the coming night. When it doesn't, I lift the top paper off the pile and start to adjust myself to searching through the life and work of Ian Healy; see what I can come up with.

Haven't got two lines when the door to Bloonsbury's office opens and the broken man walks out. There are six or seven people in the room as he walks through and every one of us stops what we're doing to stare at the guy. Bloody eyes, face streaked and ugly. A mess. Appears to be walking in a bit more of a straight line than usual but his shoulders are hunched, shuffling gait. He stops halfway across the room. Has become aware that everyone is looking at him. Knows what we're all thinking. He catches a few eyes but no one looks away. There's no one left in this station who couldn't look him straight in the eye now and tell him what they think of him.

Finally he looks at me and those eyes are bloody death; then he straightens up and walks from the room.

And if the man has any sense left whatsoever, he won't return.

*

'I've just been thinking about Evans,' says Taylor.

He looks tired. I'm not surprised. His wife has just left; he's been put in charge of a huge murder inquiry; instant results expected; under pressure. And besides, it's one thirty in the morning. And here's me, joined CID 'cause I thought it'd be nine to five.

'What about him?' I say.

End of the day. Looked through all of the papers that I'm going to. Morrow and I found a few things we'll have to check up on, but that'll be for the morning. Taylor spent a good three hours with the secretary, then sent her packing. She'd had the holidays off, then turned up for work as usual this morning. Healy was nowhere to be seen, no idea where he might have gone. And that was about it.

So. End of the day, last cigarette, last cup of coffee.

Then? Jesus. Charlotte left just after midnight, slipping me the address as she went. So I've got a choice. Charlotte or Peggy, and

I've promised them both.

Mind on the job. Evans.

'Why did he just vanish like that?' says Taylor. 'We'd started to think about him. Possible suspect, possible link between the two. Who knows? We shouldn't lose sight of things. Saturday night we charged down there, kicking the door in. The fact that the bastard had buggered off seemed to implicate him. Now, we've got Healy stamped over everything. So, do we just forget about Evans? Mark his disappearance down as coincidence?'

'There's no such thing as coincidence.'

'Exactamundo,' he says.

'So we need a connection between Evans and Healy.'

'Aye. You didn't see anything when you looked through Healy's files did you? A mention of Evans having dealt with any of Healy's clients?'

Shake my head. 'No, nothing. But then, Morrow checked half of them and he wouldn't have been looking.'

He looks at me. I know what he's thinking. See that mountain of paper that Morrow looked through. Fuck.

'Not tonight,' he says. That's big of him. 'Tomorrow morning. Have Morrow follow up whatever you dug up this evening. Don't need to tell anyone else what we're thinking. Might be a load of pish.' Champion.

Taylor rubs his eyes. Half one in the morning isn't the best time for clear and logical insight.

'I don't know, Sergeant. We're missing something here. Something obvious.'

'Come on,' I say, 'we all say that. All the time. You can't know it until you know it.'

Rests his elbows on the desk and yawns.

'Very deep, Lumberyard. Get that out of a Chinese fortune cookie?'

'Aye, I did as a matter of fact. And there's more. Always take your clothes off before you get in the shower.'

'Very funny. Piss off and we'll talk in the morning.'

He stands up. Lucky bastard is going home to an empty bed. Haven't decided where I'm going yet. Although, of course, I know exactly where I'm going.

'When's your big date with Eileen, then?' I say.

'Supposed to be tonight.' Looks at his watch. 'Bit late. Not tonight, Josephine. Plenty of time. Don't think there's a queue of guys at the door, do you?'

You never know.

'Right, I'll see you in the morning,' I say, standing up.

'See if we can sort something out from all this shite, eh?' he says.

'Aye.'

'Go home and get some sleep, Lumberyard. You look as if you need it.'

Sleep? I wish I could. And anyway, you're the man who looks as if he needs sleep.

Walk back out into the main office. The quiet of the middle of the night; CID at rest. Look at the watch. A little over five hours and the shite'll be flying once more.

Pick up the car keys and start tossing the mental coin; knowing that if it comes down on the side of Peggy I'll keep doing best of three 'til I get the right result.

34

Post sex cigarette; the best there is. It might be a cliché, but it's right up there with sex itself and watching Partick Thistle beat Celtic 4-1. Cool, bitter, biting at the inside of your throat. Like a smokey single malt by a warm fire on a cold day. Lie back, breathe it in, stare at the ceiling. Forget everything. Savour the smoke and savour the remains of the delicious sensations still lingering in your loins and stomach. You feel the tiredness, begin to give in to it, let it sweep over you. Like waves crashing on the ocean.

'What are you thinking?'

You swallow a gallon of sea water. Just as well. I was about to nod off and drop the smoking butt end onto my chest.

'Just enjoying the moment.'

She places her hand on my chest, starts drawing circles. God, she's not about to get romantic on me? She kisses my shoulder, snuggles her head next to my arm. Bloody Jesus.

'I'm really glad you've been around the past few days, Dallas. I've needed you.'

For all the bitterness and tough guy act, it still sounds good to hear it. Charlotte Miller needs Dallas Lumberyard. Sort of thing you'd scrawl on your desk at school. If you were a jessie.

Quarter past four. Just had ball-breaking sex and feel relaxed for the first time in a couple of days. Had intended going round to see Peggy when I was finished, but now that I'm here, post-sex, woman glued to my arm and absolutely exhausted, I've got a feeling I won't be going anywhere until it's time for work. Big Guilt means Big Denial. Try not to think about Peggy. There's someone else's wife to sleep with. Keep waiting for the guillotine to fall. Each time is more intimate than the last, however. Deeper into the mire. Falling in love. Me with her. Wrong person, wrong time, wrong planet.

Stopped worrying about her and Bathurst. Accepted why they slept together, although I haven't asked her about it.

A thought comes into my head as I'm drifting off; something I should ask her. And hope she's set an alarm, cause there's no way I'm waking up at seven o'clock.

Roll over on my side, away from her, and she curls her arms around me and presses against my skin, her breasts beautiful and soft against my back.

'How come you haven't got rid of Bloonsbury? The guy's a mess.' Wrong question, wrong time.

Feel it immediately. Body tensed, then relaxed. Places a slight distance between our bodies, her skin detached. I'm almost asleep. Not switched on to it. Barely notice, don't care. Her body relaxes into mine once more, her breasts flush against me. I'm tired, giving into it.

'We can talk about it later,' she says. Dreamy voice. Don't care.

She says something else, but I'm hardly aware of it, and finally I give in to the wall of sleep.

*

Shit! Tuesday morning wake up call. Don't know what drags me from sleep, but I sit straight up in bed. Already light outside, know I'm late without looking at the clock. Empty bed, bloody bitch already up and gone to work, leaving me lying here. Shit. Dare to look at the clock. Aw, shit. Shit. Half past fucking eight.

Fly into a frantic rush of cold water, toothpaste and last night's clothes. Out onto the street. Snowed in the night – a light covering. Nearly slip on the stairs. Have trouble starting the car, lurch out onto the road and within five minutes I'm stuck in traffic.

Keep looking at the clock as it gets ever later. Switch the radio on and off. Good news, boring news, weather – I know it snowed! I can see the sodding stuff – shite music.

Finally arrive well after nine-thirty. Run into the station – raised eyebrow from Ramsey – up the stairs and into the office. The usual hum of activity. In the centre of the room Taylor stands talking to Miller. They stop, look at me as I approach. Jack looks as if he wants to thump me, Miller plays the part. The disapproving superior. I shrug my shoulders. No idea what to say.

'I'll leave you to it,' says the woman who five hours ago had been writhing naked all over me, as she walks back to her office.

Taylor indicates his office and I follow him in. Realise there's a couple of DC's watching me go. Little bastards.

Taylor behind his desk. Gestures for me to close the door. Starts up. Low voice. Mad as fuck, not shouting.

'What the fuck are you doing?'

Raise the shoulders, let out a sigh. I can't explain.

'We've got a monumental case on here and you're lying in bed for fuck's sake. And by the look of you, someone else's bed. Can you not leave your dick be for two fucking days while we get some work done?'

Feel even more stupid now than I did a minute ago. Wish I had some defence.

'Bloody hell, Lumberyard, at least say something for yourself.'

I can't. He doesn't need to know about Charlotte.

He leans forward, elbows on the desk.

'Listen. Morrow's been in for the past two hours. Got some good ideas, doing some good work. Gone back out to check on some stuff. A good polis, doing a good job. Any more of this shite and it'll be your job he's doing. Get out there and get on with it.'

Stupid, humiliated, feel like saluting. Think much the better of it. Nod the head, look embarrassed.

'We're done, Sergeant,' he says.

Right. Turn to go. Wait for the quieter words that all good man managers come out with to show they're not really mad at you. They don't come. Out the door, leave it open, and then back to my desk.

The papers that Morrow checked through yesterday are all still there, a pile on Herrod's desk. I lift them over, place them in front of me. Notice beside the phone a message. *Peggy called – can you phone her*.

Push it to one side, decide to think on it before I make the call. What do I say? Just ignored the uncomfortable thought while I was with Miller. Look up at her office, the closed door. Just like the closed door of her heart.

Fuck off Lumberyard, you stupid prick. Get on with it.

Lift the first paper and begin the trawl through for any mention of Detective Chief Inspector Gerry Evans.

35

Spend three hours on it. Looking through all those papers that Morrow wasted his time on yesterday. Looking for the name of Evans, thinking about two women. It would be nice to be able to divorce your thoughts from that kind of thing, but I suppose we're all the same.

Peggy or Charlotte. Safe option against the bomb waiting to go off. Keep making mental lists with the name Evans on them both, so I don't miss him if he crops up.

Points in favour:

Peggy. History; cracking sex; mother of my children; get my family back; I'm thirty-nine and it's about time I acted it; a warm, loving relationship, especially when the relationship with Charlotte is going nowhere – it'd be foolish to lose Peggy for something that might not last 'til the end of the week; Peggy makes good Jamaica ginger cake.

Charlotte. Sex.

Try to tell myself that sex with Peggy is as good, but there's something extra with Charlotte. It could just be novelty, though. Maybe after seventeen years it wouldn't have the same bite. Nothing dulls the appetite like familiarity. You eat Cornflakes every day for seventeen years, you might prefer Rice Krispies one morning. But does it mean you really think they taste better than Cornflakes?

There isn't a problem on earth that can't be reduced to a breakfast cereal analogy.

I don't know. Head says Peggy, heart's divided, dick says Charlotte. That's about it. Know what I should do, but like the rest of us under the weight of infatuation, I'm fighting against it with all I've got.

Pick up the phone to Peggy eventually.

'Hello?' she says. Voice wary. Knows it's me.

'Don't hang up,' I say. Immediately onto the defensive before she can speak. Good move, Lumberyard, you idiot.

She doesn't say anything. Doesn't hang up either.

'Look, I'm sorry. I just couldn't come over.'

'Why? Where were you?'

Never was much of a liar, but I might as well give it a go. Easier over the phone.

'It was late. Middle of the night. And I know what you said, but there was no point. I needed the sleep, babe.' The old familiarity. I bet Brian called her darling. 'I'm sorry. It was half-four, I just went home, unplugged the phone, forgot to set the alarm and went out like a light.'

No immediate reply. Not necessarily a bad thing. Don't say anything else. Wait and see.

'I just wish,' she starts off, stops herself. 'I don't know Dallas. Just be honest, for fuck's sake.' Peggy never used to swear. Must be Brian's influence.

'I'm being honest.' Missing the point as usual. 'Look, I'll come over tonight, I promise.' Close my eyes as I say it.

'Don't, Dallas. Don't...I don't know. I still want you to come. But come when you want. When you mean it.'

'I'll try and come tonight. Promise.' There I go again.

'Don't promise, Dallas.' Click.

Phone call over, just like that. No opportunity to lie some more. Shit. Gun at my head right now, and I'd choose Peggy over Charlotte. But it won't last.

Back to work, try to think about Evans and neither of the women. Evans is just not as attractive a thought, however.

*

An hour later, and I've got it. Already early afternoon. Dying for some lunch. Morrow's been in and out, buzzing around like the good little detective. Good thing I like the guy or I'd have punched him by now.

Walk into the boss's office.

'Bingo.'

Taylor looks up. The man's actually going over some papers for once – not staring at the ceiling like he usually does. Must be taking his duties seriously. He's been out most of the morning, got in about twenty minutes ago.

'Close the door,' he says.

Do it, stand over his desk. Still feel that tension in the air. Thick like Ready Brek.

'Hope you've got something, 'cause Morrow came up empty.'

Good.

Getting as bad as Herrod. Have to stop thinking like that. It's not a competition. Hold up the file.

'Evans and Healy. Beginning of last year. Some two-bit rape charge. Evans was the arresting officer. Healy defends the guy. Somewhere along the line Evans fucks up, the guy walks on a technicality. Piece of cake. Doesn't say it, but it reeks of pay off. The rapist was some big shot banker. What's a guy like that doing going to a no-hoper like Healy? Put on to him because he knows Healy's a man to do business with, presumably. Payment to Evans, he does the necessary damage, the guy's out of jail.'

Taylor stares at his desk. Rubs his chin with one hand, indicates the chair with the other. I sit down. He's sorting it out. I've already been doing that, and although it's what we were looking for, does it actually get us anywhere?

'So what?' he says eventually. 'What do we have? Healy and Evans know each other. Know the other's bent. How does it apply here? We've got the first half of the connection, now we need the second.'

Think straight Lumberyard.

'Right. Evans and Healy worked together on at least one case. There might have been more, we don't know. The murder case last year we know was Evans. But there's no noticeable involvement from Healy.'

'Couldn't find anything on that?'

Shake the head.

'And now, we know Healy murdered Ann Keller and Bathurst,' I continue. 'We don't know if Evans has any involvement. And both men have disappeared. I talked to Evans, didn't suggest there was anything there. He did mention that he'd spoken to Herrod and Bloonsbury earlier this month, however. Now Herrod's dead too. And Bloonsbury's a mess. Might as well be dead.'

'Aye, but that's self inflicted. I don't think we can go blaming Evans for Bloonsbury's condition.'

Sit up. A cohesive thought. First for three days.

'Maybe Evans is blackmailing him. Maybe that's why Bloonsbury and Herrod went to see Evans, 'cause Evans was threatening to reveal their part in the murder case.'

Taylor shakes his head.

'How could he do that? He was guiltier than the rest of them put together. He was the murderer for God's sake.'

'Aye, but look at the guy. He's wasted, down there in his dingy little cottage. You think he's going to think straight? Maybe he threatens Jonah with it. Jonah can't pay up, he knows he's about to be found out, and he does what any self-respecting drunk does. Hits the sauce. Meanwhile, Evans clears out so that when the shit hits the fan he isn't around to catch any of it.'

'So, why hasn't the shit hit the fan yet. He's been gone three days?'

'He stopped somewhere to have a pint and is still stuck to the bar stool? Who knows? The guy's a fuck up.'

'And where does Healy killing Herrod fit in?' he says.

'I don't know. But if we can sort out the polis end, we might find out. Where is Jonah?' I ask. 'If we just come straight out and ask if Evans is blackmailing him, do you think we'll get a straight answer?'

Taylor rubs his forehead. 'Jesus, I don't know. I doubt it. Haven't seen the guy today.'

'She hasn't suspended him, has she?'

He shrugs.

'Don't know. Maybe just taken a day off to try and sober up. Who knows? Maybe he'll come in tomorrow wearing a blue and red skin tight jump suit, with big yellow pants pulled over the top.'

'So, how about we just go round there and ask him if Evans is blackmailing him over the Addison case,' I say.

'But so what if he is? Where does Healy killing Ann Keller fit into it? If there is something going on between Evans and Bloonsbury, it doesn't have to involve Healy. A connection between Healy and Evans on a small time rape charge over a year ago doesn't mean fuck all, Sergeant.'

Deep breath. He's right.

'Anyway,' he says, 'the fact is that Healy killed those two women and now he's disappeared. He's the guy we've got to find. Any connection with Evans might be entirely coincidental.'

'So where do we start looking?'

'No idea, Sergeant.'

'So, how about we go and speak to Bloonsbury about Evans. It might get us somewhere. If it doesn't, we're no worse off.'

Looks at his watch. Hope he's going to mention lunch. He doesn't.

‘All right, we’ll go with it. I’ll go and see Bloonsbury. There’s no point in us both turning up there like a delegation from Fucked Up Polis Anonymous, and if you go on your own he’ll tell you where to go.’

Nod. Fair enough. I’ll get some lunch.

‘You go and talk to your big shot banker rapist,’ he says. ‘See what he knows about Evans and Healy.’

‘He’s not going to tell me anything, is he?’

Stabs his finger at the side of his forehead.

‘Use your napper. Be subtle, for Christ’s sake.’

Subtle? I’m Scottish. What are you talking about?

Stand up, ready to go.

‘You should call Peggy. She was looking for you last night after you left.’

Shite. ‘What time?’

‘I don’t know. ‘Bout two, maybe.’

Shite. Caught with my pants down. Every time. I’m such a useless liar. Walk out. Humble pie for lunch.

36

Be subtle.

Sitting in the waiting room outside the bank manager’s office. Something like a dentist’s waiting area, except the magazines are a bit more high-falutin’ and the fish in the goldfish tank aren’t goldfish – being of an altogether more exotic nature. Thick carpet – maroon, no pattern – cream walls. Wonder how I’m going to play this if I’m to get anything out of him. As detectives go, I’ve always been reasonably good at sorting things out in my head, seeing possibilities, that kind of thing. However, when it comes to making witnesses give up that little extra, I’m useless.

The secretary appears. Late forties, hair in a bun, blue suit. Wearing four pairs of knickers, although that’s only a guess.

Leads me through the door into the banker's office, announces me as if I was attending some royal court, then closes the door behind. Doesn't offer coffee.

The banker stands up from behind his desk.

'How do you do, officer? Please come in. Sit down.'

Check out the office as I walk to the chair. Expensive paintings, big plants, massive fish tank, the same rich carpet as the waiting room. Money. This is no banker dealing with the guy on the street and his deposit account of a hundred and thirty-five quid. This is big banking.

'How can I help you, Sergeant Lumberyard?'

'Won't take much of your time, Mr Montague.' Had a geography teacher in first year called Montague. Hated him. Used to skelp you over the arse with the blackboard eraser. I could probably sue him now, if it wasn't for the fact he was murdered by one of the sixth years. 'Just like to ask you a couple of questions about Ian Healy.'

He looks vaguely like he doesn't recognise the name.

'Your lawyer,' I add.

'I think there must be some mistake, Sergeant. All my affairs are handled by Harper, McCalliog and Brown of Ingram Street.'

Affairs? Harper, McCalliog and Brown? What a load of pish. Feel like arresting him for being an annoying bastard with a posh accent.

Subtlety edged to one side.

'Rape case, last year. Janie Northolt, one of your employees. Harper, McCalliog and Brown didn't handle that affair.'

Patronising smile disappears off face.

'Oh, him,' he says. 'What about him?' Looks at his watch. 'I really am rather busy, Sergeant.'

'Perhaps then you could come down to the station later to answer some questions?'

Gives me the look. That one always shuts them up. Tries to play the big shot wanker, but he ought to know better. No one gets away with that in Glasgow.

'Very well, Sergeant. But I really don't see how I can be of any help.'

‘You know Ian Healy is wanted in connection with the murder of a woman and two police officers?’

He nods. Course he knows.

‘We’re just following up on all of his clients from the past couple of years. See what we can find.’

‘Very thorough,’ he says. Voice drips. I want to punch this guy in the face.

‘If all your affairs are handled by Harper, McCalliog and Brown, why did you go to a small time lawyer like Healy to deal with the rape charge?’

Stares down his nose at me.

‘It was a delicate matter,’ he says, voice thinner than cat gut. Looks at his watch.

‘It was also a pretty big matter. A rape charge from one of your employees. Aren’t Harper, McCalliog and Brown competent to deal with delicate matters?’

His teeth clenched behind pursed lips. Jaw pulses.

‘The law may be black and white to you Sergeant, but there are some matters which you clearly don’t understand.’

Right, that’s it. Fuck this guy; fuck subtlety. Any more of that and I’m arresting the prick.

‘Listen.’ Lean forward. His head moves an inch or two back. ‘I don’t give a fuck about your sordid little rape. We know you raped the little fucker, we know you were arrested by Chief Inspector Evans, and we know you went to Healy because you found out he was a man who could deal with Evans. Money exchanged hands, Evans screwed up intentionally, and you walked.’

He starts to object, but I’m rolling.

‘Fucking shut it. I don’t care about your rape. I don’t care about the pay off, about any of it. I’m worried about Healy. The guy’s a murderer, we need to catch him. I just need from you everything you can tell me about him. That’s it. Where you got his name, if you know why there’s a connection between him and Evans. You can tell me now, or else there are certain people who can find out about your dodgy fucking dealing with serial killers.’

Say it all in about three seconds. Feels good. That’s the thing about being a polis sometimes. You can let rip and they have to sit there and listen.

He fidgets. Fingers some papers which are lying on his desk. Toying with the idea, I suspect, of calling up some big cheese arsehole in the polis that he plays bridge with once a week on a Tuesday, and telling him to get the low-life cretin of a sergeant off his hands.

Fixes me with the look.

'I took it to Harper. He deals with my business.' That'll be Harper of Harper, McCalliog and Brown, presumably. Not Joe Harper, who used to play for Aberdeen and Hibs. 'When he heard the name of the policeman involved, he said he had a reputation. That we might be able to deal with it. However, he didn't think it would be appropriate for Harper, McCalliog and Brown to get involved.' I bet he didn't. 'They mentioned the name of Ian Healy.'

'And you know why Healy and Evans were able to do business together. Was there a history?'

Looks smug. Not getting any more.

'Businesses trust me to run their affairs and to take care of their money, Sergeant. They don't need to know how I do it, or my relationship with others in the banking world. I don't see that lawyers and policemen are any different, do you?' Point taken, but he continues to spell it out because he likes the sound of his own voice. 'I know nothing of the way these men work. I paid the money, I was released from that ridiculous and wholly unfounded charge.'

Class dismissed. The look says it all.

'Did you deal with Ian Healy on any other matters?'

Lips tighten.

'No Sergeant, I did not, and I must say I'm finding all of this rather tiring. I am a busy man, Sergeant, so if you wouldn't mind taking your leave.'

Don't know how she knows, but the Germanic weightlifter in a skirt appears at the door and stands there waiting for the uninvited guest to hoof it.

Have to accept defeat. I can't possibly arrest them both, no matter how much I'd like to. Stand up.

'Just don't think of going anywhere in case we need to speak to you again.'

His face starts to go red. With anger. Hit the mark.

'As it happens,' he says, and you can hear him struggling to control his voice, 'I'm taking my wife to Austria tomorrow night to spend New Year in Vienna.'

We stare each other down. Like in a movie. Man stuff, and a complete load of shite it is too. Decide against annoying him further and retreat slowly from the office.

Out into the cold freshness of afternoon. The snow in the centre of town has turned to slush, but it still lies on the roofs. Low cloud and cold. Looks like it might snow again.

Grab a burger, having had a totally unsatisfactory sandwich on the way there, then head back to the office. Some time after three when I walk in. Taylor's in his office, feet on the desk, staring at the ceiling. Wonder if he's found our man. Should know better.

'Hard at work?' I say as I walk in.

Takes his feet down, straightens up.

'You're a fucking idiot, aren't you Lumberyard?'

'What'd I do now?'

Looks at me. I should know. Realisation kicks in. Didn't take the wanker long to get on the phone.

'Be subtle. Remember that instruction?'

'The guy was an arsehole. He was lucky I didn't arrest him.'

'That would've been brilliant. Had Miller in here like a fucking tornado. Seemed to think it was my fault.'

'Well, if you can't control your staff,' I say, with that cheeky grin I nicked from Ally McCoist.

'Fuck off.'

Puts his feet back on the desk.

'Well, before you offended the delicate banker, did he tell you anything?'

'Nothing much. He was put onto Healy by his solicitors, Harper, McCalliog and Brown.' Taylor raises his eyebrows at the name. 'Said that he was known as someone who would do business with the polis. But that's it. Or at least, that was all he was saying. Waste of time, I suppose. Still, I enjoyed annoying him.'

'Great, Lumberyard. Well, you can go and annoy Miller now, 'cause she wanted to see you when you got in.' Looks across the desk at me. 'You've been in there a few times in the last week. You're not shagging her are you?'

'Aye, I am as a matter of fact.'

He snorts. 'Aye, you fucking wish.' Stares at the floor, runs a hand through tired hair. 'Might have a go at it myself,' he says, 'now I've no reason not to.' Don't like the thought of him moving in on my girlfriend.

'Eileen Harrison, remember?'

'Aye, well, we'll see.'

'What about Bloonsbury,' I ask. 'You see him?'

'Aye, I did,' he says.

'And?'

'Don't know. He was drunk.' Audience gasps in disbelief.

'You ask him about Evans?' I say.

'Aye. Got nowhere. Just started muttering about him being a useless bastard. The usual drunken ravings.'

'And the Addison case. You mentioned we knew about that?'

'Aye. Told me to fuck off and mind my own business,' he says, shaking his head. 'Don't know what the hell we can do. Maybe bring him in, lock him up and deprive him of drink for a couple of days. But it's Jonah Bloonsbury, for God's sake. Don't think Miller would go for it.'

'You're in charge of the investigation.'

'I'm sure there's a line in the sand, Sergeant, and arresting Jonah Bloonsbury'll be some way on the other side. We're just going to have to get our information from other sources.' He rubs his hand across his forehead. Looks tired. 'Right, Lumberyard, away and take Charlotte across her desk, or whatever it is the two of you do in there.'

'Right,' I say. 'See what I can do.'

He smiles as I walk out the room. Across the office, nod at Morrow, knee deep in documents. Wonder what Taylor's got him looking at now. Knock on Miller's door, walk in. She looks up, doesn't offer me a seat.

'Just had Jonathan Montague on the phone,' she says. Tongue coiled. About to unleash. Make a snap decision.

'Why didn't you wake me up today?'

'What?' she says, surprised.

'You left me sleeping and came into work. Knew I'd be late. What the hell d'you do that for?'

Doesn't answer. Stares back across the office. See her look behind me to make sure the door's closed.

'You do not go into the offices of people like Jonathan Montague and start mouthing off,' she says eventually. Ignoring me. Daring me. 'Especially not on ridiculous charges like the one you took to him.'

Feel stupid, but have to fight anger at the same time.

'And what was all that about Evans?' she says.

Don't answer. If I say something I'll put my foot in it. As I have been doing with some regularity. She purses her lips, taps her fingers; accepts my silence. Eyes like fire.

'Don't think you're getting any special favours, Sergeant. There's plenty more where you came from.'

Inch high. Won't have to open the door when I leave. Just crawl under it.

Stare each other down for a few seconds more. Testosterone pumping – just a lot more of it in her than in me. Nothing else to be said. Turn to go. Wonder if she'll say something to my back, but she doesn't. Open the door and out into the freedom of the main office. Breathe the fresh air. Like stepping from a lift you've been trapped in for ten hours. Escaping a straitjacket.

Walk back to my desk wondering what other no-hope lead I can follow up, and why it is that Charlotte Miller has so quickly turned against me? Look at the watch. Less than twelve hours since she was glad I'd been around the past few days.

Part of the game. And if she called up tonight and ordered my attendance at her bedside, would I have the guts to refuse? Not a chance.

37

Tuesday evening. Spend a shit night at home in front of the TV. The lot of the divorced polis. Worked 'til just after nine when I ran out of pointless things to do. Incited Taylor to go to the pub, but he stalled. Finally admitted that tonight was the night for Eileen Harrison. Wished him luck.

Asked Morrow, but said he had other things on. Wondered if he was going to be shagging Charlotte. Could hardly ask. On the way out I bumped into Alison for the first time in a couple of days. Almost asked her out, but decided not to bother. Enough women trouble at the moment as it is, and anyway she would probably have told me to piss off.

So I called up Peggy, pleased that at last I was able to honour a promise. She told me she was tired and she'd see me another night. I'd asked for that. She'd caught me lying on the phone earlier on, and had the decency not to tell me at the time. I deserved no less than to be turned away.

So that's me, back home a little before half nine. A packet of smokes, fridge full of v&t, and a couple of pieces of toast for company. Dying to call Charlotte, the thought that someone else might be in her bed, itching away at me. Need to scratch it, and so finally after an hour of shite television and wandering thoughts, I lift the phone. No answer at the flat in Kelvinside, so I try Helensburgh. Phone lifts and before my beating heart wanders casually up into my mouth, Frank says hello. I hang up without saying anything. Feel cheap, and wish I hadn't called.

So I sit for another two hours watching a load of shite and slowly getting pished out of my face. Wonder about Evans and Healy and Miller and Bloonsbury and Bathurst and every other bastard on the force, if they're all joined up in some great secret society, dedicated to murdering their own. Finally fall asleep and drift into dreams, where I'm in a church with the lot of them, and they've all got piercing red eyes; all except me. And Jack's in amongst it all, and he's one of them; Morrow at his side.

Wake up to a discussion of pre-war Spanish sculpture at a little before three o'clock in the morning. Holds my interest for a while, then I crawl off to bed. Fall asleep before I can clean my teeth. Wake up to the alarm at seven o'clock, mouth like the inside of a golf ball, face you could fry bacon on.

Miserable as fuck with it.

38

Wednesday morning. Last day of the year, and good riddance to it. Ann Keller's funeral today, nine days after the event. That's what happens with murders like this. Suppose the time of year hasn't helped. Anyway, for whatever reason, they managed to process the corpse of WPC Bathurst a little quicker. Her funeral is on Saturday morning. Herrod's will probably be on Monday. A bright start to the New Year.

Into the station at just after eight o'clock. Expect wild cheering from the studio audience that I made it in time, but silence all round. Hard little workers beavering away. Still feel as if I'm about an hour and a half late. Stopped by Ramsey as I'm about to head for the first floor. This is a man who never leaves his post.

'Aggravated assault, Sergeant. Domestic,' he says.

Shake the head. 'No way, mate. Morrow's got to be around, is he not?'

'Already handed him a burglary on Main Street. Eileen Harrison's got a couple of rapes,' he says, beating me to it, looks down his list. 'Pretty much everyone's taken. You want to speak to Taylor.'

Christ. 'Aye, all right. Give you a call.'

Up the stairs. I hate domestic assaults. Am still pondering what kind of cases I actually like investigating when I walk into Taylor's office.

'Ramsey wants me to do some domestic assault thing.'

He looks up from his desk. Clean shaven. No bags.

'Morning Lumberyard,' he says.

Nod. The guy does look as if he's had a decent night's sleep for once. Refreshed. More than can be said for me.

'Domestic assault?' I repeat.

'Got to be done. Until Healy shows his hand, there isn't much for any of us to do. You got any brilliant ideas I'll go with them, but otherwise you might as well make yourself useful.'

I've thought of going on holiday. That was brilliant.

Shake my head.

'Right then,' he says, 'you might as well get it over with. You know it anyway, so you're the best person.'

'What do you mean?'

He smiles. Don't like the look of this.

'Mr and Mrs Jenkins,' he says.

'Aw, naw, you're kidding me?'

He smiles, the bastard. The pen in the eye brigade that I spent a day on last week. The couple where one was as bad as the other.

'What is it this time?'

'To put none too fine a point on it – he kicked fuck out her. She's in the Victoria. He's got a bruise or two himself, so they say, but we don't know whether he did it to himself to make it look like she started it.'

'Christ.'

'Exactly. The quicker you see to it, the quicker you can get back to our user friendly serial killer case. If you need to bring the guy in, just do it.'

'Aye, right.' Start to head out the door. Stop. Might as well ask the question.

'What about last night, then?'

Gives me a 'what about it?' look.

'Eileen Harrison?' I say.

'It was all right,' he says. 'Nice bit of dinner. Went to a Chinky in East Kilbride.'

He's being coy. Want to ignore it, but curiosity is getting the better of me. 'And?'

'Took her home. Had a drink.' Smiles. 'Is there something

you're wanting to say, Sergeant?'

Sod it. No there isn't. Start to head out the door.

'Take someone with you in case Jenkins is still feisty,' he shouts after me. 'Edwards or someone.'

Bloody marvellous. Got a feeling the guy's only got hammer blows for his missus and confident I could take the bastard if I had to. Can't find Edwards anyway, so I head off on my own.

Beginning to think that it might be a good idea to get another job.

*

Back up to the office some hours later. Everyone looking cheesed off. End of term blues, I presume. The domestic was one of those things I wanted to wrap up as quickly as possible, but it wouldn't allow. Had to drag the guy in, spend a couple of hours on it. Booked him. Left him choking quietly with rage in a cell. Find out what the missus wants to do about it. She'll probably want him released so she can kill him.

Morrow still at Herrod's desk, doing that detective constable thing. Checking through masses of paperwork with more enthusiasm than is warranted.

Slump down behind my desk, we acknowledge each other's existence. I'm confronted with a variety of paperwork that needs sorting out. Mounting ever further as the week goes on – none of it being of any concern to the primary investigation. Stare at it for a few seconds. Decide that's all the time I've got to give to it today.

'What have you got?' I ask him.

Answers without looking up.

'Looking through all the paperwork for cases on which Justin Edwards worked. Getting nowhere,' he adds.

'Edwards? Why Edwards?'

'Haven't you heard?' he says, looking up.

Shake the head. Last man to know, me.

'I've been in with Nineties Man for the last two hours,' I say. Hairs rise on the back of neck.

'Killed in a hit and run this morning on the way in. Died on his way to hospital.'

Fuck. Stare blankly ahead, don't know what to think. Edwards.

Doesn't immediately strike me. Confused. Need more information. Gesture with my hands for him to keep talking. Where's the voice gone?

'Blue, F reg Escort. Stolen from outside a shop in Rutherglen late last night. Found abandoned on the Blantyre farm road. Don't know what the car was used for, if it was anything other than to kill Edwards. Might have been a hit, might have been an accident. I'm checking through this stuff, see if I can find anything, anyone that wanted him dead.'

His fiancée after she found out about him getting his kit off at the Christmas night out.

Stupid thought. Then, of course, I think about Evans.

Could it have been Evans? Killed Edwards for the same reason he killed Bathurst. But then, we know Healy killed Bathurst.

'Where's Taylor?' I ask.

'He and Bloonsbury have been in with Miller for about half an hour.'

'Jonah? When did he appear?'

'About an hour ago. Clean shaven, walking in a straight line, change of clothes.'

'Christ, where did that come from?' I ask and he shrugs. We stare at each other for another few seconds, then he goes back to his paperwork. Good luck to him.

Got to think, and have something sensible to say to Taylor when he emerges from the war council.

Three polis dead, and an obvious connection leaps out. The Addison case. Only Bloonsbury and Evans are left. One of them could be the killer – Evans the big favourite; Bloonsbury has had trouble taking a piss the last week – or is there someone else who knows about the five of them and is taking them out one by one?

But it doesn't make sense. We know Healy killed Bathurst and Herrod. So where does he come into it all?

The door to Miller's office opens and out come Taylor and Bloonsbury. And Morrow was right. The guy looks human. Still got the indentations on his lips where the bottle has been attached for the past week, but at least he's not staggering. He veers off to his office, Taylor heads for me. Looks extremely pissed off.

'Lunch, Lumberyard?' he barks.
'Only half eleven.'
Stops and looks down at me.
'I'm going for some fucking lunch. You coming?'
Not one to refuse a warm invitation. Drop what I'm doing – which is nothing – and walk after him as he marches out the door.

39

Sitting in a strange little café in the middle of Hamilton. Food ordered, cups of tea in front of us. Taylor didn't open his mouth on the way over here; just drove too fast.

Both ordered chicken pie and chips; presume he's as pessimistic as I am about the possibilities of getting a good result on the food front.

'So how come Bloonsbury showed up?' I say eventually. Can't sit here all day holding each other's dicks, not talking about anything.

Taylor drinks his tea, staring at the floor. Thinking.

'Maybe the bastard is Jesus after all,' he says.

Gets a disapproving glance from the waitress who places our pie and chips in front of us.

'Risen from the grave,' he adds.

Dig into the pie, delighted to find it's not too offensive. Chips are soggy though; not hot enough. A limp tomato hogs the side of the plate.

'So what's with the anger then?' I ask.

He grimaces as he tastes the chips.

'You hear about Edwards?' he says.

'Aye.'

'Think the same thing I did?'

'Evans.'

'Exactly,' he says. 'Fucking Evans.'

Crams his mouth full of chicken pie and sits chewing morosely. Washes it down eventually with some tea.

Waits until he's got more pie in his mouth before he starts up again.

'I decided I might as well raise the bloody thing with Miller. So I said, 'Heard a rumour about the Addison case.' She looks at me funny. 'I heard that rumour too,' she says. 'Don't believe everything you hear.' So I says, 'Well how do you explain the murder of three of the polis involved inside five days?' 'Coincidence,' she says, 'it does happen.' You know the tone. I mention that Evans has vanished, and that we'd found a connection between him and Healy. She says she knows, which of course she does because you blundered into Montague's office like some sort of fucking cowboy.'

Thanks.

'Bitch couldn't give a fuck. Jonah just sat there like a pile of keich. I told her I thought we should be checking it out, she says there are better things for us to spend our time on. 'Jesus has some better ideas,' she says. Used his day off to sober up and think brilliantly.'

'And what exactly might those ideas be?'

'Aw Christ, you know. The usual pish. Doppelgangers and photographs and disinformation. But you know, and they used to know 'n all, that that's not what cracks it. It's gut instinct. Jonah used to have it and so did she. Even if it was just the instinct for who the best person to shag was.'

She's certainly lost that.

'So why won't she let you get into the Evans thing?'

Continues to wolf down his chicken pie, leaving the chips where they belong. Points an angry fork.

'Why d'you think? Doesn't want to open up old wounds. If it gets out, she's going to look crap.'

Stab at the food. Chips are chips, and I'm not about to leave them, no matter how awful.

'She knows the score then?' I ask. 'The whole thing? Evans the murderer, Bloonsbury the conspirator.'

He shakes his head.

'Don't know. It would be unbelievable if she did. Even she couldn't take protecting the polis's image to those lengths, could she? Fucking hell.' Shakes his head again; finishes off the chicken pie. 'No, I don't think so. Wanting to make her station look good, fine. But the Addison thing was about Bloonsbury and Evans getting a pension.'

'What if she'd only found out in the last few days?' I say. 'She might not want to bring it all out into the open. Not at a time like this.'

'How's she going to have found out in the last few days?' he asks.

'Bathurst.'

He finishes off his tea and starts looking around for something else to eat.

'You going to eat the rest of that pie?' he says.

'Aye.'

'So we're back to Miller having been Bathurst's lover the night she died,' he says. 'I'm just not sure about that.'

Here goes. Might as well get it out there and take the flak.

'She was. I know she was.'

'How?' Looks annoyed already. Course, he's been annoyed since we left the station.

'I went down to see Charlotte on Friday night. Hodson's car was parked outside.'

'What the fuck were you going to see Charlotte for?'

I sort of shrug. Don't know how I'm going to say this without it sounding like a complete load of shite. He picks up on the hesitation, however. Makes it easier for me.

'You're not shagging her, are you, Lumberyard? Don't tell me you're shagging her?'

Just sort of nod my head. He looks at me with slightly gaping mouth. Still got a bit of chicken pie on his tongue, a couple of bits in his teeth.

'I do not believe it,' he says, and there's no doubt that's the truth. 'Am I the only bastard in that entire station who hasn't slept with that bloody woman?' The man looks incredulous. I've managed to impress him. 'How long's this been going on?'

'About a week.'

'Every night? Just the once? What?'

'Christmas Eve, Saturday, Monday.'

'Fuck.' Lets the word drift off into nothing. He lifts my cup of tea and drains it. When his mouth drops open again, the pieces of chicken have gone. 'That's where you've been all these mornings. Christ. What's she want with someone like you?'

I've been asking myself the same question of course, but there's no need for the tone of voice.

'I don't know. Probably heard how brilliant I was from all those other birds at the station.'

Shakes his head, mutters, 'Bastard.'

Stares at the floor. Runs it over in his head, what it means; see the explosion coming when the thought finally occurs to him. Looks at me. Not so impressed anymore.

'You mean we've had officers running about for the past five days trying to find out who Bathurst slept with just before she died, and you've known all along?'

Don't feel too good about that, but I can't deny it.

'Lumberyard?'

'I didn't know what to do.'

'You could've told me, even if you didn't want the rest of the station to know. Fuck's sake. Why didn't you say?'

Another inadequate shrug of the shoulders. Nothing to say for myself that isn't going to be bluster and bullshit.

'What? You wanted it to be your own little secret. Was that it? Is it more than sex, Lumberyard? What are you saying?' I'm not saying anything, you're saying it all for me. 'You think you've got some sort of chance with the bitch? Is that it? You want to be Mr Miller? Fuck's sake, Lumberyard, what are you thinking?'

He's hit the nail on the head. He is a detective after all. I just sit there looking like a lump of lard.

'When are you seeing her again?'

'Don't know. She was fucked off about the Montague business. Think she might have dumped me.'

Don't know how pathetic my voice sounded just then. He shakes his head, the anger leaves his face to be replaced by a smile. Starts to laugh. Wonder what he's doing, but it becomes infectious and I join him. He's right to laugh at me, after all, I deserve it.

'She just used me for sex,' I say, and we both end up pishing ourselves laughing for five minutes over the absurdity of me and Charlotte Miller.

If you can't laugh, what can you do? Bastard.

When we get ourselves back together he asks the obvious question.

'What was it like then?' he says. I would have asked him the same thing if the situation had been reversed.

Look for the right words, but it's hard to find them. How to encapsulate such beauty in mere language.

'It was fucking brilliant,' is as good as I can do.

He looks appreciative. 'I expect it probably would be.'

The waitress hovers nearby, Taylor orders another piece of chicken pie; no chips. She disappears again. He smiles, shakes his head, rolls his eyes, says, 'Shit, I should have ordered more tea.' Calls over to her, raises his cup. She nods at him, and there's a fifty percent chance she understood what he meant.

Glad I've told him at last. And it takes some more of the edge off this pointless infatuation. I needed a good kick in the arse to start getting over it, and her reaction to the Montague business was a reasonable start. Taylor pishing himself laughing at me is also what I needed.

'So, you think she's dumped you because of Jonathan Montague?' he asks.

'She hasn't said as much, but that's probably about it.'

'She's probably shagging him 'n all.' He smiles. 'I mean, she shags you three times in about six days, and in the middle of that she gets hold of Bathurst. Anyone else you know about?'

Begin to feel small – a minuscule part in a big plan. Just don't know what the hell that plan is. Shake the head.

'Voracious,' he says, and he's right about that. 'Wish she'd include me in it, sometime.'

'You've got Eileen Harrison?' I say, a bit weakly.

He smiles again. Stares at the floor. 'Ahh,' he says.

'What the fuck does that mean? Ahh? Ahh doesn't mean anything. What is that?'

'Look, we've got a murder inquiry here,' he says as the second piece of chicken pie arrives, 'let's concentrate on that.' There's a surprise. 'So, Charlotte's mad about you going to Montague. She knows it's because we're checking out Evans. Bathurst has told her the whole story...'

'We assume, we don't know.'

'Whatever. She doesn't think the Addison case has anything to do with this, despite the three deaths, and so she doesn't want us digging away at old wounds. Leave them be and concentrate on finding Ian Healy.'

'Or,' I say, 'she knows they're connected because she's part of it. Wants to ensure we don't discover the truth.'

'Too scary, Lumberyard. Evans, fine, 'cause the guy's sick. But Miller. If that's the case, why not just put herself in charge of the case when she removed Bloonsbury?'

'She tried that.'

'What do you mean?'

'She said she was doing it. I threatened to reveal her and Bathurst; told her to put you in charge instead.'

He looks at me, forkful of chicken pie in hand.

'You're jerking me off?' he says.

'Nope.'

'Jesus fuck, Lumberyard, you're full of little secrets. Anything else you'd like to tell me?'

I give it some thought. It's been a hectic week.

'Don't think so.'

'Good. You haven't shagged Jonah then?'

'Har, har.'

'Well, bloody hell, nothing would surprise me now.'

Starts munching the pie which had taken half a minute to get to his mouth, and I gesture to the waitress that I'd like some more tea.

'So what are we going to do?' I ask.

He spears another piece of pie.

'We're going to ignore her and go after Evans. Go back down

to Arocher later this afternoon. Speak to a few people, do a more thorough search of that horrible little house of his, and we're going to work out where he went.'

The tea arrives.

'Stoatir,' I say.

40

Some time after four o'clock. The evening has already arrived, but still the country is bright with the low cloud and the snow lying on the ground. Hogmanay, the usual busy night ahead. Still, it isn't like it used to be around here, that's for sure. Anyone's granny will tell you that. All that charging around and first footing; turning up at the house of total strangers with a bottle of White & McKay at your armpit; singing strange songs without words which might be Cole Porter or might be Harry Lauder or might be some complete load of pish; all that has gone. We've become a nation of people who sit and watch Bill McCue and the Alexander Brothers, and complain endlessly about how bloody awful it is and how New Year just isn't what it used to be. As if it's everybody else's fault but our own.

No crap TV for us tonight, though. We're on the hunt for Evans, and after a few hours wasting time chasing reported sightings of Ian Healy, we're back on track. Might be the wrong track, but I have a feeling.

In the last two days nearly ninety people have reported seeing Ian Healy. Sounds good? Rubbish. If they'd all come from the same place, we'd be fine. But, as is always the case, we've had calls from everywhere. Down south as well, as his picture went out on the national news.

So Ian Healy is this week's Elvis. Working a petrol pump in Wolverhampton; sitting on a bench in Hyde Park; throwing up over the side of the Mull ferry in choppy seas; playing golf in

Nairn.

That's the trouble with putting out photographs – you get all sorts of dunderheids calling in. Same last week with the photofit, which turned out to be a pretty poor resemblance of our man. Every poor bastard with no one to talk to wants to phone the polis.

Problem is that it only takes one of those calls to be right, so you can't ignore any of them. So I had four hours checking up on spurious calls from around Glasgow.

Bloonsbury charged around for a few hours until he hit the wall about three o'clock. Didn't see him do it, but you could smell the whisky on his breath, see it in his eyes. Can't keep a fuck-up away from his drink for long.

Just before I left I got another call on the Batphone from Charlotte. What are you doing tonight, Dallas? Frank's in Poland. Why don't you come down? She's taking the piss. Must be. Toying with me. Fortunately, however, I'm not going to fall for it as badly as I was. Doesn't mean I'm not going to go down there, of course.

Anyway, the waste of an afternoon is behind us and we head on down to Evans' house. Talk to a few of the people around and not just the repugnant neighbour. Do a more thorough investigation of the house, try and see beyond the porn and empty beer cans, see if there's any note of where his ex might be.

We get to the house not long after five. Step out of the warmth of the car into the chill of night. Stop and look out over the loch. No cars on the road, low cloud and the snow muffling any sound. Silence. Snow in the air, but it hasn't started to fall with any force. The loch is still, hardly a wave washes upon the shore. The mountains covered in white. Beautiful. Scotland in all its silent, scenic grandeur. Clean and fresh.

Hear the faint murmur of the TV set from the house next door. Wild cheering from some ridiculous quiz show. The moment is gone. We turn back to Evans' house. The snow covered path virginal. He hasn't been about today, but then we hardly expected that.

'Right then,' says Taylor, 'let's get it over with.'

Up to the front door, push it open, and into the house of fun.

Lights on. Doesn't look as if anyone else has been in the place since we were here on Saturday night, which is good.

And so for another hour and a half we plunge back into the seedy world of Detective Chief Inspector Gerry Evans. Go over everything, a much more thorough search than before. Look for scraps of paper, address books, telephone numbers, anything. Down the back of sofa and armchairs, clearing out drawers, every filthy nook and every revolting cranny trying to find what we can. And at the end of it we've got an old book with old numbers of people he probably hasn't spoken to in years, plus a couple of addresses and numbers on bits of paper which long ago fell behind cushions and into holes. The sad state of Gerry Evans – no friends, and no life barring the putrid collection of illegal pornography.

Sitting in the lounge at the end of it. Lights on, watching the snow fall. Dying to step out into the cold.

'Almost feel sorry for the bastard,' says Taylor, and I know what he means. But, as I've said before, he's not a man to inspire much sympathy.

'Aye. Still like to stick him in jail, mind.'

'Aye. Right, I'm going to make some of these calls, if this idiot's phone is still connected. Big surprise if he actually pays the bills.' He lifts the receiver, raises his eyebrows. 'We're on. Obviously a conscientious citizen. While I'm doing this you can start the house to house. Begin with next door if you like.'

'Can I arrest him?'

'Feel free. Just remember you'll have to fill out a report.'

Good point. How many bastards who should be in the nick get off because of that?

Taylor starts to dial the first number, I head out into the cold. Snowing quite hard. Feels clean. Almost seven o'clock; wonder what the idiot with bad hair is going to be watching on the TV tonight. Haven't watched Hogmanay tele in about six years, so I wouldn't know.

Ring the bell, wait for the explosion. Wish I'd brought my truncheon.

Ring the bell again. Can picture the old man inside, tutting and cursing, swearing at his missus. If he knew it was me he probably wouldn't even answer; then I'd get the chance to break the door in, wave a piece of paper at him pretending it's a warrant, and ransack the place. Might do that anyway.

Door opens. Hold out the badge.

'Detective Sergeant Lumberyard, CID. We spoke on Saturday.'

He looks at me funny. That well-practiced 'who the fuck are you?' stare which might just work with a constable with no testicles questioning a member of the public for the first time.

'About your neighbour, Evans.'

Lets out a long breath. 'Och aye, that eejit,' he says.

'Aye, that eejit. You seen him recently?'

Shakes his head.

'I told you before, did I no'? He fucked off. And I wish you'd do the same. Fucking polis.'

He starts to close the door. Pissed me off just a little too much. Put my foot across the line, hand to the door.

'Listen you old git, you either answer my questions properly this time, or I'll get a warrant and a team from Special Branch and we'll come down here and rip your fucking house to shreds.'

He hesitates. The cry comes from the living room – 'What the fuck are you doing, you stupid eejit. Close the fucking door!' – glances over his shoulder, then comes out onto the front step, closing the door behind him.

'Right, what do you need, 'cause I'm watching the tele?'

It worked. Some people realise you're bullshitting and threats don't get you anywhere. Not this comedian.

'No shite now, or you're in trouble, all right? I need to know the last time you saw Evans, exactly what he said when he called you, if he'd had any visitors, anything. Think about it, take your time, I need to know everything.'

'What's that useless bastard been up to, then?'

'It doesn't matter. Just answer the questions, please.' Bit of civility never did anyone any harm. The urbane polis, that's me.

He breathes out; big sigh. Wants to show what a huge favour he's doing me. Probably thinks he'll get a mention in the Honour's List.

'Me and the missus don't sleep so good, you know? Me with

the sciatica, and her with the arthritis. Right bastard that sciatica, I'll tell you, and they doctors don't know shite, so they don't.' I'm about to punch him. 'So we're quite often awake in the middle of the night, you know. So Saturday morning, I don't know what time it was, maybe one o'clock, something like that, I hears a noise, you know. Something going on next door.'

'What kind of noise?'

'I don't know, do I? I wasn't in there, was I, you stupid bastard? So, whatever. I hears the door slam and I looks out the window. Seen him drive off up the road.'

'Which way?'

'Up yon. Loch Fyne way, you know.'

Right. Getting somewhere. Didn't head back to Glasgow.

'So when did he call you?'

'In the morning sometime. Can't remember exactly when, you know. Eight o'clock or something like that. Maybe earlier. Bastard got me out of my bed.'

'What did he say?'

Shakes his head, sucks his teeth. I hate this guy. But then, I hate most of the people I have to question.

'No' much. Says he was going away for a few weeks, could I look after the place. I mean, what a load of shite. That bastard couldn't look after his own prick.'

'OK. How'd he sound?'

'How did he sound? Fucking hell.' Looks over his shoulder at the closed door, a wistful glance. '*Lethal Weapon 3*'s on, you know,' he says.

'Come on, Gramps, it's a load of shite. You're involved in the real thing here. Much more interesting.'

He thinks about this. At least his facial gyrations suggest he's thinking.

'So how did he sound?' I repeat.

'I don't know. I didn't speak to him much, you know, but he sounded a bit different. Hard to describe. With a cold, or breathless or something. Ach, I'm no one of they psychiatrist bastards, one of they educated bastards. I'm a working man. Forty year in the postal trade.'

'That'll explain the sciatica.'

'Aye, it does, but d'you think the Post Office wants to know about it? Do they fuck, mate.'

Nod, look sympathetic. The New Policeman.

'So, is there anything else you can tell me?'

'Aye, there is. My fucking bollocks are getting frozen off. Can I go back inside now?'

Sometimes you just know when you've reached the limit of all you're going to get.

'Aye, right, on you go.'

He grunts something in fluent Neanderthal and slams the door. Away back to Mel Gibson, you sad bastard.

Turn away from the door just as Taylor emerges from Evans' place. Looks none too happy, but he rarely does.

'Get anywhere?' I ask.

He shrugs his shoulders.

'Spoke to three people. Julia, the ex. Hasn't heard a thing from the guy in five or six years. Says that if we find him we've to remind him of his alimony payments.'

'Some chance.'

'Aye. The other two, don't know who the hell they were. Wouldn't say, but we can check up on them. Just a couple of shady sleazoids that Evans does his dirty work with, I suspect. They both sounded pissed off at the mention of his name. I'd guess he owes them money, and neither of them know where he is. What about you?'

That's polis work for you. Hours of crap for little reward. Point in the direction of the Rest and be Thankful.

'Left at about one in the morning and went that way.'

He looks into the snow, along the road which runs beside Loch Long; which rises up the hill away from the loch, and then gives way to turn offs which offer at least three choices of what route to take. The snow is already thick on the road and hardly a car has passed along it since we arrived. Only a fool would head up into the hills on a night like this; particularly when the man we're following went five days ago, and his trail will be colder than the water in the loch we're standing at the head of.

'You're going to follow him, aren't you?' I say.

He grunts and looks at me as if I'm an idiot.

'Get out of here, Lumberyard, it was five days ago for God's sake.'

Oh. 'What then?'

'You're going to go and interview some more of the neighbours, while I go back inside and watch the tele. *Lethal Weapon 3*'s on apparently.'

Bloody marvellous. The usual division of labour.

'And Lumberyard,' he says, 'brush the snow off your hair. You look like an idiot.'

41

Get back into the house half an hour later. Frozen to the bones; in need of a hot drink. Or alcohol. Find Taylor with his feet up watching one of those lousy sitcoms that pepper the TV schedules.

'Anything?' he says.

'They all thought he was a creep. Some of them had stories to tell, but nothing relevant.'

He grunts a reply, keeps watching the TV.

'What about you?' I say. 'You find out who the bad guys were in *Lethal Weapon 3*?'

'You might be surprised to hear I've been working.'

'I'm shocked.'

'Piss off. Put a call through to all the polis in the surrounding area. Asked them to go out looking for Evans' car, and to phone here if they found anything.'

'God, I'll bet you were popular.'

'Just used my natural authority.'

Have a picture of fifteen desk cops trudging out into the snow, cursing him extravagantly.

'So what if he drove outwith the surrounding area?'

He looks at me. 'We do it tomorrow. But if it's nearby we can go looking for it tonight. So we sit and wait. Give them an hour or two. Told them to call in with nil returns. Fine, he could be anywhere, but if his car's in one of the smaller towns out west here, then we might get him.'

Fair point. Might work.

'Couldn't we go and sit in a bar somewhere?'

'Don't be a jessie, Lumberyard. Park your arse. There's some warm McEwan's beside the settee.'

Thanks.

And that's it for a long time. We sit and wait, enduring awful television as we go. The phone rings every now and again with some polis informing us he's checked the one car park in his one car park town; but the rest of the time we're quiet, too numbed by shit TV to have anything to say to each other.

About an hour and a half into the ordeal, when we're on the point of giving up, we get the one we're waiting for. Dunoon. The local Feds have found his car parked up a small street away from the residential area. Taylor gets the location, tells them to leave it as it is; says they can bugger off and we'll be along to check it out ourselves.

So, a few quick calls to warn off the rest of the search party, and then we're back out into the snow. Along Loch Long away from Arocher, slither up the Rest and Be Thankful, down and along Loch Fyne, past Strachur.

The snow lessens as we go, but Taylor is concentrating on not driving off the road, while I let my mind wander through a variety of women. Peggy, Charlotte, Alison, and the enigma of Eileen Harrison. Even think of Jean Fryar for some reason. More women than you could shake a stick at. The mind rambles on.

Get to Dunoon, drive past a chippie on the way in, and the smell proves too intoxicating. Fish suppers all round, and then we start driving around looking for the street where they said we'd find Evans' car. Takes us a while to find it as there just aren't any polis to stop and ask the way.

So we step out into the snow and the cold, still finishing off our dinner. Good fish supper too – crispy batter, tasty piece of fish, right amount of salt and vinegar, chips deep-fried to perfection.

We stand looking at the car. Kicking the tyres, various other forms of external examination, while we eat the last of the meal – Taylor a little behind 'cause he was driving.

'So what?' I say to him. 'He got the ferry over to Gourock? Got the train up to Glasgow.'

'Shite,' says Taylor as he drops a piece of fish into the snow. Takes more care with the next piece. 'No, doesn't sound right. What would be the point?'

'Trying to throw us off his trail.' I say.

'Don't know,' he says. 'Who can figure out the mind of someone like Gerry Evans? Need to speak to one of the had-his-teddy-bear-stolen-at-the-age-of-five brigade.'

Finish off the fish supper, stuff the paper into my coat pocket and wash my hands in the snow. Light up a cigarette. That post-fish supper nicotine experience.

Taylor fishes around in his pocket and tosses me a small black book. Evans' life in sixty small pages.

'Check through that. Look for anything in this area.'

Get to it in the dim light of the street lamps, while Taylor continues to circle the car kicking at various parts, nothing left of his dinner but chips. Finally says, 'You any good at breaking into these things?'

Look up from Evans' seedy list of acquaintances. Horrified to see that I'm down there.

'Naw. Herrod was your man for that.'

'Well he's not here, is he?'

Good point. Lose interest in the book because I'm not getting anywhere; wander around the car. The lock on the boot looks pretty rusty, and since it's a hatchback that'll allow us access to the whole thing.

'Get a crowbar and jemmy the boot lock, or put in a window,' I say.

He finishes off his chips, tosses the paper onto the ground. The perfect citizen.

'Good fish supper,' he says. 'Right, I've got something in the boot you can use for that. Break the lock, it'll make less noise. No point in arousing the suspicions of the local constabulary if we don't have to. I expect Charlotte's slept with most of them as well.'

Very cutting. Pick up the paper he tossed on the ground and put it into a bin along with my own. Retrieve the small crowbar from the boot of Taylor's car.

'I could eat another one of those,' he says, as I return laden with crime committing goods.

'A second fish supper?'

'Aye.'

I think about it as I get to work. Two fish suppers in the quick succession. Greedy but not outlandish. However, no matter the temptation, the second one is always a disappointment. Never quite matches the pleasure of the first. Be it fish suppers or bowls of cornflakes. This golden rule does not apply to vodka tonic, of course.

Hold the cigarette between my lips, speak without managing to drop it into the snow.

'Aye, maybe you're right. A second fish supper...,' pause for that bit of extra effort, 'might just be called for,' I say as the lock springs open.

Take another long draw on the smoke, remove the cigarette from my mouth.

'Might have a haggis supper this time,' I say.

'Aye, we can get them in a minute. Stop salivating and open the boot.'

It was your suggestion you bastard. Put the cigarette back in my mouth, lift the boot...need both hands, it's so rusted and stiff.

The boot opens, we stare at the contents; obvious despite the dim light. A vaguely unpleasant smell drifts out. The cigarette falls from my mouth into the snow.

'Fuck.'

'Fucking right,' says Taylor.

He reaches forward and pulls at the head of the corpse which is lying bundled in the back of the car. It does not move to his touch, so we both pull at the body more vigorously. It is stiff and unyielding, but eventually we manage to pull it over, and the head comes round to meet us. Eyes and mouth open.

We stare at it for a while. Neither of us knows what to say. We've spent the last week and a half not having any idea what's going on. We pieced together what we could, and came up with some sort of connection. And now everything we thought made sense has been tossed out the window.

'Fucking hell,' says Taylor.

'Aye,' I say in reply.

'I could use that fish supper now,' he says.

42

Still thinking of Emma. Always thinking of Emma. Doesn't realise that Christmas has passed, such labyrinthine paths has his mind wandered down; through valleys of gold, up mountains of green, hand in hand with Emma.

Still sees himself giving Emma a Christmas present, cuddling Emma under the duvet on a cold Christmas night, the lights of the tree twinkling in the corner. *All I want for Christmas is Emma.*

Head twitches.

He is cold, cold to the bones. Hasn't had anything to eat for three days. He was fed at first, but now that's drifted off. Forgotten what food tastes like, forgotten the warmth of it as it slides down his throat. Water and the occasional shot of J&B is not enough. The whisky burns and warms, but still he does not like the taste; nothing can change that.

His wrists were sore, but eventually the numbness came to take the pain away and now he feels nothing; except for the occasional trickle of blood down his arms after he tries to wrestle himself free. Knows the way to no pain is to stay still, but sometimes he is gripped with a desperation to get away. Emma is out there – sweet Emma – and she needs him. He knows she aches for him the same as he aches for her. Imagines all kinds of things happening to her, and the anger wells within him at the thought of what might happen to her without him to protect her.

There are so many weirdoes and idiots out there. And here he is, imprisoned, and there's nothing he can do about it.

The anger passes. He thinks of a quiet Christmas afternoon. Lights sparkling on the tree, Bing Crosby crooning. The egg is in the nog, whatever the Hell that means; coal crackling in the fire. Holding hands, his ring around her finger.

His hands around her throat.

43

There's never a ferry when you need one.

Heading back to Glasgow, the long way round from Dunoon; back the way we came. It's going to take at least a couple of hours in this weather, and we could call someone in Glasgow to do our work for us; but who's that going to be? Who do you call when you've just found your prime suspect dead in his own car, leaving you suspicious of the two most senior officers at the station?

Evans had looked as ugly in death as in life. I can't think of anyone I'd feel less sorry for, having found them long dead in the back of their own car. Alerted the locals, but asked them to keep it under their hats for a few hours. Do the necessary, but don't go phoning Glasgow with the news, 'cause Glasgow already knows.

Still plenty of snow on the ground, no talk in the car. Taylor concentrating on not driving too fast for the conditions, leaving me to concentrate on what the hell is going on. Can think of only two available options.

Out onto the dual carriageway past Balloch before the snow gives a temporary respite, and driving becomes easier. About twenty minutes left of the year, and I can't wait to be done with it.

Taylor speeds through the night. Decides it's time we talked about it. Gerry Evans, dead in his own car.

'You worked any of it out, Lumberyard?' he says.

Gather the thoughts, try not to say them all at once.

'If Evans had anything to do with the other deaths, there must have been some accomplice who's now taken care of him. Alternatively, and more likely, he had nothing to do with it and has been dealt with like the others as part of the same deal. Forgetting Ian Healy for a second, 'cause I've no idea where he fits in, of the original gang of five only Bloonsbury is left.'

He nods. 'Aye, you're right.'

'So, is it that Jonah's been taking care of all his co-conspirators, or does it mean that someone else is going after them all and Jonah's next in line?'

'Miller for instance,' he says. 'Or, fuck, I don't know. Since she knows about the Addison case then maybe she's going to be the next victim.'

'So who do we warn? Bloonsbury or Miller?'

'No idea, Lumberyard. Maybe they're in it together.'

Jesus, maybe they are. Nothing would surprise me now.

'And what about Healy?' I say.

He shakes his head.

'I can't work that out. We know he killed Ann Keller and Bathurst. Herrod was killed at his place. I don't know. Maybe he's working with Bloonsbury. Jonah did let him go after all. Maybe they did a deal.'

Stare ahead into the thick mist of night. Can't think straight without at least two v&t's inside me. Fish suppers aren't any good for the brain. Especially when we didn't get the chance to have that second one.

'He realises Healy's the killer,' I say. 'At the same time he's wanting to get rid of all his co-conspirators, so he enlists Healy's help. Threatens to arrest him if he doesn't do his dirty work for him, something like that.'

'Fucking Jonah Bloonsbury,' says Taylor. 'Still don't believe it. That theory's still got to be on the sidelines. If he was going to shaft them, why get the help of a psycho? How are you going to control a guy like that? Why not just do it himself?'

We pass through Dumbarton – city of magic – still not much traffic, a few flakes of snow in the air, half an hour short of our destination. Bloonsbury's house; although what will we say if we find him sitting there, a wee dram in his hand and angrily proclaiming his innocence?

'No proof,' I say to him.

'What?'

'We've no proof. Of any of it. It's all speculation.'

He nods. 'I know. That's why it's a pain in the arse.'

'We could be miles off the mark, pishing in the wind. Here's a scenario: Healy kills Keller, then Bathurst. Just in the natural course of his duties as a loony. Maretta Johnson puts Herrod onto Healy, and he gets his comeuppance when he goes to see him. Healy, realising the polis are on to him, buggers off. The next day, Edwards is killed in a hit and run. It happens. Pretty big coincidence, but why not? Meanwhile, some scum confederate of Evans with whom he does business, gets fed up with our slime ex-polis and does away with the guy. There are probably a thousand people out there who wanted to see Evans dead. So, five deaths and Jonah Bloonsbury has nothing to do with any of them.'

Taylor stares into the white gloom. Thinking. Likes the sound of it, I can see that. And it doesn't sound too far fetched either. A little, perhaps, but not as outlandish as Jonah Bloonsbury enlisting the help of a psychopath.

Nods his head eventually.

'You're probably right. Hope you're right. Can you imagine the stench of this if Bloonsbury's our man?'

'Maybe we've been getting ahead of ourselves,' I say. 'So, there's been a coincidence or two. It happens. We'll charge in there to find Jonah sitting getting quietly pished along with Bill McCue, and we're going to look stupid.'

Drums his fingers on the steering wheel.

'Fuck, I don't know, Sergeant. We could talk ourselves in circles. We'll just go and see the guy, midnight or not, and we'll tell him about Evans. See his reaction, or something like that. We're certainly not dropping it now just because it might all be a big coincidence.'

Fair enough.

'All right,' I say. 'Then I've got Charlotte Miller to think about.'

'What do you mean?'

Hit the Erskine Bridge; and somewhere bells are ringing to herald the arrival of the New Year. Party. The snow starts to thicken once again.

'She asked me down there tonight. Frank's in Poland, apparently. I mean, who the hell goes to Poland?'

He looks at me. Fortunately not for too long, and turns back to the road.

'And were you going to tell me this sometime?'

'I'm telling you now.'

'God's sake, Lumberyard.'

'What's the problem? You jealous?'

'Fucking hell. Where were we ten minutes ago with this discussion? There are four polis dead. If it's not coincidence, if they're all dead for the same reason; if it's not Bloonsbury who's done it and he's next on the list, it could be Miller. She knows we know. Why else would she ask you down there?'

Get out of my face with that crap, you idiot. He pisses me off sometimes. Just cause his wife's left him for someone half his age and twice his penis size, he can't handle me getting laid by the boss.

'If she was going to do it,' I protest, 'then why not do it before now, for fuck's sake? She's had plenty of opportunity.'

'Fuck, I don't know, Lumberyard. Just ask yourself why she's shagging you in the first place.'

And that remark drops out into silence. He's right. I've no idea. But it still doesn't make sense that it should be to keep me quiet. I didn't know a thing about all of this when I first went down there on Christmas Eve. Maybe she just thought I knew.

Nothing to say. The journey continues in silence; and the snow falls in ever more furious flurries, so that by the time we arrive in Hamilton we're driving through a white mass.

Haven't been at Bloonsbury's house since he had a bachelor poker party two weeks after Beattie moved out. Really it was a poker/fuck movie/drugs/alcohol/whore party. The standard polis fare. Filled the house up with a bunch of us, raided the warehouse and got what he could, dragged in a couple of tarts that they'd picked up specially the night before. You know the deal: 'come round and shag the lot of us tomorrow night or you're nicked.' Happens all the time. Anyway, sad to say, Detective Sergeant Lumberyard was in the midst of it all. Steaming out of my face, losing a shit load of cash at the cards, standing in the queue for the women. Jesus knows what number I was in line. Not a proud moment in my career. Some things are best forgotten.

Pull up outside the house, get out of the car into the cold. Up the path, the tangled mass of vegetation that is the garden still evident despite the snow. Wonder what state of decay the house is going to be in.

The house is quiet. Dead. No lights, no sound.

'He's either out, or he's collapsed on the floor,' says Taylor as he rings the bell.

'Probably out somewhere collapsed on the floor,' I say. Pull my coat closer around me; makes no difference. It's bloody freezing. Scottish weather at it's most eloquent.

He rings the bell again and we stand and wait. In vain. Tries the door handle. Locked.

'You ready to put the door in again?' he says.

'You're kidding?'

'Come on, Lumberyard, don't be a jessie. We're not standing out here all night waiting for the guy to wake up or come home.'

'But he could have nothing to do with it. He might just be a drunken pish head. How's it going to look if we go breaking into his house and nothing comes out of it?'

He looks at me – the Chief Inspector look.

'Lumberyard, break the fucking door down. I'll take the responsibility. Just do it. If someone is taking them all out, Bloonsbury could be lying in there dead, anyway.'

Let out a long breath. Bloody hell, here goes. I'll be getting my Door-Kicking Proficiency Badge at least. Glad I've got my boots on.

Foot up, kick hard at the lock with the soul of my boot. The door gives slightly, while I lose my balance, slip and fall on my backside. Into a soft bed of snow. Taylor ignores me, puts his shoulder to the weakened door, and pushes it open. Looks back.

'Come on, Lumberyard. Get up off your arse,' he says, and walks into the house. Puts on the hall light, looks up the stairs.

'Jonah!'

I dig myself out the snow, brush it off best I can, walk into the house.

'Jonah!' he shouts again.

Dead quiet.

'Right, up the stairs Lumberyard, I'll do down here.'

Taylor walks off into the sitting room – the scene of a vast majority of the poker party – while I head up to the bedrooms; scene for another part of the poker party. Two bedrooms and a bathroom at the end is all there is up here, if I remember correctly.

Have a vaguely embarrassed feeling, walking into the house of someone who may well be perfectly innocent. Half expect to find him in bed with someone from the station, and I'm going to feel like an idiot.

To the top of the stairs, stop and listen. Nothing.

'Jonah, you there?'

No reply. Feels a bit creepy now that I'm here, even with the lights on. Vaguely unpleasant smell in the air. Wonder if it's death. Don't think so. Assume that anywhere Bloonsbury lives is going to smell vaguely unpleasant.

Walk along the top landing, floorboards creak beneath my feet. Past the regulation polis photo – the young Jonah with the Secretary of State for Scotland of the day. Bruce Millan by the looks of things. His glory days were that long ago.

Push open the door to the front bedroom.

'Jonah?'

Turn on the light. The place is a shit tip. The sort of state your room is in when you're twelve and your mother's forgotten to tell you to clean it up for the last year. The man lives like a pig. Hate to think what sort of lifeforms Taylor's going to come across in the kitchen.

Walk into the room, start poking around his things. Clothes

everywhere, blankets tossed off the side of the bed. Sheets and pillows stained. Wonder if he's changed them since the whores were here along with all the guys from the station. By the looks of things, not.

Think I feel it first, rather than hear it. A noise; a whisper of sound. Niggling. Feel it in the shiver down my back. Drop the jacket, the pockets of which I've been looking through. Stand still. Silent. Taylor maybe.

It comes again. A murmur of noise. The next bedroom. A strange sound. Not like a man or woman's voice, but still human. A whimper.

Wish I had a gun again. Ought to start carrying these things around, but still the noise is not threatening. Out into the hall, and now I can hear it more clearly. Feel the pain of it. Hairs rise on the back of my neck.

A noise from downstairs. Taylor stumbling into something, a low curse; calls out for Bloonsbury again.

Stand outside the other bedroom. A second's hesitation. Wonder. Push the door open, no idea what I'm going to find. Half expecting to see a dog whimpering in the corner.

Light on.

Jesus Christ. The smell hits me as much as the sight of what is in front of me; get that instant shock like needles of water under a freezing shower.

Ian Healy, manacled to the wall. Unshaven, cheeks drawn, barely recognisable from the man I spoke to a week ago. He is naked, his arms attached to the wall above him, and from these he hangs limply. His feet can touch the floor, but they offer no support. And around his feet are several days worth of his own faeces and urine and vomit.

Take a step back, try to ignore the smell. He squints from the light, and then looks at me. Acknowledgement flickers across his face, a word tumbles almost silently from his lips.

'Jack!' I shout, 'think you'd better get up here.'

44

Can hear Taylor labouring up the stairs. I'm about to plough my way through the human detritus on the floor to let Healy down, when I decide to wait for the boss. He might look like a pathetic shambles of a human being, but he's still a killer. Ann Keller at least, although the truth of the second and third murders is beginning to kick in. Taylor arrives, stands at my shoulder.

'Fuck,' he says to my back.

Finally, after a week and a half of speculation and haphazard supposition, we have something concrete. A piece of living evidence up on the wall which is all the proof we need of Jonah Bloonsbury's involvement in the murders of three other polis. 'Fuck' just about hits the nail on the head.

Taylor comes into the room, walks up to Healy. The smell hits him.

'Jesus Christ,' he says. 'This is unbelievable. Medieval for God's sake. You got your keys, Lumberyard?'

'Aye, but remember what this guy did to Ann Keller.'

'We don't know he did anything to anyone,' he says.

'Come on. Maybe the rest was a set up, but how did Bloonsbury get on to him in the first place? This guy killed Ann Keller. Think about what he did to her, before you go letting him down.'

He looks at Healy who stares blankly back. At a guess I'd say he has no idea what we've just been talking about. Dead eyes, mouth attempting to smile.

'How long have you been here?' says Taylor.

Nothing. The guy doesn't have a clue.

'Healy, how long?'

A whispered word passes his lips, drops out into the room, unintelligible.

'What was that?' says Taylor. Voice still harsh. No time for naked psychopaths on walls.

Healy's lips move again, and this time we can hear it. The chill, croaking voice.

‘Mother,’ he says. ‘Tell Mother.’

Loony.

*

The threads of a story come from time to time together and make a picture in the web.

Another one of Charlotte’s favourites. Very appropriate.

Half an hour later and we’re back on the road. Called Ramsey and told him to get a few of the lads round. Impressed the delicacy of it all upon him. No one’s going to like the truth of this. Got him to start the search for Bloonsbury and to have the guy brought in. Who knows what gutter he’ll be lying in at the moment? Also told him that we’d take care of telling Miller, which is where we’re heading right now. Down to Helensburgh, back the way we just came. Stopped for petrol and provisions in case we get stuck in the snow, and on our way.

Eileen Harrison showed up at Bloonsbury’s place before we left, looking extremely hacked off, but all that went when she saw what we had. There were three of those Neanderthal constables with her to take care of Healy, just in case the guy decided to get funny.

Brief discussion in the car before Taylor shut up to concentrate on driving through the blizzard. We’d asked a few questions of Healy, but he was in no fit state to answer anything.

The pieces fall together, scraps of rubbish into a bin. Maybe it all starts when Evans tries to bribe Bloonsbury. That’s a guess, but we know they had dealings in the last month, and it’s a reasonable stab at it. Bloonsbury begins to panic about the truth of the Addison case getting out. Great career finally flushed down the toilet, starts to wonder what to do about it.

Meanwhile, Healy murders Ann Keller. The same night, Bathurst finds out the truth of the Addison case. Maybe Bloonsbury gets wind of that, maybe not. Maybe he knows she goes to see Miller. Anyway, I put him on to Healy, he talks to the guy, realises he’s our killer. Hatches his plan. Decides he’ll get rid of all his co-conspirators. Who knows how quickly he worked it all out? So he gets hold of Healy some time after he’d tried it on with that stupid tart in Rutherglen.

Early hours of Saturday morning he goes down to Arocher, takes care of Evans. Bundles him into the back of the car, drives it to Dunoon. Gets back to Arocher and his own car somehow. Stole another motor perhaps. Having dealt with Evans he then comes up to Glasgow and kills Evelyn Bathurst. Not sure how he knows where to find her, but then she was between her home and the station; not that much of a stretch. Does to her what Healy did to Ann Keller, planting evidence to incriminate Healy.

Next up, he knows somehow that Herrod has been put onto Healy by Maretta Johnson. He waits for him, stabs him through the chest. Then the following day he does for Edwards in a drive-by murder.

The story so far. Don't have too much proof of it all, but it falls into place. Feels right. Jonah Bloonsbury, come to this; and the confirmation of that hanging on the wall in his spare bedroom. The guy had been there a few days, Jonah's been at his house in that time. No set up, no bullshit, Bloonsbury's our man.

Feel empty. Hollow. Don't want to be in the polis tonight. Every one of us is going to look bloody awful when this gets out, and there'll be no one on the force thanking Taylor and me for having discovered it.

Which brings us to the last big question. The involvement of Charlotte Miller. Which side of the tracks are we going to find her on? We could have phoned her, but this is the sort of thing you have to say to someone's face. See the reaction.

Don't really start talking about it until we're over the Erskine bridge, the snow has cleared and we're both chewing on nasty ham and cheese sandwiches we picked up at the petrol station. Nearly two o'clock.

'How we going to play this?' I say eventually.

He waves the sandwich at me.

'What the fuck you buy these for, Lumberyard? They're minging.'

'It was after midnight for God's sake. What choice d'you think there was?'

He grumbles, continues to eat the sandwich.

'Not sure, is the answer to your question,' he says. 'Been

considering letting you go in yourself as planned.'

'What? You mean to see if she kills me?'

'Aye.'

'Thanks.'

'Don't think it'll work,' he says. 'I mean, if she doesn't know anything about it, then she'll shag you and I'll be left sitting in the car freezing my balls off. And we'll both look like idiots when we have to tell her the truth. So, we'll just go in there, tell her what we've found. We think Jonah's been killing off everyone who knows about the Addison business, which means that she might be next on the list.'

'And what if she's in on it and pulls a gun?'

'Don't see it. What's her motive? Sure, if the Addison stuff got out it'd look bad, set her back a year or two, but how is she supposed to know if some of her officers are murderers? And she's Charlotte Miller, for fuck's sake. She can shag and connive her way out of anything. She doesn't need to conspire to murder her own officers.'

Takes the left fork at the lights, heads down towards Helensburgh. I have to agree with him. The woman I've got close to in the last week isn't any confederate of Bloonsbury. What he's done is sickening, but he's such a mess of a man that however much your belief is stretched, there's still some credibility about it. But Charlotte Miller?

'And if she is in on it,' he continues, 'which I really doubt, what's she to gain from doing anything to us? It's already out about Bloonsbury, everyone knows. No, if she's implicated she'll deny everything, get hold of Jonah and kill him so that he can't talk. That way, she suffers minimum damage.'

Sounds right, but this is such a mess you never know.

'So where's Jonah got to?' I say.

He shrugs. 'Who knows? Lying in a ditch, maybe. If he realised from what I said earlier today that we were on to Evans, maybe he's just done a runner. Off to London to sleep under a bag with the rest of his peers.'

'Or he could have come down to Helensburgh to kill off Miller. The last of the people who know.'

‘We know,’ he says. ‘He’s still got us to take care of.’

Given the alacrity he’s shown in polishing off the others, that is not a comforting thought. Imagine my death at the hands of a crazed Jonah Bloonsbury. Start to have this morbid rumination over which of the four deaths we’ve had so far I would choose for myself. Decide on the strangling that Evans received, despite trying not to think about it.

Still pondering what it would be like to have a sword driven up through your insides, embedding you to a wall in the manner of the late and little-missed Herrod, when Taylor pulls up outside the mansion. Stops the car, switches off the engine. Looks at me.

‘This is it, Lumberyard. Is she is, or is she ain’t?’

Get out the car, once again feel the cold cut through the thin lining of the jacket. Boots crunch into the snow, an icy crust having formed on the top. Look up the path at the house. A couple of lights on, but don’t see her face pressed against a window watching out for me. If she was expecting me, I’m a good deal later than she’d have thought I was going to be.

Push open the gate at the bottom of the garden, start the long walk up the path.

‘Hope she’s in,’ says Taylor.

‘And alone,’ I add. ‘And unarmed.’

‘Jessie,’ he says.

45

Stand on the doorstep, where I’ve been twice in the last week. Feel a bit nervous, like I have the previous occasions. Different reason now. Almost at the end of the rainbow. Don’t know whether it’s going to be a bloody swamp, or a firing squad. Certainly won’t be any pot of gold or loony tune wizards.

About to ring the bell.

‘Wait,’ says Taylor.

Look at him.

'Second thoughts?' I ask.

'Got a feeling in your guts, Sergeant?' he says.

'What do you mean? Because of the ham sandwich?'

'You know what I mean.'

He's right. Polis instinct. There's something wrong. Don't know what, don't know how. Just a feeling, but there's so much work done on the back of feelings like this. Something in your stomach; the hairs on the back of your neck; that extra sense that stops you walking into the unexpected, stops you getting a knife in the belly.

'You want me to kick the door down again? That'll keep our arrival a secret.'

He gives me his Chief Inspector look, reaches out, tries the door handle. The door, in mockery of my dramatic suggestion, clicks open. That's my trick.

Give each other a 'right, keep your gob shut' look, and walk into the house. Close the door silently behind and stop and listen.

Nothing.

Lights are on in the hall. Door to the lounge is open and we can see the faint red of the Christmas lights, although the tree is out of sight. He gestures to me to check out the rooms on the other side of the hall and I start tentatively looking in the first one, as he goes into the lounge.

A library, the sort of room that normal people just don't have in the house. Rows of books that will remain forever unread; a writing desk untouched by human hand; an old-fashioned globe from a time when the Far East was just a vague mass, and Manhattan was a swamp; a small lamp burns in the corner, for whatever reason. To aid the investigating officer, perhaps.

Walk through the room to the door at the far end. Gently. Open it, into the next. In the dim light cast by the small lamp in the library I can see the outline of the billiards table. The overhanging light above the board dominates the room in its shady darkness. Nothing to look at here. Through the room and into the one behind – the room at the back of the house.

It's dark in here, the dim light from the library not penetrating.

Looks like a sitting room, the large TV set in the corner. Must be a 36” screen. Size is important after all. Nothing to see. Through the room to the door on the other side, after a cursory glance. We’re looking for Charlotte, not carrying out a close scrutiny of the place.

Back out into the hall. Taylor already coming out of the kitchen. Shakes his head, indicates up the stairs with his thumb. Either that or he’s giving me a thumbs up sign. ‘It’s all right – she’s in the kitchen impaled on a bread knife.’

‘Upstairs,’ he says quietly to me as he walks past. Knew that was what he meant.

It’s a big hall, allowing a large sweeping staircase to run up the right hand side; elaborate balustrade, which includes a figurehead at the top of the stairs. You’d think it might be a composer or something pretentious like that. But it’s even worse – it’s some old Rangers player from the forties or fifties. George Young, or someone like that. Christ but Frank’s a sad bastard. I nearly burst out laughing the first time I saw it. Decided that he deserved to have had me shag his wife. Walk up behind Taylor – not a creaking floorboard to be heard – and he stops for a look at the small figure. Not a word, shakes his head, walks on.

Stops on the landing and we stand and listen. Nothing again, the house still silent. Don’t know exactly what it is we’re looking for. The sound of someone being murdered? The screaming sounds of sex? Can’t be that – I was the one lined up for the job.

‘Bedroom?’ he says very quietly to me.

Point along the hall. Feel a tingle of excitement at the very mention of it. The thought that Charlotte will be lying in there waiting for me. Don’t think she’s going to be too impressed with me turning up with company. Can hear her saying, ‘Think you couldn’t cope, Sergeant?’ in a mock patronising voice. Can also hear her losing her temper and telling us where to go. Begin to have my doubts about just walking into the house unannounced. The gut feeling is still there, but Charlotte Miller is the boss after all, and she’s about to have two great galoots standing on the threshold of her bedroom. Uninvited.

‘You sure about this?’ I say to him, voice as low as I can get it.

'Think we should go back and ring the bell.'

'Don't be a jessie, Lumberyard,' he says.

Stand outside the door. Look at Taylor. For all his hard words, can see he's not quite as sure as he wants to be. Not a sound from within. What if we just barge in there and all she's doing is sleeping? We're going to look like idiots. And I'm definitely killing off any chance that I've got; although my brief infatuation has already burned at its brightest and is waning.

'What are you expecting to find?' I whisper.

Looks at me. Can see he's definitely not as sure as he wants to be. But still, the guy's wife has only recently left him, and we're all at our most reckless when that happens. Just looking for something else to go wrong.

Shrugs the shoulders. This is it.

'Just tell me something before we ruin the rest of our lives,' I say.

He raises his eyebrows in question.

'Did you shag Eileen?'

Looks blankly back. Completely ignores me.

He opens the door, hand to the light switch, steps into the room. I blunder in behind, and the two of us stand there like a couple of Action Men in the middle of the room.

Except there is no Action Man outfit for making a complete arse of yourself.

Charlotte stirs in her bed, raises her head. Her eyes blink the sleep away and she sits up. Looks at us as if we're aliens. The sheets fall away from her and she's wearing the same top she wore the first night I came here. Can see the swelling of her breasts, but embarrassment prevents me from getting too excited.

We stand there like a couple of great puddings waiting for her to say something, even though the onus is really on us.

'Chief Inspector?' she says eventually. The look on her face is moving slowly from surprise to lack of understanding, on its way to outrage. Taylor better make this good, 'cause I'm keeping my mouth shut.

He hesitates, but knows he has to say something.

'We've got to speak to you about Bloonsbury,' he says.

Interesting. Good, but not quite good enough.

She stares at him; the withering, reduces constables to jelly stare. Taylor's got an in-built force field against it, but I'm not so lucky. Feel like a total moron.

She pushes the sheets away and stands up out the bed. The top slithers down her thighs, but not before she's allowed us the briefest glimpse of pubic hair; smooth and sensual thigh. Get that weird feeling at the back of my throat. Right place, wrong time.

Shakes her head, eyes still squinting into the light.

'What the fuck are you doing, Jack? What time is it?'

'About two,' he says. Good command in the voice. The guy is not a bit intimidated. Balls of steel.

She looks at me, reducing me to gravy. Turns back to Taylor.

'And you couldn't phone?'

Doesn't bat an eyelid, Taylor. Very impressive.

'It's pretty big. Thought we should see you in person.'

She stares at him again. Giving it her best, but she must know it doesn't work with him.

'The doorbell?'

He doesn't immediately answer. Come on, Jack, think of a good one. Have no idea what he's going to say, and then he does the obvious and completely ignores the question.

'We found Ian Healy,' he says.

The eyes light up, the face does a variety of different things. Takes a step forward.

'Where?' she says.

'Bloonsbury's house.'

Brow furrows. Don't blame her.

'What do you mean?'

'Bloonsbury had him prisoner in his house. Had him there for a few days by the looks of things.'

She stares at him for a while, a different kind of stare now. Sits down on the bed, shaking her head. Then the hand goes to the forehead and she starts rubbing. Stress. The bane of our times. This is a reasonable time to be stressed, however. Can hear all that this piece of information entails running through her head. Or maybe she's already thinking of her own position. How she's going to explain it to the media, to the Chief Constable; how much will she have to bear the burden of responsibility? If she already knows that Healy's been imprisoned at Bloonsbury's house, as one of our theories went, this is a command performance. Meryl Streep.

Looks up after a while. Can see the panic in her eyes. Already ageing.

'Right, go downstairs and wait in the lounge. I'll be down in a minute,' she says. 'Fix yourselves a drink,' comes as an afterthought. A good afterthought. Need that v&t.

We stand there staring at her, but we're already dismissed. The allure of a woman in her pyjamas, or a reluctance to let her out of our sight. Don't know. Finally Taylor leads and we walk out. Miller and I exchange a glance, but I'm an idiot. Absolutely no idea what it says.

Surprised to find my legs are still fully functional. Along the hall and down the stairs, past the bust of Wullie Thornton or whoever the hell it is.

'Don't know how you do it,' I say to him, when I presume we're well out of earshot. 'I've shagged her and she still intimidates the hell out of me.'

'Piece of pish, Sergeant,' he says as we walk into the lounge. 'You've just got to remember which one of you has the balls.'

Shake my head. 'I always have my doubts about that.'

'Got to use your napper. If we'd discovered nothing amiss, the minute it got nasty I just needed to drop in the bit about Healy and Bloonsbury. The shock of that was always going to completely alter the situation.' He raises his eyebrows at me to get my approval. I stare at him. Good point, but it wouldn't have stopped my legs from being jelly even if I'd thought of it. 'She's just a wee woman, Lumberyard, remember that.'

Head for the alcohol.

'I need a drink,' I say. 'Want a single malt, they've got some good stuff here?'

He stands in the middle of the room, staring at the remains of the fire – a single low flame still struggling to escape the ashes – illuminated by nothing but the red glow from the Christmas lights.

Check the ice bucket and find it fully equipped; make myself a v&t. Half and half. Take a long swallow. Cold and warm and smooth and sharp, the perfect drink.

'They've got some Lagavulin here,' I say. 'You like that shit, don't you?'

He's staring at me, forehead knotted, eyes squinting in the dim light.

'There's something not right,' he says.

'What do you mean?'

He looks around the room, but mostly it is in warm darkness. Red glow, faint shadows. Still.

'Don't know. Just something...' Lets his voice trail off.

Looks away, into dark corners. Forget the drink for a second, follow his gaze. Have the first inclination of tension; a shiver down the spine. A suspicion of sound, of movement. Swallow. Muscles tense. Waiting.

'Get the light, Lumberyard,' he says.

And then the movement from behind the seat by the tree. The words barely uttered, no time for me to get to the light switch. A brief agitation in the dark, the flurry of an arm, and something flies through the air and thuds into the side of Taylor's head before he can duck out of the way.

He falls back, crumples to the floor. The chair is pushed aside into the tree, the figure appears from behind. Heading for Taylor, knife glinting red in the dull light. The tree topples over, all tinkling balls and rustling tinsel; the shadows roll around the room with the falling light.

Can make out the ugly face of Jonah Bloonsbury, contorted in exertion; can smell the whisky as his breath is angrily exhaled. He is almost on top of Taylor, unmoving on the floor. Throw the drink at him. The weight of the liquid shifts the flight of the glass, but still it hits him on the side of the head. Makes him turn, stumble, and before he can attack Taylor I'm on top of the guy, hand to his wrist, lifting it up, stopping him stabbing the knife.

Fall back, wrestle each other onto the floor. Gritted teeth, can smell the man. Still not thinking straight, propelled unprepared into the middle of the fight. He starts to drag the knife down.

Stronger than me, always knew that. Brings it closer, and now all my efforts and thoughts are at stopping it. Six inches from the top of my head, even closer to his. But he has control, I'm totally defensive. Defensive. Think of the best way to play football, the best way to do anything. Go on the attack. Risk it. For an instant. Switch energies, and with everything I've got I bring my head up into his face. Miss the knife by a fraction. His nose and teeth crunch under my forehead, and I feel it as much as he does. But I'm ready for the shock, he isn't. The briefest second, that's all I have. Control his wrists, bring the knife down sharply. Feel the warm embrace of his neck around the blade as it plunges into him just beneath the chin. Instantly the fight goes from him, the body rests heavily on top of me. The chest still heaves, can feel the warmth of the blood begin to pulse from his neck. Sickening, dark, tepid. Push him off me, and struggle to my feet. Can hear his gasping on the floor, the deep breaths, low moans from Taylor lying next to him.

Light.

The room is full of it and Miller is standing in the doorway looking at the scene in the wasted middle of her sitting room. Taylor struggling to sit up, blood running down his face from a healthy wound; Bloonsbury lying on the floor, hand over the wound in his neck, the knife still cradled in the hand which stabbed him – I should take it off him, not thinking straight, don't do it; and me standing over them, blood across my face and the top of my coat.

Her mouth is open, but there's nothing coming out. Nothing to say. A well-placed profanity might be in order. She looks scared, I'll give her that. Taylor starts to struggle to his feet and I step over Bloonsbury towards him.

'I'm all right,' he says, holding his hand up. 'You'd better call an ambulance for him.'

'What happened?' says Miller eventually. Voice shattered. Bloonsbury continues to moan on the floor. Should be more wary of him, but he's been knifed in the neck. Still not thinking straight.

'He attacked us,' I say. 'It's him who's been killing off the others. Bathurst, Edwards, Herrod. Even that bastard Evans.'

‘Evans?’ she says. Completely lost. Close to panic.

‘Everyone that knew about the Addison case. Presumably you were next.’

She stares down at him, open mouthed.

‘Jonah?’ she says. Thinks he’s dying.

His head lifts for the first time. Ignores me and Taylor, looks straight at her. The movement of his neck starts the blood flow off again. Steady pulse. His voice, when it comes, is hoarse, choking with blood. Hate-filled.

‘Fucking bitch,’ he says. ‘Bitch.’ Blood spits from his mouth.

The look on her face changes. Shock to anger. Eyes burn. Seen the look before.

‘Christ,’ she says. ‘I knew I should have done something about him ages ago. Jesus. Look at the state of this. I’ll get an ambulance.’

Look at the state of this? What? The carpet?

She begins to walk from the room.

‘Don’t you turn your back on me, you bitch. Don’t you run my life for me, then turn your fucking back.’

She hesitates, turns. Bloonsbury has hauled himself onto his elbows, breaths coming from him in great gasps; panting; gurgling. Taylor and I watch it, uninvited guests.

‘Get back here you fucker,’ he wheezes at her, voice seemingly on the point of giving up. She stares down at him, all the contempt that anyone could muster in those eyes.

‘Fuck off, Jonah,’ she says. Words spat out, and she starts to turn away.

I look at him, not really sure what’s going on. He’s still got the knife in his hands. Have a brief moment, see what’s going to happen. Strange vision. And it paralyses me for a hundredth of a second.

From nowhere Bloonsbury finds the strength. Picks himself up, knife clutched firmly in his hands. Almost slow motion. Blood spills from the wound in his throat, he is covered in it. Leaps towards Charlotte, knife back, every last effort into taking his revenge. She senses the rush of movement behind her, turns her head. Time for the briefest flash of panic across her face.

But he's a dying man. As the knife is on its downward sweep towards the middle of Charlotte's back, I'm on top of him, wrestling him to the floor, and he collapses under my weight. The knife falls from his hands, lies useless and blunt on the carpet.

I look up at her, at that impassive face. Panic gone, no trace of fear. Dead. Can't read a thing into it. Push myself off Bloonsbury, and the blood gurgles in his throat from some desperate breath. Pick up the knife; Taylor and I stand and stare at Charlotte.

She gives all she gets. Bloonsbury might just have implicated her in all of his crimes, but she'll know whether there's any proof out there. The actions of a drunk psychotic aren't going to see anyone incriminated.

'Thank you,' she says. Small voice, but steady. 'You saved my life.'

I nod. Don't say anything. Taylor and I just stare at her in the brightly lit silence. He fingers the wound on his head.

A bauble topples from the Christmas tree with a tinsel shiver, settles on the carpet. Bloonsbury suddenly coughs a bloody cough, a strangulated breath wheezes from his body. Silence broken, the spell dispersed.

'I'll call an ambulance,' she says, because she has to. Although, might she not want Bloonsbury to die where he lies?

There's something in her eyes, then she's turned and is gone from the room.

Look down at Bloonsbury. Too late for an ambulance anyway; the man is dying. From the hands of Detective Sergeant Lumberyard. For all my mindless thuggery of the last twenty years, I've never killed a man before.

Don't think about it. Stare at Taylor, and we're both left with the same question. Uninvited guests we are indeed. Silence over the house. A clock ticking somewhere. For some reason I start wondering what Frank is doing, and will he care?

Poland, that was it. Knee deep in gorgeous Central European women.

'Go and listen, Lumberyard. Make sure she calls an ambulance. And the local polis 'n all,' says Taylor.

'Aye,' I say.

46

Three o'clock, New Year's Day. Watery sun low in the sky; bright afternoon with the snow still thick on the ground, frost already in the air for the night ahead. Clear, chill, fresh, a beautiful day.

Standing on the doorstep of the old family home. Haven't bothered to call in case I was rejected. Gone for turning up and not giving her the choice. Course, she doesn't have to let me in, but I'm counting on my charm to see me through. Small bunch of flowers in my right hand – nothing ostentatious, no attempt to make up for a week of lies. A gesture, that's all. What else can I do? I can ask for forgiveness, and while you might think I've got a bloody cheek, she was the one who threw me out for another man three years ago. There's forgiving to be done on both sides. That's how I like to look at it. See where it gets me.

Ring the bell and wait.

A couple of hours sleep, some time between five and eight. Still woke up feeling a million times fresher than I have for weeks. Case closed. It'll take a long time before the stench of this vanishes, but we'll get there.

The Great Detective, Glasgow's cross between Sherlock Holmes and Batman, lies in the morgue at the Victoria. Died on his way to hospital, and they brought his body up this morning; died at the hands of Detective Sergeant Lumberyard. First man I ever killed. Once the full truth is out, don't think anyone will be resenting me for it.

Checked out some things this morning. Our suspicions were pretty close to the mark, and anything new we've discovered has confirmed our theory.

Found out from Maretta Johnson that she spoke to Bloonsbury first on Saturday. He told her to call Herrod the following day. Set him up right from the off. Poor lassie unknowingly played her part, Herrod walked straight into it. Bloonsbury knew his man, knew he would charge round there on his own. White knight. Waited for him, then butchered him. His own man. Can't understand it, because I would've thought Herrod would've been all right to keep his gob shut. But who knows what was going through Bloonsbury's mind the last few weeks?

Found details of a car stolen from Dunoon late Friday night or early Saturday morning. Turned up in Arocher. Fits the bill for Bloonsbury having dealt with Evans.

What else do we have? They're going back over the body of Bathurst, see if they can find any trace of Bloonsbury on there; now that they know what they're looking for.

Taylor interviewed Healy for a couple of hours. Didn't sit in on it. He wavered all over the place; psychotic to reasonable to switched on lawyer to deranged killer. And through it all, an obsession with a variety of women. An obsessive personality, which had needed an outlet, and had finally got it. Tipped over the edge by a really shit movie, but why not? We've all come out of movies thinking we're cooler than we are, or wanting to beat the fuck out of someone, or wanting to be an astronaut. Why not, if you're the appropriate loony personality type, come out of the flics so traumatised you want to stab someone's face in. It's the modern way.

So, can you believe anything such a man tells you? Said that he was taken by Bloonsbury after he blundered into the flat of that stupid tart in Rutherglen. Thought he must have been followed. Pretty messed up in those manacles, so he lost track of night and day, but we know how long he was there.

Ian Healy should be locked up for the rest of his life, but who knows these days? Gets a decent lawyer and he'll probably have the jury feeling sorry for him because he was kidnapped by the polis; and they'll let him off. We'll get enough evidence on the guy to convict a multitude of murderers, but you never can tell. Fucking lawyers.

Found Bloonsbury's prints in Evans' house and on the car that was used in the Edwards hit and run. Pished Jonah; didn't even think to wear gloves. You just don't do it as a polis, do you? When you get prints, you check them against those of known criminals – not against your own men.

So Bloonsbury is guilty as charged on all counts. And dead with it, which is good. All the best scum get killed at the end. Saves on the trial costs, and means there isn't going to be any screw-up in the courtroom with some bloody stupid jury.

Which leaves us where? Bloonsbury's gone to Hell and taken his secret with him. Charlotte Miller.

She sat watching it all in the middle of the night, as the ambulance arrived and whisked away the dying man. Guzzled expensive brandy; bottled in Roman times. Hid behind her masque of wealth and shock, all carefully constructed. Safe in what knowledge? That there was no connection between her and Bloonsbury, or this: every step of the way, after every action she has taken, she has wiped the board. There will be nothing out there to point the finger in her direction.

Can you convict anyone on the actions of someone like Jonah Bloonsbury? Maybe it was the final act of petty revenge from a dying man. To make it look as if she'd colluded with him all along. Because what other proof do we have? We had our suspicions before we went down there, and the way Bloonsbury acted suggested she was part of it. But that was it. It could be that our continuing investigations will unearth something, but we both know she'll have been more thorough than that.

And so, today, she left us to it. No attempt at interference. Appeared at the station for twenty minutes. The Chief Constable turned up – all shiny buttons and stinking of drink – then left with a smile far from his face, ten minutes later.

She called me into her office just before she went. Stood in front of her in that office for the fifth time in a week. Wary rather than nervous. Wondered if I was going to hear a confession.

Not a chance.

'I'm going away for a few days,' she said.

Oh aye? I thought. Nodded, didn't say anything.

'Just need time to think. Get my head together. Chief Constable thinks it would be a good idea. Let things settle. The last few days have been rather hard on the station,' she said. Rather hard? Go on, Charlotte, tell it how it is. 'It all seems like some great conspiracy.'

That's exactly what it is, Hen. And there's a good chance

you're at the centre of it all.

She looked at me for a few seconds. Don't know what she was expecting me to say. Was she looking for sympathy? But I didn't give her anything. There was nothing to say. Taylor and I both suspect her of involvement and we'll do everything to get evidence of it. However, until then we're not about to go mouthing off. She knew it, knew exactly what we were both thinking.

And we are left to wonder what went on between her and Jonah Bloonsbury. Maybe it goes back all the way. Twenty-one years ago to a guy called Dixie Klondyke and a chase across open moorland. Must have started sometime. The two of them have been in it together all along, riding the back of the other. And while Bloonsbury couldn't cope and floundered in an ocean of whisky, Charlotte Miller rode the high seas. Was going to go all the way.

'Would you come with me?' she said. A quiet, nervous voice, but I wouldn't believe that voice now no matter what the tone. Still, that request was out the blue. An electric shock. But whereas before it would have been a shock from an entire power grid, now it was like static off a jumper. Nothing at all. 'Now that it's over, you should be able to get some time off. I'm sure Jack wouldn't mind.'

Jack would go fucking mental, Hen. But there was nothing to worry about. There was no way I was going anywhere else with Charlotte Miller. Standing in front of her desk was as far as she was ever going to get me to go.

Shook my head. 'Don't think so,' I said. Still too many things to sort out. And even if there weren't...

She swallowed. Took it well. Knew what I was thinking, I'm sure.

And that was that. She didn't say anything else, I turned my back on my infatuation of the past week and walked from her office. Closed the door behind me.

A couple of minutes later she swept out of the station. No goodbyes. We couldn't exactly lock her up just because Bloonsbury tried to kill her, but I would bet now if we find something and want to bring her in, she'll be very difficult to get hold of. Got a feeling that a few days might turn into weeks and months. Off somewhere with her bank account and silk pyjamas.

And that's just about it. Some questions answered, some not. Still haven't found out if Taylor slept with Eileen Harrison; a crucial part of the investigation. But they're seeing each other tonight, and he did have more of a smile on his face than the night's events warranted. What else? The man who currently rots in prison on the Addison murder charges from last year. The crimes of Gerry Evans – although that's all hearsay. Maybe it was Bloonsbury all along. Who knows? It'll be for someone else to work out what to do with the guy.

The door opens. Rebecca. Tentatively smiles. Not sure whether she should be pleased to see me. Stares at me, doesn't say anything.

'Happy New Year, Becky,' I say. On instinct I hold out the flowers. If she was six years younger that would be a sure fire winner, but she's twelve; well into maturity and cynicism these days. Looks wary.

'Mum! Dad's at the door.'

Thanks.

About to withdraw the flowers when she takes them from me. Smells them. Looks curious. Wondering where I got flowers on New Year's Day. Probably thinks I stole them from a hospital.

'They're nice,' she says. 'Where'd you get them?'

I knew it.

Peggy appears behind her, puts her hand on her shoulder. We look at each other. No words. Like a scene in a movie. I hate it when my life looks like a scene in a movie. Feel like there's someone watching.

'We're just about to have lunch,' she says.

Look at the watch. 'Bit late,' I say.

'We were down seeing mum this morning. She's gone to Billy's for dinner.'

'You not invited?'

She laughs. Old joke, not worth explaining.

'You all right?' she says. 'Saw what happened on the news.'

‘Aye. No problem. Jack’s got an ashtray injury, mind you.’

She laughs again, the face warms. Might be getting somewhere, but there’s always something below the surface. Know her well enough, but then we’re all the same. You can never really tell.

‘You going to come in then?’ she says.

Nod, take the step up into the house. Come in from the cold. Rebecca steps back, hands the flowers to her mum. She closes the door, looks at them.

‘Nice flowers,’ she says. ‘Where did you get them?’

Andy appears from the living room kicking a football at his feet. Pleased to see he’s shaved off the fusty moustache. Gives me the chance to change the subject.

‘See you got rid of that thing on your face,’ I say to him.

‘Didn’t do it because of you,’ he says. Of course not. ‘You staying for dinner?’

Peggy closes the door and looks at me. Wary.

‘Yes, he is,’ she says. ‘But he’s got some explaining to do.’

I shrug and follow Andy back into the sitting room. The smell of lunch is in the air, the fire is going and the old family home feels warm and comfortable.

‘So where d’you get the flowers, Dad?’ says Rebecca to my back.